MY
Clarity

M. CLARKE

This is a work of fiction. Names, characters, places, and incidents are products of the author's imagination or are used fictitiously and are not to be construed as real. Any resemblance to actual events, locations, organizations, or person, living or dead, is entirely coincidental.

To my husband and my children,
Thank you for showing me there is no limit to love. It grows everyday, with every new experience, with every new hope and dream. I love you to the moon and back.

Books by M. Clarke (NA)
Something Great
Something Wonderful
Something Forever-8/25/2014

Books by Mary Ting (YA)
Crossroads Saga:
Crossroads (Book 1)
Between (Book 2)
Beyond (Book 3)
Eternity (Book 4)
Halo City (Book 4.5)

From Gods

Enjoy excerpts at the back from:
Angela Corbett
Jennifer Miller
Cory Cyr

Thank you Myra Espino for creating an awesome book trailer.
I can't thank you enough! http://youtu.be/pun8Ly6W9r4

To Love A Woman
Download song from Amazon

Lyrics by M. Clarke/Mary Ting
Produced by Aaron Martinez

Verse 1:
You see her across the room.
Every other face disappears.
The Earth shakes inside of you.
Her smile crawls into your skin,

Chorus:
Touching your heart,
your soul,
your can do nothing,
but dream of her.
All you want to do
is hold her in your arms.

Verse 2:
You want to breathe her in,
and taste every word on her lips.
You long to touch her,
taste her,
give your heart to her,
until you can feel her in your blood.

Bridge:
With every kiss,
and every touch,
she takes away pieces of you
With every breath,
till there's nothing left
but you need her
so you let her.
Cause you love her
and cannot breathe without her.

Praises for:
MY CLARITY

"My Clarity is refreshing, beautiful, and tugged at each of my heart strings. I loved it!" **Toni Aleo New York Times & USA Today Bestselling author of the Assassins Series.**

"At first glance, no one would believe Elijah's tough guy exterior hides a genuine and giving heart. But, you cannot help whom you fall in love with and when opposites attract, the chemistry is undeniable!" **InD'tale Magazine**

"M. Clarke/Mary Ting blew me out of the water with this book. I am in awe and in love with this epic tale. Elijah Cooper is now my #1 book boyfriend." **Sammie's Book Club, for book lovers**

"M. Clarke has done it again! My Clarity is a magnificent well written story. You will cry, you will laugh, you will fall in love, but the best part you will not want to put the book down until you have read the last word!" **Books and Beyond Fifty Shades.**

"My Clairty will give you the best book hangover ever because you're not going to be able to put it down. You'll love it to the moon and back. Just like I did." **Fairiechick's Fantasy Book Reader**

"Through the darkness of our pasts, we are all looking for a little clarity. For Alexandria, Elijah could be just that. My Clarity is a story of love and hope, that through the hardest times we find clarity in each other." **Spare Time Book Blog**

"Elijah and Alex sizzle in this wonderful page-turner by M. Clarke. I absolutely couldn't put it down! This book was 5 stars amazing!" **CrossAngeles**

Dedication

I can't tell you enough how much this story means to me, but at the same time, I can't tell you enough how much your support and friendship means to me. I feel humbled and honored that you are reading My Clarity. You give me the fuel to continue my passion.

Damaris Cardinali—Thank you for being my awesome PR. Words cannot describe our friendship and how much you have done for me.

Kim Rinaldi and Jen Joanisse—What can I say? Thank you for guiding me to make this book the BEST that it can be. Love you both very much!

Alexandrea Weis—Thank you for EVERYTHING. Your guidance and support has helped me become a better writer.

Vanessa Strickler—My angel sister, thank you for all your support and for running My Clarity and From Gods pages. And thank you for being there for me when I needed to vent.

Janie Iturralde—My Street team admin. Your friendship means so much to me. Thank you for all your help, but most of all, your friendship and for always being there for me.

Sam Stettner—Your enthusiasm, and love for Elijah fills my heart. I can't thank you enough for all you do. Love you to the moon and back, Sun!!!

Kitty Bowers—As I have said many times before, thank you for being my number #1 fan and cheerleader. You pick me up when I am down.

Lisa from The Rock Star of Romance—For all your support and setting up an awesome blog tour.

Street Team—You're my other family. I don't even know how to thank you. Words are not enough for all your time and energy. You are simply the best!!!

Laura Hidalgo—For your friendship, and for creating an awesome covers. And for always looking after me.

Joann Buchanan—You are amazing! Thank you for all your input and for loving my books.

To all the **authors** and **bloggers** that have been beyond supportive and have become my friends. I can't thank you enough. There are too many to make a list. I'm very grateful for your support and friendship.

7

Prologue

Alexandria

Life presents you with many roads, but two things remain constant: you're born, and when it's your time, you die. Struck by cancer, my father had traveled his last road. I knew someday he would get really sick from smoking, and no matter how hard I tried to convince him, he didn't listen. He would rather smoke than live a longer, healthy life with me. That's the way I saw it.

Wheezing, my dad looked at me. "Alexandria," he started to say. With a faint smile, he pulled my ear closer to his lips. He was having a difficult time getting his words out. "Don't. Date. Guys. Who. Smoke." He tried to laugh, but ended up coughing instead.

"Okay, Dad," I said softly with a light laugh. I wanted to get mad at him for joking at a time like this, but the irony of his words lightened the mood.

Mom looked like she was going to lose it. Unable to wipe her tears fast enough, she turned away. "I'll be right back," she said quickly, heading out of the hospital room to give us space, most likely into the arms of her current husband.

Trying hard not to break down as I wiped my tears, I didn't see my dad. I saw a man who suffered because of his chosen path. And I saw a man who was going to give his daughter some last words of wisdom.

Suddenly, the urgency of this situation hit me fast and hard. I'd kept myself so closed off from talking about my dad's cancer that seeing reality in front of me was like hearing the news for the first time. I had a difficult time dealing with the situation. So much so, that I couldn't even talk about it with my best friend. The word cancer was a death sentence, and I didn't know how to deal with it. Before I knew it, tears started to stream down my cheeks. My gut told me today was his last day. I just knew. I was lucky though. Most people don't get to say good-bye.

"Alex, I'm sorry. I wish I had stopped for you," he said as he struggled with his breath.

I wanted to yell at him, remind him that I had tried to tell him many times that I felt like he chose smoking over me. It didn't mean he was a bad dad. In fact, he was a wonderful one. I wasn't sure about being a good husband since my parents had divorced long ago, but as a dad, he was involved in every part of my life. He was an active dad who knew everything that was going on with me, and even knew my friends by name.

Most of my friends didn't feel close to their fathers, but my dad and I bonded through music. We would spend hours singing karaoke together. He said I had a beautiful voice and wanted me to try out for American Idol, but I was too shy. Despite all the good points, what good was it when he wouldn't be around?

Placing his hand on my cheeks, he started to whisper. "Sunshine…my only sunshine…." He paused. It was a song he sang to me growing up. I can clearly remember the first time he sang it to me. I was five years old.

"Sunshine, why are you crying," my dad asked, placing me on his lap.

Instead of answering, I showed him my cut finger that was slightly bleeding.

"What happened to this little finger?" he said in the sweetest, caring tone.

"I fell." I pursed my lips as tears welled in my eyes.

"Let's go clean that up. I'll make it feel better. But before we do that, can you smile for me?"

9

I shook my head with a pouting face, still holding up my index finger. It was my way of reminding him what I needed.

I heard a light chuckle, but when I looked at him, he hid his humorous expression. "Do you know why I call you sunshine?"

"No." I arched my brows in curiosity.

"When you smile, you light up the whoooole room." He extended his arms out, and then dropped them to embrace me. "You're like the sun, glowing, warming up my heart."

My eyes grew wide in wonderment. "I glow like the sun?" My tone went up a notch in excitement.

"Yes, you do," he nodded, holding my other hand. "I can't see it, but I can sure feel it. It makes me happy. When I have a bad day, all I have to do is look at your smile." Then he started to sing the song. I watched his lips part as I gazed in amazement.

When the song was over, I had forgotten about my cut. I had forgotten about the pain. I was the sun that gave him warmth on his cold days and it was the coolest thing. From then on, he would sing to me when I was feeling sad.

The song will always remind me of him. Suddenly, that song meant more to me than it had before, knowing it could possibly be the last time I heard him sing it.

After he closed his eyes, as if to clear his mind, he opened them and continued. "I'm sorry I won't be there to see you graduate from high school and college, and I won't be there to walk you down the aisle." Tears poured down the corners of his eyes. "I'm sorry I won't know the guy who will one day think of you as his sunshine." He paused. "No matter where I am, I'll always watch over you." My dad stroked my cheeks.

I couldn't take it anymore. As uncontrolled tears poured down my face, his words engulfed me in a darkness I had never felt before. "Okay," I nodded, looking anywhere but his eyes as I gasped for air. I wanted to tell him so much. I wanted to apologize for being mad when he became sick, blaming him for his choices when I should have accepted it and tried to spend quality time with him instead. But I thought I'd have more time with him. I didn't realize that the thing I feared the most would happen this fast.

"Shhh...." he whispered, wiping my tears before they fell. "This isn't goodbye. I'll see you one day, but not too soon, okay? You're only eighteen. You have a long life ahead of you."

I nodded, whimpering.

"I love you, Sunshine. I always will. I'll always live in your heart. Look for me there when you need me. You keep me there until you can replace me with a guy who will love you as much as I do. Who will love you for all your goodness and your faults. Who will make you feel like you're the center of his world. Who will give you the best of him and all of him. Promise me."

Nodding to confirm since speaking was out of the question at this point, I wrapped my arms around my dad's chest and felt it rise and fall. I was a little girl all over again as he stroked my hair with his hand. As we held each other tight, all went silent. I didn't know how long we stayed that way; I just knew I wanted it to last. The last thing I remembered before I let out a gut-wrenching cry was his barely audible voice. "Please don't take my sunshine away." I felt his hand slide off my back and there was no movement on his chest.

"No, Daddy. Don't leave me," I whimpered repeatedly, holding onto him. I cried so loud, my mom and the nurses rushed in. It took the three of them to peel me off my dad. Holding onto my mom, my body shook with shock and regret, thinking I should have spent more time with him, and shouldn't have been so mad at him. Now it was too late. He was gone.

I didn't know watching someone you love die would be like this. How do you prepare for it? How do you prepare for the hole left inside by their silenced body? No longer would I hear his laughter. Gone were the lectures I often hated to hear. Now, I would give anything to hear him say I was messing up. Something. Anything. No, there is no preparing. The pain and the sorrow hits you so hard even when you know it's happening.

Finally calming down, I raised my hand to my heart. The hole in my chest felt empty. The pain of loss had replaced it. I had made a promise. "You'll be right here, Dad." My lips quivered, unable to stop my tears again. "You'll always be here."

Chapter 1

Alexandria

Three months later.

"Don't cry," Emma said, wiping her tears. "Look, you're making me cry."

Leaning on the side of her car, I nodded to answer, but snorted at the same time when she gave me a dorky face. Emma was such a great friend. She was my cheerleader when I first found out about my dad's cancer and she was there for me after he passed away. Emma checked up on me by calling and coming over after school to make sure I was okay. She was the sister I wish I had. I wish she could come with me.

"This isn't good-bye forever. It's see you later, okay?" she continued, shifting her eyes to see the people waiting for the same bus, and then she turned back to me. "Your dad is so proud of you right now; his little girl is going off to college. I bet he's smiling down at you."

I nodded to agree. I almost lost it when she brought up my dad. Every time he was mentioned in conversations, my heart felt like it was on fire, scorched by the memory of him. It was as though I was burying him all over again. His name, the word Dad, our home together, his friends, his favorite food, our love for singing, everything we shared was a constant stab to my heart.

I wanted to forget, hoping it would make the pain bearable, but the burning sensation pulled me back to reality, reminding me. The thought of never seeing him again was pure devastation. Most people I knew could only empathize because they had never felt this degree of loss. It wasn't that I didn't appreciate their efforts, they just didn't understand.

Emma started to caress my arm to comfort me, but the tears kept coming. "I'm sorry," I sniffed. "I told myself I wasn't going to cry." I fanned my hand as if it would make them stop, but it also gave me some relief from this humid, sweltering weather. Finally, after several deep breaths and short gasps, I buried the tears deep into the recesses of my heart.

"You don't need to apologize." She paused. Her eyes danced, as if to gather her thoughts, searching for the perfect words. "You're going to have a great experience. It will do some good for you to leave this town. Leave the memories behind you and make new ones. Hell...if I could go with you, I would. I would feel better if I did, especially since it's only been three months since your dad passed away. It's okay to cry when you miss him. It's also okay to call me when you want to talk about him, ya hear? You don't have to be strong by yourself. You know you have me to lean on, even if it's just over the phone."

I nodded because words failed me. I was afraid I would bawl like crazy in front of her.

Emma continued, looking at me with hope in her eyes. "Maybe you'll meet someone who will sweep you off your feet. And do try to hang out and not be such a nerd. You only get this experience once. You're supposed to find yourself."

After Emma graduated from high school, she continued to work for a clothing store. She said the pay was good and she was going to be a manager in a few months, so she decided that was the road she was going to take. As for me, I wanted to go to college, preferably out of this town.

I had already said good-bye to my mom and my stepdad before Emma picked me up to take me to the bus station. Mom offered to take me, but I told her Emma would take me instead. Ever since Mom remarried five years ago, our relationship hadn't been the same. I'm glad I only had to live in the same house with them for three months. I couldn't help it. I was so mad at her for leaving Dad, and for not doing everything she could to try and keep the family together.

Living away from home plus paying college tuition was going to be expensive. Since I didn't want any of my stepdad's money, I insisted that I use the college fund Dad had saved up for me. The rest had to come from the part-time jobs that I would have to get once I was there. It wasn't so much that I disliked my stepdad. It was just strange to think of him as a dad since he hardly knew me at all.

Lung cancer stole my dad's life. He fought till the very end, but the odds were not in his favor. I can still recall his last words to me: *Alexandria, make sure to give your heart to the guy who will love you for all your goodness and your faults, who will make you feel like you're the center of his world.* What did he mean by that anyway?

"The bus should be here in five minutes," Emma said somberly, opening the trunk of her car.

Excitement and sadness rushed through me as I took out my suitcase, a small duffle bag, and my purse. This was it—my freedom, my independence, and my new life. Though I was scared out of my mind and heartbroken, I had to do this. Turning to Emma, I gave her a big smile and another tight squeeze. "I'll text you when I get there."

"You better. And you better keep in touch and not forget about me," Emma started to tear up again.

It was difficult to say goodbye to the best friend I've had since kindergarten. Being an only child, she was like a sister to me. We

14

did all sorts of crazy stuff together and we knew each other's deepest secrets—which wasn't much, since we weren't the rebel types. The only bad thing we did together was sneak out of the house to go to parties.

"Now who's the one crying," I said as my lips quivered.

"I'm going to be jealous of your new roommate. What was her name again?"

"Jimmy told me her name is Ellie. Well, he texted me. I was lucky I even got a text from my cousin, let alone a phone call. You know how he is."

"I can't believe Jimmy had a female roommate. Not that there is anything wrong with that, but personally, I would prefer to live with the same gender."

"I know, right? But I'm sure they worked it out. Who's to say opposite sexes can't be roommates?"

"True. But you better not like her more than me," she scowled playfully, trying to lighten the mood.

"I could never. I'm only three hours away. Maybe you can visit."

Emma's eyes lit up and shifted to her car. "I would love to, but I don't think this clunker could make the long drive. And don't let Liam visit you."

"Emma," I said her name a bit too loud. "He's not as bad as you think."

"That's right. He's actually worse. If he really cared, he would be driving you to your new place."

"He's busy. And he lives too freakin' far. I'm lucky to even get a visit from him."

"It still isn't a good excuse. If he cared enough to try to get into your pants, he should care enough to drive you there instead of making you take the bus. Your dad wouldn't have liked him."

When my eyes widened in surprise, she spoke again. "I'm sorry. I only want the best for you, and I don't think he's it."

"You can't help whom you fall in love with," I commented, but what I really wanted to say was that I didn't know if I loved Liam. It was too much to think about...too much to admit on top of my already broken heart.

Liam and I started dating several months before Dad passed away. Dad never got to meet him. I wanted to wait until things got serious, because I knew no matter whom I brought home, he wouldn't have been good enough for his *sunshine.* "I'm a big girl. I'll be the judge, but I thank you for caring," I stated with a smile.

Not wanting to be the type of girl who needed a guy to take care of her, it had never crossed my mind to have Liam drive me. I didn't want to be like my mom. I could tell my stepdad took good care of her. Perhaps it's the reason why she left Dad.

With a heavy sigh, Emma turned to the sound of the bus slowing down. "Next stop is to begin your new adventure."

"I'll come back for Christmas, and I'll text you as often as I can." My tone was full of promise, but we both knew that the distance was going to be a killer. I already felt it with Liam. I was hoping it would be different between us.

"Go...before I don't let you," she said when the door to the bus opened. A few passengers already placed their bags inside the storage compartment. I decided I should do the same. After Emma helped me, she gave me another hug and backed away.

Giving her my pouty face, I headed up the bus steps.

"If you ever want something from a guy, make sure to pout. You have one hell of a sexy pout."

"Yeah, right," I laughed, waving to her as I handed the driver my ticket. The air-conditioned bus immediately cooled me down, giving me shivers. I found a window seat and sat down. I looked out the window and saw Emma still standing there, so I gave her a reassuring smile and waved. She appeared smaller and smaller until she was nothing but a tiny blur.

I turned to face the front, but kept my eyes staring out the window. I couldn't believe I was actually doing this. I was going to live out on my own and create my own adventure. I was an open book, blank pages yet to be written on. How cool was that!

Well Dad, I thought to myself. *I'm really doing this. I'm really excited and nervous, but I know you're with me. You're always with*

16

me. Then somehow, I felt a sense of ease trickle through me, slowly releasing the tension I'd felt since getting on the bus. Talking to my dad, even though he wasn't here, always helped me through whatever I was facing.

Chapter 2

Alexandria

As the party music rang in my ears, I couldn't help but sway a little to the rhythm of the melody as I headed to my destination. Wheeling a suitcase behind me, a small duffel bag in my other hand and a purse strap over my shoulder, I searched for 48 Dartmouth Court. I prayed that the party was not at the condo I would be staying at.

The exterior of the buildings all looked the same, with the same beige paint. You couldn't tell them apart, except for the address. It looked to be a single-level condo with each unit attached side by side. As long as it was in a livable condition, I didn't care.

The streetlights provided enough light, and the numbers getting higher indicated I was getting closer. Finding a place to live near the college was not an easy thing to do. Lucky for me, my cousin Jimmy graduated and told me I could take his old room. I was hesitant, but I had no other choice since my funds were limited.

One of the perks was that the furniture and basic appliances were already provided and all I had to do was move in. There was only one condition; I had to live with a roommate. From what my cousin said in his text, she seemed like a really nice person. No biggie. I could handle a roommate, I hoped.

Looking at the address on my text again just to confirm, I knew today wasn't my lucky day. The music was blasting out of 48. Great! Approaching the doorway, there were two guys and a girl with their backs to me.

When the first guy turned, my heart skipped a beat and our eyes locked for who knew how long. With dark brown hair and piercing, beautiful eyes that twinkled just underneath the light, he was attractive. I could even tell he had a nice, toned body from the gray tank top he was wearing.

I didn't know what to do. I lost my words. His stare became intense. I waited for any type of greeting, but he continued to stare in silence. With a fast sweep of his eyes from my head to my toes, he finally shifted them away from me. Maybe he didn't like what he saw, but I didn't care.

"Lookie here," the second guy said, breaking my trance. "Hello, sweetheart. How can I help you?" His words came out too playful.

"I…umm. Is this 48 Dartmouth Court?" I asked shyly, wringing a strand of my hair around my index finger, then quickly dropped it when I saw his eyes widen with amusement.

"It sure is. Are you here to party or spend the night?" His eyes fell to my suitcase.

"Oh…I'm Jimmy's cousin. I'm taking over his room. I'm Alexandria, but he calls me Alex."

"You're Alex?" the second guy said too excitedly, laughing out loud. "I thought Alex was a guy. How about that?" He nudged the first guy, but he didn't bother to reply.

"Oh My God! You're Alex? I should've known." The pretty brunette's tone rose with elation. With beautiful green eyes, her soft curls passed her shoulders. Wearing shorts and a black tank top, I didn't blame her. We were dressed similar. The blistering heat was unbearable today and it carried over into the night.

"I'm Lexy," she said, extending her hand to shake mine. "Jimmy is a good friend of mine. Actually, a good friend to all of us." She gestured to the guys.

"Lexy," I repeated, returning the heartfelt smile, releasing her hand. "Jimmy told me to get in touch with you. He spoke highly of you."

"I don't know about that," the second guy teased, chuckling. "Unless you want a good time." He got a good smack from Lexy. "I'm Seth. If I knew you were Alex, I would have told Jimmy to send you my way. I have a spare room if you change your mind about this place, or if you don't like your roommate," he winked.

Seth had that kind of baby face that would make you trust him easily. The look you could warm up to, because he had a sweet smile. But knowing him for only a couple of minutes, he was obviously a big flirt.

"I...um...thanks," I said quickly, feeling my face warm up. I didn't want to be rude, but I wasn't sure if I should have said that since he was flirting.

The first guy hadn't said a word. I glanced up to see if he would introduce himself, but he wasn't even looking my way. He just lit a cigarette and puffed away. Only when I started coughing from the horrid smell, he look at me with a short, irritated sigh. It was a fast glance, and then he turned his back to me. Great! I just got here and I already met someone who doesn't like me.

"Let me take you to your room," Seth said, taking my suitcase.

"I'll see you inside," Lexy muttered. "Say hi to your roommate, Ellie, for me." Lexy let out a hearty laugh as she accentuated the word "Ellie."

It only made me wonder if this Ellie was going to be a friend or a nightmare. "I will," I said, and then followed behind Seth. I turned when I heard a low grumble sound from the smoker. He looked surprised when my eyes caught his, most likely thinking I wouldn't have turned. I just hoped I didn't have to see him around any time soon.

It was difficult to follow Seth through the mass of people inside, but I couldn't miss him. He was taller than most of the people in the crowd, so I could see the tips of his blond hair. There were several small groups of guests talking and holding red plastic cups. Someone was behind the dining table making drinks. Several couples were making out on the couch. They seriously needed to get a room. Others were near the DJ and on the balcony, shaking and grinding their bodies against each other to the music.

Pushing through while bumping into bodies, I managed to catch up to Seth, who looked over his shoulder to see if I was following.

"Here's your room," he said, opening the door.

"Oh God!" I yelped, covering my mouth from saying anything else. A couple was having sex.

Seth slammed the door. "I'm sorry. I'll be right back."

He went inside and shut the door behind him. Cursing and shouting penetrated through the door, even with the loud music. He was kicking the two naked people out of my room. I guess I'm shopping for new sheets...or better yet, a brand new bed. Gross! The couple was still making out as they chuckled and left the room without showing any hint of embarrassment. At least they had put their clothes on.

"Let's try this again." Seth gestured for me to go in first. "Ellie kept this part of the condo pretty clean."

Seth was right, but I couldn't tell from his tone if it was a question or a comment. There was a bed, a dresser, and a desk. It was pretty empty, so I didn't know what Seth was talking about. How could you make a mess when there is nothing to make a mess with? I was more than happy to see that this room was in good condition. The white walls and the carpet met my standards.

"Did you drive here?" he asked, breaking my observation.

"No. I took the bus and walked the rest of the way. It wasn't too far from the bus stop."

"You should've called one of us. Did Jimmy give you our numbers?"

"He gave me Lexy's, but I didn't want to bother her."

"Give me your phone," he demanded, but his tone was polite.

So I did. Seth punched the keys away and gave it back to me. "I've set my number. Call me if you need anything. Jimmy and I are fraternity brothers. Actually, he's my big bro, so that makes you like my little sis." He lit a quick grin, a way of confirming I would be fine, and then continued. "If you need anything, don't hesitate to call."

"Thanks, Seth. I appreciate it."

"Do you want to come out and meet my friends? Actually, I only know a few of them. I have no idea who the rest of these people are," he chuckled. "If I introduce you as Jimmy's cousin, they won't try to hit on you. And please don't walk alone on campus at night. Pretty girls such as yourself can get into a whole lot of trouble around here. Crazy people come out at night."

"Okay," I replied, blushing from him calling me pretty. He was very forward. "Let me wash up first. I feel all sticky."

"I'll wait for you by the kitchen."

"Thanks."

"By the way. There is only one bathroom so make sure to lock the doors on either side. I know this because I practically live here," he informed with a shrug.

"I'll remember to do that." Before Seth could step out of the room, I asked him a question. "Do you know where Ellie is?"

"Oh." He seemed a bit nervous or amused. I couldn't tell. "I'm sure Ellie is around here, somewhere. Don't worry about it. You'll meet Ellie soon."

"Okay." It was all I could say, but I did worry about it. Why wouldn't she be at her own party? I hoped she didn't like to throw parties on a regular basis. From what Jimmy texted me, she seemed really nice. I was actually looking forward to getting to know her. I prayed we would get along.

Chapter 3

Alexandria

After I texted my mom, Emma, and Liam that I had arrived safely, I took a quick shower. I didn't even bother to dry my hair or put on makeup. What was the point? I wasn't trying to impress anyone. Slipping on another pair of shorts and the white tank top with the pretty little designs, I was refreshed and ready.

Not wanting anyone else to come and look through my stuff, I shoved my belongings inside the empty closet. Who knew who else would come in here when I left the room? Suddenly, nervousness settled through me. I dragged in a deep breath as I wondered if I would fit in. It was always difficult being the new person.

Since I didn't want Seth waiting for me too long, I rushed out the door, making sure to close it behind me. Feeling the bass of the music drumming against my chest, I headed to the kitchen. On the way, I got comments like, "Hey baby, come drink with me." Seth was right. Standing alone, I was being hit on left and right; most of them were drunk and probably looking to get laid.

"Alex...here." Seth waved his beer bottle, yelling over the music. He was standing near the dining area.

I waved back letting him know I saw him.

"This is Dean." He pointed to his friend, standing next to him. Dean was shorter than Seth with warm hazel eyes.

"Hi," I smiled.

"Hey," he grinned, taking my hand to shake. "You're Jimmy's cousin. I've heard so much about you."

My eyes were wide with curiosity. Had Jimmy been talking about me?

"Shut up," Seth chuckled. "I just told him that you were a minute ago." He rolled his eyes. "Would you like anything to drink?"

"No thanks. I mean…not beer. But could I have some water?" I replied, observing the hard-core party that was happening right in front of my eyes.

"I'll be right back." When Seth left, I suddenly felt alone, even with Dean beside me. Knowing Seth was a good friend of Jimmy gave me a sense of security and comfort since I was new here.

Jimmy must have been a partier, but at least he had a good head on his shoulders. He got into UC Berkeley Business Graduate School. That made me wonder about the people around me though.

I was stunned into silence by the number of wasted girls. I didn't want to judge, but why would they do that? Although, I did give them some credit for not giving a damn. Sometimes I wish I didn't care so much. I'd like to be a little more adventurous and do something I wouldn't normally do, live a little more on the daring side.

"Where did you come from?" Dean asked, breaking me away from the uncomfortable setting.

"I'm from a small town about three hours from here."

"Seth tells me you're a freshman."

"Yes." My answer was short. I didn't want him to ask me questions. I didn't want to share.

"So, did you leave a boyfriend behind?"

"Yes, sort of." I didn't know why I hesitated.

"Oh, one of those situations." He took a sip from his red cup.

"What do you mean 'one of those'?" Though I was a bit offended, I hoped my tone didn't give him that impression.

"It just sounded like you weren't sure. You know, like I'm with someone, but I don't know if it will last."

I smiled in understanding. "Actually, it's more like I'm in a relationship with this guy, but don't know what's going on. So, I guess you're right on the spot." I'm an idiot.

"Here you go. Sorry, I had to step out for a sec," Seth said, thankfully breaking up our conversation, handing me a bottle of water. I was beginning to wonder if he was ever coming back.

"Thanks." Unscrewing the cap, I took a sip. It felt refreshing going down my throat, cooling me from this wretched heat. With so many people in the condo, the air-conditioner did little to cool the place down.

"When do your parties usually end?" I asked, trying not to sound like a party pooper.

"Sometimes they go all night," Seth answered. "But I'll shoo them out earlier since tonight is your first time here."

"No, it's okay." I was thankful that he would do such a thing, but at the same time, I didn't want him to change anything because of me. "I'll just close my door and turn off the lights. I'm so tired, I'm sure I'll just fall asleep." I hoped.

"Hey! You washed up and changed," Lexy cheered, appearing suddenly, pushing aside the people in her way. "Sorry about the party. We didn't know you were coming today."

When I turned to her, I saw the smoker. My eyes had a mind of their own. I didn't mean to glance his way, but his presence demanded attention. I thought the first time my heart fluttered mercilessly was due to heat, but it did it again when I looked at him. His eyes met mine longer than I wanted them to, but he broke away first. That's when I saw the beautiful black dragon tattoo on his right arm, enclosed by a circular shape. The body of the dragon swirled, like a snake. The design was exquisite, etched on the curve of his tanned, toned bicep. It made him appear dangerous, badass; my curiosity kicked in. It was way too sexy for my eyes.

A part of me wanted to get to know him better, like why he got that particular tattoo, what it meant to him. Most people get them for sentimental reasons, like to honor a loved one. For others, it was simply for the art or to make a statement. I couldn't help but wonder what inspired his ink. However, he seemed closed off and judgmental, not to mention he smoked. Major turn off.

I didn't want him to catch me staring at his tattoo, so I flashed my eyes to Lexy. Trying to recall what she had said, I was almost certain she saw me staring at *him* since her eyes were already on me. Crap! "That's okay," I said, hoping I wasn't too off on our conversation. At least if I sounded like I knew what we were talking about, I wouldn't appear like a girl who was drooling. Was I? "I guess there was a misunderstanding," I continued. "I thought Jimmy would've texted you to let you know I would be coming today."

"No worries, hun. We are closing down the party early. As for Jimmy, he doesn't communicate very well with me."

"I know the feeling. But seriously, it's okay. I don't mind at all. Really. There is no need to kick everyone out on my account." I was feeling terrible. I didn't want everyone looking at me accusingly or to be known as the girl who killed the party. Wanting to disappear before they could put their words to action, I excused myself and headed to my room. As I did, I asked, "Where's Ellie? Is she around?" Again, I thought it was strange for her not to be at her own party.

"Oh." Lexy curled her lips slowly. "You'll meet Ellie soon enough. I'll stop by tomorrow before noon, but if you need anything, don't hesitate to call."

What did she mean by "I'll meet her soon?" I didn't want to sound nosy my first day here, so I didn't pursue the questions I wanted to ask. "Thanks," I waved.

"See you in the morning," Seth said, raising his beer bottle.

"It was nice meeting you," Dean said next.

After I gave them each a warm smile, I peered up to see the smoker. I didn't want to, but I couldn't help myself. His existence made me feel a dangerous heat I didn't want to feel, especially when

I could sense his eyes on me. It was odd, since he also scared the crap out of me.

Maybe it was his drop-dead gorgeous grin that I observed him offer to his friends, or the fact that he seemed so mysterious. Or was it his deliciously toned body you don't see in most guys? Whatever the reason, this feeling latched on to me, making me too aware of *him*. I didn't like this feeling at all.

"Elijah," a girl with auburn hair called, wrapping her arms around his chest—a chest any guy would want and any girl would want to touch.

"Where have you been? I've been looking for you," she flirted in that squeaky tone I couldn't stand.

"Heather, where's my hug?" Seth pouted with his arms extended.

Not wanting to see anymore, I headed for my room. *Elijah*. I repeated his name in my mind as I turned the knob, and then closed the door behind me. It did hardly any good at drowning out the noise. Elijah…what a sweet name for a hot guy. Too bad he didn't seem all that nice. It didn't matter anyhow. It wasn't as if I was remotely interested in him that way. I was seeing someone.

I figured that since I would be hanging out with Lexy and Seth, I should try to get to know their group of friends, which included Elijah. My heart pounded hard against my chest when I thought of his name, and I wanted this unnerving feeling to go away. My dad had told me many times before not to judge a person by their looks, and sometimes not even by first impressions. Maybe Elijah will surprise me. And where in the heck was Ellie?

Chapter 4

Alexandria

With a stretch and a yawn, I woke up the next morning feeling groggy and tired. I tossed and turned on the bed last night before I finally fell asleep. I wondered how long the party lasted. After a night filled with murmured voices and muffled music from the party, I felt like I hadn't slept a wink. The intensity of the heat in the room indicated that it was going to be another scorching day. I could feel the warm, soft breeze blowing in from the window I had opened last night to let in some air.

I was quickly reminded of my new room. The first thing I saw was the wooden desk and a dresser by the closet. Thankfully, the heat made a blanket unnecessary. Recalling the couple having sex on the bed last night, a new blanket and sheets were the first thing on my list to buy.

I planned to ask Lexy to take me to Target so I could buy all my necessities. Thinking about Ellie and wondering what she looked like, I dragged across the carpet to the bathroom with the towel and toiletries I had unpacked last night. As soon as I walked in, the other door to the bathroom opened. I had forgotten that there were two doors, but what caught me by surprise was seeing Elijah standing there. I completely froze.

I think both of our eyes popped out, but maybe mine even more. He looked sexy as hell with disheveled hair, black shorts, and a tank top he was just pulling down. I got a glimpse of flesh and a tattoo on the left side of his chest...the letters C-L-A-R, and the rest disappeared under his shirt.

"Hey," he mumbled. Running his fingers through his hair, he gave me a shy, half-smile as he turned back around. After he walked out, he shut the door behind him.

I had an "Oh My God" moment. He actually spoke to me. Just then, I guessed he was Ellie's boyfriend since he spent the night. Disappointment struck me. He had been here with Ellie. He took my breath away and made me feel things I didn't want to feel. Sure, Liam gave me butterflies in my stomach, but this was different—naughty different—physical attraction different. A huge part of me felt guilty toward Liam and my new roommate.

Ellie and Elijah most likely needed to use the bathroom, so I took the world's shortest shower and unlocked their side when I was done. I rushed out the door and closed my side. This was very inconvenient, especially since I assumed Elijah would be spending the night here often. I would not only have to think about Ellie's schedule, but Elijah's as well. Having a roommate was hard enough, but adding a third person to the picture, especially a guy, was not what I had in mind.

My mind drifted back to yesterday. Maybe he was giving me strange looks because he found out I was the new roommate. A third person he didn't want, especially since they were used to living together without a roommate for the summer. This was only an assumption; however, if it were true, everything seemed clearer. Maybe he wasn't a jerk after all, especially now that I could understand where he was coming from...I think.

Before falling asleep last night, I had unpacked, somewhat. With a towel around my naked body and wet hair dripping water down my back, I walked to the dresser, and took out my shorts and the pink tank with lace trim at the bottom.

After I got ready, I walked out the door to a mess—an unbelievable freakin' mess. Don't people believe in cleaning up after themselves? I'd been to parties before, but it had never been like this.

The entire sofa cushion was out of place. There were spilled drinks and crumbs on the coffee table, not to mention the obvious gross stains on the carpet. This was not the ideal living situation I had in mind. Not a great start. Though I was disappointed, I needed to take one day at a time and make this work. I had no choice.

Digging through the kitchen cabinets, I found what I was looking for. With a trash bag in my hand, I started picking up beer cans, bottles, napkins, chips and peanuts.

Crinkling my nose and passing judgments against those who left a mess, I heard Ellie's doorknob turn. Finally, I would get to meet her. I looked up as excitement burst through me, but it was short lived. A different kind of exhilaration flushed through me. My pulse escalated and I felt heat on my face.

I gulped from nervousness. "Hi…Elijah, right?" I knew his name, but I didn't want him to think I was eavesdropping last night when Heather practically threw herself at him.

"Hey," he grinned. With a quick flash to my eyes, he dropped his, as if he were embarrassed. Certainly, he wasn't shy. There was something different about his attitude toward me. With his hands inside his pants pockets, he stood watching me, making me uneasy until he asked a question. "What are you doing?"

Hearing a full sentence out of him gave me the quivers. He had a deep, manly voice. The same tone you would imagine hearing from a hot guy. "I'm picking this stuff up for my collection. I collect trash." I don't know why I said that, but it broke the ice.

Seeing his lips curve up and hearing the sound of his laughter made me do the same.

"Cute." His brows twitched in amusement. "Sorry about the mess. You don't need to clean up. Let me do it."

He extended his arms to reach for the bag, but I pulled away before he could. Again, I noticed his tattoo and looked away when he noted my eyes on it. "That's okay. I'm just waiting for Lexy to come by. I really don't have much to do." I had to unpack the rest of my belongings, but there wasn't much.

Elijah went to the kitchen, came out with another trash bag, and started cleaning on the opposite side of me. I turned toward Ellie's door. The sound of the toilet flushing was a sign she was awake. As I wondered when Ellie would make an appearance, I decided just to ask instead of waiting. "Do you think Ellie will come out soon?"

Elijah stiffened and turned toward me. Racking his hair back, he looked flustered. "About that…what did Jimmy tell you about Ellie?"

At this point, I was really getting annoyed. "What do you mean? When Jimmy found out I was coming here, he told me that his old room was available. That Ellie was really nice and he thought we would get along. Then he texted me the address and said he would take care of the details. He texted me the date I could move in. That's all. Jimmy is always busy so I didn't want to call and bug him. In fact, he never answers his phone anyway, but his texts were clear enough."

Elijah raised his brows, crossing his arms in front. "That's it?" He sounded irate. "That's all he told you? You two didn't bother to talk on the phone, to talk about the little details?"

I crossed my arms and held my guarded stance. Why was he mad at me and why did he care that we hadn't talked about details? What little details? There was nothing to discuss. "I don't understand why you're upset. This isn't your place. I mean…I kind of understand because Ellie is your…girlfriend?" My tone ended with a question and the word "girlfriend" came out hesitantly. I knew I was assuming.

Elijah laughed out loud. "Ellie is not my girlfriend. Having a girlfriend is not my thing."

"Oh." It was all I could say at that moment. I guess they were just having sex or maybe it was a one-night stand.

"Look." His tone was soft and low. "After I tell you who Ellie is, you don't have to live here if you don't want to. I can help you find another place."

"Okay," I said, narrowing my eyes on him in confusion. I decide to sit on the sofa while Elijah remained standing.

"Jimmy and I were fraternity brothers. He rushed a year ahead of me. Being roommates, he would bug the hell out of me to rush. I thought I'd give it a try, but I knew right away it wasn't for me, so I got out. For that short amount of time, Seth and I shared Jimmy as big bro. One of the things they did at the frat was call us by girls' names. You get the picture?"

When I didn't respond, he continued. "Ellie is a guy, not a girl."

Then it hit me. I have a guy roommate and seeing Elijah come out of Ellie's room half naked only meant.... "So you're trying to tell me that you're gay?" I shrugged sheepishly, praying that I was right.

Elijah's eyes practically rolled back into his sockets as he slowly dragged his hand down his face in frustration. His tone clearly stated that he was. "Alex, I'm not gay. I'm faaaar from being gay. I love women. I have sex with them…lots of sex."

Holy shit! He did not just say that to me. Blushing from his words, I shot my eyes down to my fingers folding into each other. I couldn't look at him. I didn't want him to see how embarrassed I was. Nobody ever confessed to me that they had lots of sex with women and that they loved it.

"Alex," he called softly with a smooth, seductive tone. At least that is how it rang in my ears.

Slowly gazing up, I jerked back and hit the back part of the sofa when I saw his face far too close to mine. With his knees bent, his hands were planted on either side of the sofa cushion near my thighs. My heart went into overdrive as my eyes outlined his muscular biceps, up to his shoulder, his dark stubbles, and then…bam! My eyes were deadlocked on his.

Frozen in place, I was mesmerized. His piercing brown eyes sucked me in. I wanted to trace his thick brows with the tips of my fingers, down to the perfect base of his nose, around his high

32

Clarity

cheekbones, and across his smooth, kissable lips. I swallowed a nervous gulp, feeling little tremors rush through every part of me. I swear I felt like I was shrinking...dissolving into the sofa...melting into his scent. Though I had expected him to smell like cigarettes being this close to him, he actually smelled nice—minty.

Holding me captive with that look, I knew at that moment he would be my fantasy, the one I would dream about in bed...the bad boy with the tattoos, with that arrogant attitude, the heartbreaker. If only he drove a motorcycle and wore a leather jacket, he would be the complete badass package.

"Yes," I think I answered. I couldn't remember.

Still looking into my eyes, he said slowly, "I...am...Ellie."

"Ellie." I repeated, soaking in his words. "Uh...hi, Ellie," I said in monotone. I didn't know why I said that, but it was all I could think of to say at that moment. What could I say when Ellie turned out to be...well, a he and not a she. "Elijah...Ellie." I understood now. I finally figured out what he was trying to tell me all this time. Why didn't he just come out and say that in the first place? And who was in his room? Then the shock wore off and it hit me hard. Oh My God! I had a hottie for a roommate. This was bad. VERY BAD!

Chapter 5

Elijah

Alex didn't look shocked. In fact, she didn't show much expression at all. The way she said, "Hi, Ellie" was just too damn sexy, even though she sounded more like a robot. She might make a good roommate after all, except I was not prepared for these unwanted feelings—purely physical attraction. She was hot! I had to dismiss that, more so because she was Jimmy's cousin—the main reason she was off limits. Not to mention, she was my roommate now.

If we were going out, I would've wrapped my hands through her long, blonde hair and pulled her in for a kiss. But first, I would have kissed those faint freckles on her nose. Being this close up, they were more apparent. And her beautiful blue eyes just sucked me in, making me feel like I was looking up at the sky.

To top it all off, she looked so adorable with her shorts and pink tank top that clung to every one of her curves. Her lightly tanned skin looked like it would be silky smooth to touch. I was already envisioning myself stroking her. If she continued to dress like that, she was going to be a huge distraction.

As I continued to look at her, her eyes shyly broke away from mine. She pressed her lips together tightly, seemingly uncomfortable by my proximity. I couldn't help it. I loved the way she smelled—lavender and honey. It was intoxicating and I wanted more. I had to move. If I stayed here any longer, I was going to do something really stupid—like kiss her. That would have been a great slap-in-my-face introduction.

I was picking up the soda cans and beer bottles that were on the table when, from the corner of my eye, I saw Alex get up to help. I didn't want her help. After all, she wasn't even at the party, though I'd wished she stayed a little longer. It was a sweet gesture on her part, and it clearly showed what kind of person she was.

I felt horrible for having her see the place in this condition, but it wasn't my fault. I had no idea she was coming. In fact, I had no idea Alex was even a girl. I had to have a serious talk with Jimmy. I doubt he wanted his angelic-looking cousin to be sleeping under the same roof with someone like me.

A part of me wanted to welcome her with open arms, but a part of me was mad as hell. I was going to bring whomever home with me and she would see all of that. Still, why did I care what she thought? We were just roommates.

"Alex," I muttered. Suddenly, her name meant more to me than just a name.

"Yes?" Shoving the last bottle into the trash bag, she looked up at me.

"Please don't call me Ellie. Call me Elijah." My tone was serious, but gentle.

"Sure thing, Ellie." She looked at me with a challenging gaze and a cute smile. I liked the humorous side of her.

I tried to hold my hard stare, but lost it when her eyes grew wide with an apology. Immediately, my heart softened. I wanted to release her worry, so I gave her a huge, impish grin that was way too playful.

Exchanging a flirtatious moment made me nervous and I needed a cigarette. Now that I knew she didn't like the smell of it, I should smoke outside. Shit! Something else I wasn't used to. This was the part of having a new roommate I didn't like. Since Jimmy smoked too, we smoked inside, sometimes. He was the one that got me hooked in the first place.

I was just about to go outside when there was loud knocking—three steady knocks and two short ones following after. It was Seth. I opened the door. Blinded by the sunlight, I covered my eyes.

"Good morning, Ellie. Does she know yet?" Seth brushed past me to enter and stopped in his tracks in front of Alex, who was standing behind me. "Uh…hi, Alex." His greeting sounded a bit off, most likely thinking he should have kept his mouth shut. His eyes were greedily taking in her beauty, and I don't know why that bothered me.

"Hi, Seth," Alex giggled, wearing a huge smile on her face. "I just found out."

"You're up early," Lexy said to me as she entered. "Hey, Alex. How did you sleep last night?"

"Great, thank you. And thanks for offering to take me shopping."

I guess I should've offered, being her roommate and all, but I wasn't thinking straight. Not that I could, since my mode of transportation wasn't conducive for a shopping trip. My motorcycle didn't have much storage.

"Not a problem," Lexy replied, heading to the kitchen. "Yuck! Gross! I guess you guys didn't clean the kitchen yet."

"We just woke up. I mean…I just woke up. You could've helped last night," I stated.

"You know I don't clean. At least this place looks better than last night," Lexy scoffed.

Lexy was attractive and an awesome friend, but she could be a total bitch. Not my type, though she tried to kiss me one time. She played if off like she was buzzed, but I'm not stupid. I loved our friendship too much, so I wasn't going to let her have me for one night. Not to mention, she and Jimmy had dated, and fraternity brothers don't date each other's girls, sisters, or cousins.

"Then I guess Alex didn't have breakfast yet?" Lexy asked, grimacing by the sink. "Eww…it looks like someone puked in here and forgot to rinse."

Shit! I forgot to offer. She must be hungry, but I didn't have much in the fridge or in the cabinet. We were too busy talking about whom Ellie was. "I haven't gone grocery shopping and I didn't know you were coming—" I started to say, but Alex cut me off.

"It's okay. You certainly don't need to feel like you have to take care of me. Lexy was going to take me out today anyway," she smiled. Her smile was too sweet and she looked like an angel. Damn, it felt like she drugged me with just her smile. I was feeling high from it and I couldn't look away. My first impression was that she was a good girl with a good head on her shoulders, but we'll see.

"This is just gross." Seth took the milk carton out of the fridge and examined it. "It's outdated by weeks. Don't you look at the date? You don't even drink milk. Don't tell me this was Jimmy's milk."

Seth snapped me out of it. I knew I was staring at Alex's smile longer than I should have, but I couldn't help myself. Seth was fucking unbelievable, trying to make me look bad. Even if I was a slob, he didn't have to point it out in front of Alex.

"Come on, Alex, you must be starving. I'll take you grocery shopping." Lexy tugged Alex along.

"Wait," Alex halted, causing Lexy to jerk back. "I need to get my purse." After a few minutes, she came back out from her room and stood in front of me. "Elijah, do you think I could have my own set of keys?" she asked timidly. "Unless…." She cleared her throat and looked down at her nails. "…unless you'd rather have me move out. I mean, unless you don't want me as your roommate. I know you thought I was a guy, but obviously, I'm not. I'll understand."

While she was talking away, I reached inside my pocket and took out the spare key I was going to give her if she'd decided to stay after I had the talk with her. Knowing that she did made me happy—I think. "Here."

She peered up, trying to hide the biggest smile I knew she would've given me, but she contained herself. "Thanks."

When she picked up the key, her fingertips brushed against my hand. I felt that touch tingle up my arm and travel throughout my body. Holy shit! What she could do to me with just that simple touch was very unnerving. I wished the situation was different. I could indulge myself, and then let her go.

Seth looked at me strangely while he plopped on the sofa. Did I do something wrong?

"Hey, Alex. Do we get to meet your boyfriend?" Seth asked while looking at me as if to prove a point.

Alex turned to Seth. "I think he's coming next week, and we're just seeing each other."

Of course, she was taken. Someone like her would be snatched up quickly. Did she know "seeing each other" really meant the guy was free to date others while the girl was usually the one that was faithful? I could already imagine this guy in my head—intelligent, loaded, arrogant, then imagining the worst—a dick. Maybe I just wanted him to be one.

"Are you going with them?" I asked Seth. "And don't put your feet on the coffee table."

Seth dropped his feet. "Nope. I just came here to get a good laugh, Ellie."

"You're wonderful, Sally," I teased back.

"Sally?" Alex laughed, and started to walk out the door with Lexy.

"Shut up." Seth threw a pillow at me before turning to Alex. "Call me Seth, Alex."

"Okay, Sally. I mean…Seth."

I enjoyed her humor and so did Seth. My chuckling stopped and my attention went to my bedroom door being opened. Shit! I forgot Heather was in there and even if I had remembered, I didn't think she would come out. She looked baffled to see all of us staring at her. She was wearing the shorts and T-shirt she had on last night.

Clarity

I don't know why, but my eyes shifted to Alex. She looked like the blood had drained out of her, and she was as pale as the wall behind her. I could see it in her face, passing judgment on me, especially since I told her that I didn't have a girlfriend.

Brushing aside my guilty feelings—I don't know why I even felt that way—I casually pushed Lexy and Alex out the door. Just before I closed it, Lexy looked at me and mouthed, "I don't like her. She isn't good for you."

I knew that, but she was attractive and she practically jumped on me, so what was a guy to do? After all, Heather knew I didn't date and didn't care about the "forever." It was mutual.

Chapter 6

Alex

Lexy went to grab a cart while I waited for her by the entrance. Being that it was the weekend, the store was crowded. I didn't mind. I was just glad to get out of the heat as we entered the store together. Glancing at the list I pulled out of my purse, I made a mental note of the items I needed to buy, and shoved the paper back in while Lexy pushed the cart.

"I just want you to know that you can always hang out at my place if things get weird."

"Weird?" I questioned as we headed down the aisle.

"I mean, if there are too many parties or if too many girls wind up hanging out at your place." Her voice trailed off, sounding as if she was uncomfortable.

"Don't worry, Lexy. I can hold my own, but thank you. If I need a place, I'll let you know."

"Elijah has a big heart. He's just been through some rough times." Lexy steered the cart to the right and I followed. "You said you needed bedding, right?"

"Yes, bedding. Like what, if you don't mind me asking?" Ignoring me, she pointed to the left. "Here we are." Looking for something simple, I walked down the aisle. About mid-way, a lavender comforter set caught my eye. "What do you think of this one?" I asked, placing it in the cart.

"Love the color," Lexy smiled, and then placed a hand on my shoulder. "Listen, I didn't mean to ignore your question earlier. It's just that Elijah is like a brother to me. We've been friends since…I don't know if you knew Jimmy and I used to date."

My eyes grew wide from this news. "I never knew. Jimmy and I rarely spoke after he went to college." I suddenly felt bad.

"That's okay. We went out for a couple of months. We both knew that it wasn't going to work out, especially since I started liking someone else…which he didn't know, but anyway…." She brushed that subject off with a roll of her eyes. "So what I was trying to tell you is that I've gotten to know Elijah very well. The four of us, Jimmy, Elijah, Seth, and I became like the four musketeers."

"This way," I interrupted, pushing the cart toward the food section. Recalling the refrigerator being empty, and needing supplies of my own, it was the second thing on my list. I changed the subject. "Elijah said he didn't have a girlfriend, so is he dating the girl that came out of his room? What's her name? Heather?" I was trying not to sound nosy or too interested.

Lexy rested her hand on my arm to get my attention while I was shoving apples into the plastic bag. "Alex, you should think of Elijah as being off limits."

I started laughing. "Oh, no." I shook my head. "Don't get me wrong. I'm asking these questions because he's my roommate and I want to know what to watch out for. I'm already seeing someone, and to tell you the truth, I don't date guys that smoke. I'm sure he's nice and all, and I don't mean to sound like a snob, but…." Thinking of my dad, I stopped.

Lexy snorted and her brown eyes twinkled with amusement. "Well, it doesn't stop other girls from wanting him, even if they have a boyfriend. And yes, I knew. Seth mentioned it. What's his name, and when do I get to meet him? Details." She didn't wait for my reply. "Since Jimmy isn't here to play the big brother role, I'm your big sister now."

I was grateful for what she said. Though she had been nice since we met, hearing her words meant the world to me. I didn't feel so alone.

"His name is Liam," I started to say as we headed to another aisle. "We've been in a relationship for six months. He wants to go to law school. My best friend from home and I would sneak out to parties, and that's how I met him. He was at his friend's house during spring break." I shrugged my shoulders and gave her an innocent smile.

Lexy shook her head. "My parents would have freaked out if they knew the things I did. Anyway…go on."

"Liam is sweet and…." I didn't know what else to say. "He's a senior, like you." Putting boxes of cereal in the cart reminded me I needed to buy milk. "Do you have a boyfriend?" I asked, diverting the attention away from me.

"No, I don't want anything serious right now. Who knows where I'll end up after graduation?"

"I know what you mean." Then I began to think about my relationship. I knew Liam wanted to go to graduate school. How would this affect our relationship? I wondered how serious he was about us? I didn't want to admit it, but Emma was right. He could have driven me to the condo, but at the same time, I'm glad he didn't. He would've seen how crazy it was here. Would he have cared?

"Do you need anything else?" Lexy asked, pulling me out of my thoughts.

Closing my eyes, I tried to remember the things on my list without taking it out. Giving up, I peered down at the items I bought. "I just need to swing by the other section to get some towels, shampoo, and toilet paper."

"I'm sure Elijah has them." Lexy gave me a funny look.

"I'm sure he does, but I don't want to use his stuff."

42

Lexy's eyes shifted to the cart. "Don't tell me you're buying all that food for yourself. You barely ate anything for lunch. If you plan to share with Elijah, then I'm sure he won't have a problem sharing toilet paper."

"Lexy, please. I don't mind giving. I'm just not good at taking," I pouted.

Lexy rolled her eyes playfully. "Great…you're one of *those*." She wheeled the cart as I followed behind, glancing from aisle to aisle to make sure I didn't forget anything. Since I didn't have a car, I didn't want to bother her again if I didn't have to.

"What do you mean, 'one of those'?" I asked, feeling worried. Had I offended her?

"The giver and the pouter. I bet you get away with anything you want when you pout like that with Liam."

"Emma always did tell me I had a killer pout," I laughed.

Seth and Elijah weren't around when we got home. Lexy helped me bring the groceries inside, and we put everything away in the refrigerator and the cabinets. Since the kitchen had been pretty much empty, it was easy to toss them in. Then we went back out in the dreadful heat and brought the rest of the bags into my room. She went out of her way for me today, and the only way I could think of to thank her was to invite her to dinner.

"Wow! I've never seen this refrigerator full…like ever, even when Jimmy was around. Elijah would cook for us once in a while, but he's a guy. They eat out all the time," she laughed lightly, wiping sweat off her forehead.

"I guess all guys are like that," I shrugged and changed the subject as I did the same. "Are you free tomorrow?"

"Depends on what time?" Lexy paced toward the living room. "Since school starts next Monday, I'm going back to work. I work at the food court."

"You do?" That piqued my interest since I needed a job. "Do you know if they're hiring?" I followed behind her with two bottles of water. "Want one?"

43

"Thanks." She took it from my hand and sat on the sofa. "I could ask for you."

"That would be great." Both of us chugged down our water.

Lexy got up and turned on the air conditioner. "It's so freakin' hot. Don't mind me, I practically live here."

I didn't mind it at all. According to everything she had told me, they all acted like family. "Anyway, Lexy, I want to thank you for helping me out and I would like to make dinner for you, Seth, and Elijah too, tomorrow if you can make it."

"Really?" She looked at her watch. "Uh oh, I gotta go. I have an orientation in half an hour for work. We do this every freakin' year. They should cut me some slack. I've been there for the three years. Anyway, sure…thanks. I would love a home-cooked meal." Lexy sounded excited. After grabbing her keys and purse, she paced toward the front door. Just then, the doorknob rattled slightly and Elijah walked in, all sweaty.

His tank top clung to his chest, framing his toned abs; his workout shorts did the same. The vision of him walking in hot and sweaty, the sun beaming perfectly around him as if God had presented a gift at the front door, was a heart fluttering moment. I could tell Lexy was captivated, too. I don't know how long he stood there as I stared at him, but I broke out of my trance when Lexy spoke.

"Hey, Elijah. Did you go to the gym?"

"Lexy, what do you think?" he chuckled as if she should have known. Little did he know that Lexy was possibly tongue twisted from the sight of him.

"Come here and give me a hug." Just as he reached for her, Lexy jerked back.

"Hell no. You're all sweaty."

Elijah cut his laugh short when he saw me. "Hey," he said in monotone. That was all he had to say to me as he walked into the kitchen.

"I gotta go, Ellie," Lexy laughed, halfway out the door.

"Bye, Lexy. And don't call me that." Elijah's good-bye was somewhat muffled from his face being inside the refrigerator.

"By the way, Alex is going to cook dinner for the three of us tomorrow night. I'll let Seth know." Looking over her shoulder to me, she asked, "What time?"

"How about six?"

"Perfect. Seth and I will bring beer and if we have time, we'll get dessert. What do you like?"

"How about ice cream? Any kind except for vanilla, unless you bring some sprinkles or hot fudge syrup."

"Damn girl, you sound just like Ellie. See you tomorrow," she waved and left.

The sound of the front door and the refrigerator door closing simultaneously startled me. They were both loud. Elijah turned to me with a frown.

"Alex, you bought so much. That's fine. I'm not going to tell you what to buy or how much to buy, but you need to save some room for me. Not that I buy much." His tone was loud, but it sure wasn't friendly.

Suddenly, I got nervous and couldn't look at him. What he said was so weird and awkward, as if I would be that selfish and take up all the room. I should have thought about what he would have thought, but never having a roommate, how the hell was I supposed to know? He didn't mention anything about sharing space before I left.

"I'm sorry. I know I bought a lot but I was actually thinking that we could share. I don't expect you to pay me a penny for it. Lexy told me that you can cook, so I thought maybe if there was more food in the refrigerator, you would eat more home-cooked meals instead of eating out so often. It's not good for you." Oh God! I said too much. When I get nervous, I just spit out whatever I'm thinking. It was a bad habit of mine.

The awkward silence made me look up at him. I could tell he didn't like what I had said. Elijah's head tilted and he was narrowing his eyes on me. They flickered, as if he couldn't believe what I had just said. Then he opened his mouth to speak. "Just because Jimmy and I are good friends, you don't have to feel obligated to take care of me. I'm more than capable of taking care

45

of myself and I don't need anyone to tell me what I should or shouldn't eat." Though his tone was soft, it was stone cold.

I couldn't believe his reaction. Anger and embarrassment shot through me. I knew he didn't like me when we first met, but I thought he would at least have the decency to be nice to me since I was his roommate. He had painfully twisted my heart with his words. We were off to a great start! Not what I had in mind when I thought about having a roommate, imagining how much fun Ellie and I would have together. How ironic.

Elijah didn't move, but he looked away. I could have told him off, but it would have made things worse, so I decided to bite my tongue. Though a huge part of me wanted to yell at him for being a jerk, I knew once I said something, I couldn't take it back. I also didn't want to get kicked out. Not having another place to live, I had to stay calm.

I wasn't mad at Jimmy for not letting me know Ellie was really Elijah, but he was going to hear from me…today. Making sure I had a water bottle in my hand because I had no intention of coming out of my room as long as he was here, I stormed to my bedroom. Instead of slamming the door, I closed it softly behind me.

Chapter 7

Elijah

What the fuck did I just say? I couldn't believe the words that flew out of my mouth. Shit! I had practically yelled at her. For what? For doing something so sweet, it actually surprised me. Brushing my hair back with my hand, I contemplated what to do. Do I knock on her door and apologize or do I just forget about it? Either way, I felt like shit, especially when I saw her eyes glisten. Hopefully, those weren't actual tears.

What was wrong with me? I had to keep reminding myself she wasn't like Clara. My ex-girlfriend would manipulate me to get what she wanted. There should be rules against dating older women. I thought I was in love. I don't know if it was our age difference or her being older than me, but she controlled me, like she had a whip in her hand. Of course I didn't realize it at that time, but my friends saw it. They warned me many times, but I didn't listen.

Their warnings didn't even faze me because she had me wrapped around her finger. She told me what to wear, what to eat, and even threatened to break up with me if I didn't stop smoking. I never quit for her, but she thought I did. When I finally realized how ridiculously possessive she was, we had been together for over a year.

Jimmy, Seth, and especially Lexy did not like her at all. I should have seen the reason, but I had been sucked in so deep that I couldn't get out. I swore off relationships the day I broke it off with her. I had no problem just sleeping with a girl, as long as she knew I wasn't going to date her afterward.

Speaking of being sucked in, I had dug myself into a hole and I didn't know how I was going to get out. I was just about to knock on Alex's door when I heard her leave a message to someone…Jimmy, I think. Maybe she was calling the guy she was dating to come pick her up. I also heard her blowing her nose. I hoped she wasn't crying. I'm just guessing, but girls cry easily when they get upset or when they're sad. I could imagine her doing it and that made me feel like crap.

Assuming she wouldn't come out of her room unless I was gone, that is exactly what I decided to do. She would need to come out to eat, so I decided to head to Seth or Lexy's place. I'd make up an excuse as to why I was over there, but they wouldn't believe my lies. They knew me too well. Hell, I'll just go to the school café instead. After I grabbed my wallet, I slammed the front door so she would know I had left.

Alexandria

I had just left a message for Jimmy to call me when I heard the front door slam. It indicated how pissed off he was. Must he slam the door that hard? That fueled my rage even more. Not knowing if Jimmy would call back, I texted him, too.

You didn't tell me Ellie was a guy! Call me!!!

Instead of waiting for a response, I called Emma, and then I called my mom, since that was long overdue.

"Alexandria, you were supposed to call me as soon as you got there," Mom scolded.

"Sorry, Mom," I said, feeling awful for making her worry, but she could have called me, too.

"How are you? How's your roommate?"

"Great," I lied. "Ellie is really nice." I had to tell a fib to cover up what Jimmy had done. Mom would have flipped out and called her sister right away.

"I'm so glad to hear that. William and I will try to come visit when he gets a chance to get away. He's been very busy at his firm."

I heard her words, but I didn't believe them. I could say with certainty that William and Mom would never come to visit me.

"How are your classes?"

Yup, asking me about classes when I had told her I was going a week before school started was an indication she hadn't listened, nor would she be coming anytime soon. I had gotten used to her not being all there after she remarried. I grew up quick and at times, it didn't feel like I had a mother.

"They're fine. It's all great," I tried to sound cheerful. "Anyway, I better go now. I need to get to class." It was a little lie, but I felt bad for saying it when I could have reminded her about school starting next week.

"Call me soon, Sunshine." Her words stung my heart. Was it intentional?

Mom had never called me by that nickname before, only Dad had. What possessed her to call me that? She opened a wound I was trying to close. Being upset already didn't help the situation either, and tears started to pour down my cheeks.

"Talk to you later, Mom." I shut the phone and didn't wait for her response. I didn't want her to know that I was crying. Missing my dad terribly, I hugged my pillow tightly and let the tears flow. I had already felt the loss of what "home" meant when my dad passed away, but I felt it even more so today. I didn't want to pity myself, but I felt utterly alone. It had been a while since I heard the word "sunshine" and it had been a while since I cried so much.

Chapter 8

Alexandria

I woke up to the smell of eggs and ham. Assuming Elijah was cooking breakfast put a smile on my face, but when I thought about how he pissed me off last night, I frowned. Then my heart softened. Talking to Dad last night, as if he were here, helped me clear away the anger. It always did. After I showered, changed and looked presentable, I walked out of my room feeling a little edgy and uncertain.

"You're up. Just in time," Elijah said cheerfully. "I hope you don't mind, but I thought I'd cook us some breakfast."

I almost dropped my jaw. What a turnaround from last night. If this was his way of apologizing, then I happily accept. Actions spoke louder than words anyway. "Thanks," I said with a smile. Since he was pretending we were fine, I decided to do the same.

"I'm going to assume you like eggs and ham since you bought them. I also washed some blueberries," he said, taking the plates to the table.

"Sure. I can eat anything since I didn't have dinner last night." After my words came out, I froze. "I mean…since I wasn't hungry last night. I was so tired, I just slept." Oh God! Here I go with my rambling again. I didn't want him to think that I was so upset over our argument that I didn't eat because of him. Losing my appetite was solely about me missing my dad.

I don't think my words fazed him since he didn't say a word. I was glad it didn't. Instead of sitting down, I went straight for the refrigerator to take the juice carton out. Closing the door, I almost smacked into Elijah.

"Sorry," I said, moving to my left, but he moved to his right and we bumped again.

"Excuse me," Elijah said lightly. "It seems we need a bigger kitchen."

"Sorry," I said, moving to my right without thinking. As he moved to his left, we collided again. It was as if we were an uncoordinated couple doing a tango.

Elijah placed his hands on my shoulders, causing me to stay in place. Looking into his eyes intimidated me, so I quickly shifted my eyes to his arms. They were flexed and nicely toned, and I got a closer looked at his dragon tattoo. When he swung me to his right, I snapped out of it. We finally got it right.

Pouring two glasses of juice, I took them to the table.

"I think we need to talk about a few things," he said casually. Sitting across from me, he handed me a fork.

Instead of replying, I let him know I was ready to listen by gazing into his eyes with a quick smile. He had the most beautiful piercing eyes and long eyelashes. I couldn't stop staring at them as we sat in silence.

Elijah finally cleared his throat and sat up straight while he continuously twisted the fork in his hand. "I think that we should each let the other person know when we ask someone over. Like your boyfriend, for example."

"He's not officially my boyfriend. We're in a relationship, or seeing each, or whatever you call it," I interrupted.

"Okay, whomever you date," he said, taking a bite of his scrambled eggs. "If I decide to bring someone back here, I'll let you know ahead of time so you can decide if you want to go out for a bit or stay in your room."

I quickly swallowed so I could repeat what he'd said, to be sure there were no misunderstandings. "So if I want Liam to come over, I should let you know. Is it okay if he spends the night, since he'll have to drive several hours to see me?"

"Sure, I don't see a problem with that. You don't have to ask for my permission, Alex. I didn't mean it that way." He took a sip of his drink. That only made me thirsty, so I took a sip of mine, too.

I nodded in understanding. "Then, I'm letting you know now that Liam will be coming this Saturday and he'll be spending the night."

Elijah blinked his eyes, as if he needed to register what I had just said. "Sure. I have plans anyway, and I plan to stay out pretty late so that will work out just fine."

"Anything else?"

"When Jimmy and I were roommates, we made sure to wash our own dishes and clean up after ourselves. We also left our school schedule on the fridge, just in case. I also need your cell number, since we don't have a landline. I'll put a small magnetic whiteboard on the fridge. We can communicate that way, too. The rent is due at the end of the month and I'll let you know how much the utilities cost, since we split them. If you decide you want to move out, I need a month's notice, along with the rent. Also, if you didn't know, there's a washer and dryer in the room next to the bathroom. I think that's about it."

"Okay, easy enough. And don't forget, I'm making dinner tonight."

"Alex, you don't have to make dinner just because I made breakfast."

Elijah had the wrong idea. I'm pretty sure he hadn't heard Lexy tell him last night that I was making dinner, since he was too busy being mad at me and his head was stuck in the fridge at the time. "I'm actually making dinner for Lexy to thank her for yesterday, and for all the trouble to come. Since I don't have a car, I'm going to have to ask her for more favors. I've been saving up for my own, so hopefully I'll have one soon."

"Oh." Elijah looked confused or stunned. I wasn't sure which.

After we had finished talking, I thanked him for breakfast, excused myself to check my phone, and then came back. Lexy had told me she would let me know in the morning if there was a job for me, and there was. Feeling elated, I told Elijah that I would clean up since he cooked. He had no problem with that since he didn't like doing the dishes. That worked out just fine.

Thinking back, I'm glad I'd bought more than my share of food. Though I didn't know Elijah that well, he was one of Jimmy's good friends. That alone was enough reason to want to share, to give. Even if he weren't Jimmy's friend, that wouldn't have changed.

Elijah

I hadn't seen Alex at home lately. Since I was in training to work in the Administration Office during the late afternoons, I hadn't really seen her the past couple of days. Not that I was waiting for her or anything. I was just curious as to where she went since she didn't have a car. I should have told her that she could ask me for a ride as well instead of always having to ask Lexy, but I didn't feel like it. Besides, I didn't know how she would feel about riding on my motorcycle. I also didn't want that responsibility hanging over my head.

Not wanting to eat more of Alex's food and feeling like I wanted a burrito, I decided to go to the campus dining hall. I hated long lines, so I went after the lunch rush. Not only that, but knowing that Lexy worked there was an added bonus. Wearing a baseball cap backwards, since I had just gotten out of the shower after working out at the gym, I headed out the door.

"What can I get you, hot stuff?" Lexy giggled.

"How about wrap yourself naked in a tortilla with all the fixings," I winked. Lexy and I were so comfortable with each other that even when I flirted, she took it as a joke.

"One special ultimate Lexy burrito coming up." As I watched her create my special burrito, dumping in chicken, beef, lettuce, and everything that was in front of her, I spotted Nolan, the guy I loathed, and his group.

How could anyone not notice them? They had a way of making heads turn by being loud when they entered. At least they settled down at a table and only one stood in line to order lunch for all five of them. I guess he was the unlucky one who had to pay today. Being in the same room with them was not how I wanted to spend my lunchtime. "Lexy, make that to go, please."

Lexy's vision followed mine. She understood. "Sure. I'll make it to go. I hope those assholes won't stay too long. I can't stand them."

After she slid my tray to the cashier, I flipped open my wallet, ready to pay.

"That'll be seven dollars, please. Would you like something to drink?"

Wait a minute. I knew that sweet voice. With a flash, I peered up to see the most beautiful, angelic smile. Her smile temporarily took me to a happy place, the smile that I couldn't seem to turn away from. "Alex?" She was standing next to another girl. It looked like the girl was training her.

"Hi, Elijah," Alex waved, flashing that innocent smile again. She looked shy and happy at the same time. I think the girl beside her said hello. I wasn't sure. I only had my eyes on Alex, so I just smiled at both of them. I had no idea who the other girl was. Many girls I didn't know said hi to me, so it wasn't anything new.

"You work here? When did you start?"

"Two days ago. I wrote it on the whiteboard. I guess you didn't see it."

She just answered my question about her whereabouts. "Oh, yeah…the whiteboard." I arched my brows and nodded in a way of apologizing. I'm an idiot. I told her the purpose of the whiteboard and I dismissed it. "I must have missed it. Sorry about that. I'll make sure to check it daily. It's been a while since I had a roommate."

"That's okay," she shrugged sheepishly. "Lexy got me the job."

"I'm sure they hired you because of who you are." I wasn't sure if that was the right thing to say when I saw her tilt her head sideways, looking baffled. After I paid, I decided to stick around so I found the table furthest from Nolan. Bringing my cap forward, I tilted it lower, hoping to become invisible so I could enjoy my burrito, but that didn't last very long.

From the corner of my eye, I spotted Alex walking around with a tray in her hand. She wore longer shorts than what I was used to seeing her in, and a fitted T-shirt that conformed to the curves of her breasts. She was picking up the trash from the tables that the lazy people didn't throw away. That reminded me of when she told me that she collected trash and it made me laugh.

Because she was new, she got to be the gopher. Poor Alex. It was one of the drawbacks of working in the school's dining hall. I casually observed her from a distance and ate my lunch. I didn't think much of it until she stood in front of Nolan's table. That got my attention big time.

"Are you finished with your drinks?" Alex asked.

"You must be new. What's your name sweetheart?" Nolan's smile was too big. I wanted to erase the perverted expression that was smeared on his face.

"Alexandria," she said quickly. "If those are trash, please throw them away, thank you." Then she started to walk away. Alex suddenly swung around from Nolan's grip, causing me to stand up. I had an urge to protect my roommate, who had somehow become my responsibility now. I didn't want another confrontation with Nolan, but I swore that if he did anything to piss me off, I was going to break one of his bones.

"Don't walk away, Alexandria." He took the tray she was holding out of her hand, placed it on the table, and pulled her tightly to his chest.

Seeing Lexy was ready to make her move, I sat back down so I wouldn't make a scene. It was better to be scolded by the manager rather than by me. At least he would listen to her.

"What do you want?" Alex huffed. I couldn't tell if she was afraid.

Nolan loosened his grip. "How about you and I go out?"

"Sorry, but I'm taken." Alex pushed his hands off her.

"Do you know who I am? Let me start over. My name is Nolan Smith, and these are my friends." He didn't ask her to shake his hand; he just shook hers.

"It's nice to meet you and your friends, Nolan, but I need to get back to work."

I liked how she played it off cool, not affected by him at all.

"Do you know how many girls want to go out with me? No, let me rephrase that. Do you know how many girls want to sleep with me?"

Alex gawked at him, most likely unbelieving what she heard from this arrogant bastard. "That's nice, Nolan, but like I said before. I'm already taken."

"And I don't take no for an answer," he huffed, sitting back down on his chair. "Why don't you give me a chance? I promise you, you'll be leaving your boyfriend after I show you the best time of your life."

"And I don't say yes after I say no. I really don't care who you are, but no means no. And please get your hand off my ass." Alex meant business by the sound of her voice and her facial expression. Her cheeks were pinched in and her lips protruded out.

Alex had the finest ass I'd laid eyes on, and to see it being groped by Nolan infused me with anger. I was just about to go over, unable to handle seeing his hands on her like that, but I was beyond stunned to hear what she said and did next.

"If you don't stop squeezing my ass like you're milking a cow, I'm going to have to cool you down."

His group of friends started to laugh and Nolan thought it was funny too, until Alex made her move. Grabbing a cup off the tray, she dumped soda over his head. "Oops, I'm so sorry. Clumsy me."

It was epic! I had to give her credit for being so brave, doing what she did. Grabbing her tray, she paced back to her station with that sexy catwalk, and the "I don't care what you think of me" attitude in her stride. Lexy's mouth dropped before she busted out with laughter.

Nolan stood up as if he'd been bitten on his ass, liquid dripping down his head. It mostly soaked into his T-shirt, and what hadn't pooled around his feet. When he curled his fingers into a tight fist, I got up too, ready to step in. Surrounded by students, I knew he wouldn't dare hit her, but regardless, Nolan was unpredictable.

Thankfully, he just growled and wiped himself with the napkins his friends gave him. "What are you looking at?" he shouted to the students at the nearby tables, and then sat back down. Everyone around cowardly turned away. Lexy, on the other hand, was smiling behind the counter. As of right now, Alex was on my best friend list. After I let out a hearty laugh, I threw my trash away, turned my cap back the way it was, and headed toward Nolan's table.

"Just get out of the shower, Nolan?"

Nolan pushed back his chair so fast that it slid across the floor. Putting his face right in front of mine, he gritted his teeth. "I hope I get to race you next time, pretty boy. I'm going to break your record."

"Yeah, that's what they all say. As far as the record book shows, I'm still number one. And next time I see you put your hands on Alex, I'll break every one of your fingers."

It took all four of his friends to stop him from coming after me. As he cursed and flailed his arms, I casually strutted toward the door. Just before I exited, knowing his eyes were still on me fuming with rage, I flipped him my favorite finger. I'm almost certain God created the middle finger longer on purpose, for assholes like him.

Chapter 9

Alexandria

I couldn't believe I had just dumped soda on that jerk. I was so nervous and annoyed that he had his hand on my ass. I didn't know what else to do. It was the first time I had ever been assaulted like that. Thank God I didn't slap him or I'm sure I would've been fired.

When I saw Elijah stand up out of the corner of my eye, I felt a sense of courage. Knowing he would come to my rescue like that made my heart flutter. He looked so damn good in his jeans, T-shirt, and baseball cap. It took some willpower to concentrate on what I was doing, even though I was just picking up trash.

Guilty as charged, I watched him walk away. I had thought he was leaving, since he told Lexy he wanted his order to go. I wondered what changed his mind. When I saw him confront Nolan face-to-face about something, I was curious about that, too.

"I can't believe you dumped soda on Nolan," Tracy, the girl who was training me, exclaimed.

"I can't either." I shook my head.

"And how do you know Elijah? Aren't you a freshman? He was talking to you like he knew you."

"Oh." I didn't know why I suddenly felt embarrassed. "It's kind of a long story, but he's my roommate."

Tracy's eyes popped open, and at the same time, she practically dropped her mouth to the floor. "Shut up. No way. Are you kidding?"

I didn't know what to make of what she was saying. Why would I lie about it? "Elijah's old roommate Jimmy is my cousin and when he left, I took his room."

"Jimmy's your cousin? Why didn't you tell me? He's one of the coolest guys I've met. I was actually sad to see him graduate. I was happy for him, of course. But wow…Elijah is your roommate. How the hell do you sleep at night knowing one of the hottest guys on campus is possibly naked in the next room?" she snorted.

I never thought about what she said, but now it was on my mind. Crap! I was just thinking about Liam this morning and now Elijah's naked body was filling my head.

"I sleep fine," I shrugged, turning toward the next customer.

"Lexy, I don't think I want to go. Thanks for inviting me, but I don't even have a broom and I've never played broom hockey before," I laughed softly.

"Don't laugh. It's a lot of fun. It's a great way to exercise and a great way to meet guys," she informed, looking at her watch. She pulled out a mirror from her purse and glided gloss on her lips. "Plus, the frat boys always bring extras." She smacked her lips and stuffed everything back in her purse, looking up at me for a response.

"Maybe I'll go with you and just watch first instead. And did you say frat boys?"

"Yes I did, but it's not a fraternity function so don't worry. We wouldn't be invited if it were. And you should see Elijah. He's really good."

I bet he is. He took care of himself unlike most guys I knew. He was double the size of Liam. Since school hadn't started yet and I had nothing better to do, I decided to go.

"I need to text my friend, Emma, and Liam. By the way, Liam will be here sometime tomorrow. He didn't give me a specific time, but maybe you'll get to meet him," I said, walking to my room. "I'll be right out. I left my phone in my room."

"Alex, don't forget to bring a sweater and you need to put on your tennis shoes."

"Why?" I asked, sticking my head out from my bedroom, looking down at my flip-flops.

"We don't use skates. We wear tennis shoes."

"Okay, and why is the game so late?"

"It's cheaper, plus we get the whole ice rink to ourselves."

The music blasted as soon as Lexy opened the door, and the change in temperature from hot to cold made me shiver. Slipping my arms through the sleeves of the sweater, I followed right behind her. I didn't know why, but having so many eyes checking me out made me uncomfortable, especially since I didn't know most of the guys.

"Hey, Lexy, Alex," Seth greeted, giving us each a hug. "Everyone, this is Alex, and you know Lexy."

"Hi," they said. A group of guys surrounded Lexy and me, mostly wanting to shake my hand since they already knew Lexy. I recognized Dean.

"Alex, I didn't know you played broom hockey," Dean said excitedly.

"I actually don't. Lexy talked me into coming. I'm just going to watch. I don't have a broom." I glanced around for Elijah, trying not to make it obvious I was looking for someone.

"Well, I'm glad you're here. We have plenty of sticks."

"Want a long one or a short one?" one of his friends asked.

"Alex, I can give you mine. It's long, thick, and hard," Seth said, laughing.

"Yours has no endurance," one of his friends joked and I could hear the laughing comments from his other friends.

"Yours is the smallest," Seth fired back. "And it's been handled way too much by your own hands."

Everyone started to laugh again. Oh God! Lexy and I looked at each other and shook our heads in laughter. Why did guys have such perverted minds and why did they like to compare the size of their dicks?

"Don't touch any of theirs. They're not good enough for you," a guy said in a deep, sexy tone that demanded my attention, making me feel those guilty tingles I didn't want to have. When I turned, my heart took a nosedive and this cool rink just got hot. Elijah was standing before me and the room became silent.

"Let's see what you've got," he challenged, handing me a broom.

"Thanks, but I don't know how to play."

"There's nothing to it if you know how to play hockey. Shoot the puck into the goal."

After Lexy and I put our purses together into one locker, the teams were picked, and we headed onto the ice. Lexy and I were on opposite teams, and somehow I ended up on Elijah's.

I held onto the rail and slowly made my way onto the ice. It was smooth and not as slippery as if you were on skates, but I almost fell a couple of times. It had been a while since I had been on the ice, but I got used to it very quickly. It almost felt like I was gliding on air, but cool underneath my shoes. As I carefully walked across the rink to my team, mist escaped my mouth with each breath I took.

Elijah gave me a red bandana to wrap around my broom. This was a way to distinguish the teams. I was more than happy about this, especially since I didn't know most of the players.

"Stand behind me, Alex," Elijah demanded. "They can get pretty rough. The losers pay the rental fee and believe me, no one wants to pay."

I saw what Elijah meant. When the whistle blew to start the game, everyone became aggressive all of sudden, putting on a different face. Eyes were fierce and focused, and lips were pressed into a thin, hard line. Winning was the one thing on all their minds, and they were going to make that goal one way or another. The tightly gripped broom was no longer a household item. It became a weapon. Watching the guys sweep the broom across the ice as if their lives depended on it, made me laugh hard.

I looked for Lexy. She was determined as well. I could tell she'd played many times before, just from the way she moved across the ice and the way she handled her broom like a pro. She wasn't a female sticking out like a sore thumb like I was. I stayed back to observe, to scope out the ones to fear.

It happened in blink of an eye; the other team stole the puck from us. The puck was passed to one of my team members, but Seth stole it to score. Their team cheered and gave high fives to each other, while our team frowned and cursed. Quickly, we all met at the center to start the game again.

Elijah turned to me. "Alex, stay close to me."

I didn't understand why he felt the need to protect me. Sure, this was my first time, but I could hold my own. I didn't listen to Elijah, of course. He didn't know I had a competitive side to me, too. As the opponent came toward us, I had a couple of advantages. I was a female and I was smaller. I may have never played this game before, but I knew what needed to be done.

I lagged behind and observed who the more aggressive ones were and who I could take advantage of—the ones that would go soft on me because of my gender. And there was my first victim.

Dean tried to maneuver around me, but lost concentration when I gave him a seductive smile. I ducked low, placed my broom in the perfect position, and stole the puck from him. I wished I could have framed the look on his face.

"What the fuck!" he said out loud, looking dumbfounded.

His teammates didn't look or sound happy when they shouted at him—*Get your mind in the game. Dean got pussy whipped.* Poor Dean! Seeing the opposite team come at me all at once, I screamed as my teammates shouted at me to pass the puck to them. Not knowing who to pass it to, I hesitated, but when I heard Elijah's voice and saw him running toward me, I passed it to him fast and hard.

With a slam from the bristles of his broom, he dead-stopped the puck and dashed away. Swiftly moving the broom from side to side, his body was hard at work, and so was his fine ass. It was hard not to look. Flexing his muscles, he was smooth and graceful, as if his body was one with the ice. I now understood what Lexy meant when she said he was really good. I couldn't peel my eyes off him. With a quick sideways turn, dodging a broom that was meant to trip him, he scored.

Elijah

"Score," I hollered, giving high fives to my friends around me. Feeling the rush and the excitement, I looked for Alex. Without thinking, I ran to her and swung her around. "That was a perfect pass for a newbie," I said out of breath, giving her a kiss on the cheek. That kiss was so spontaneous that I was shocked at myself. Oh hell. It was an innocent kiss. I'm sure she's had guys kiss her cheeks many times before.

When I placed her down, her cheeks flushed. I couldn't tell if it was because she was cold or…was it from my kiss?

"That was awesome, Ellie," she nudged me.

Before I could remind her not to call me by that name, I heard someone yell, "Watch out!" Too busy paying attention to Alex, I didn't realize the game had started again. Next thing I knew a puck was headed our way. Someone had hit it way too high. Out of instinct, I grabbed Alex. I think she was trying to get me out of the way, too. We were both pulling on each other, but in opposite directions. We both lost traction and I fell on top of her.

On our way down, I managed to support her head and bent my knees in an effort not to crush her. That didn't feel good to my knees or my hands at all. Since Alex didn't move a muscle, I didn't know how much of my weight landed on her or if she was hurt. All I felt now was my upper body touching hers.

"Alex, you okay? Did I hurt you?" I murmured, looking at her.

She didn't answer. Instead, her shocked eyes stared back at me. Those angelic blue eyes sucked me in so deep; I became lost in them. I was hypnotized, spellbound by her beauty and the eyes that held so much mystery, making me want to get to know her.

When her eyes shifted to my lips, I could feel my dick straining against my pants. Cool, small breaths escaped her mouth into mine, and I swallowed them up—every single breath. Her body entangled in my arms, her breath became ragged. Her chest rose and fell quickly, and mine was doing the same. I'd like to think I was the cause of her rapid breathing. In that moment, I lost all sense of time…space…and reality.

I don't know how long we were connected like that, but I almost lost my self-control when my lips headed towards hers as if they had a mind of their own. Fuck! I wanted to kiss her. We were in another world and everyone around us disappeared, but then, a part of my conscience reminded me that she was off limits. God I really hated that voice right now!

Thank goodness Seth broke our link. "You guys okay? And would you stop molesting her on the ice?"

I rolled my eyes at him. "Shut up and help me. I hurt my knees," I said out loud, so the crowd around us could hear me. I had to make an excuse as to why I stayed on top of her so long when I could have gotten up.

Seth rolled me over, and Lexy helped Alex up. Sprawled on my back, I took in the cold. No amount of ice would have cooled down the heated feeling I was trying so hard to avoid with her. I had even been trying to stay away from our place as long as I could, so I didn't have to be around her too much. Finally standing up, I rubbed and stretched my arms. The numbness disappeared as I walked out of the rink.

I didn't understand this hold she had on me. I didn't like it one bit. Not only was she seeing someone, but I didn't want to have a relationship; she was making me so confused. A part of me felt like I wasn't good enough for her. And a huge part of this was that she was Jimmy's cousin. If I screwed up, it would just be too weird for our friendship, for all of us.

"I'm sorry, Elijah, are you okay?" Alex sat next to me on the sideline bench. She was sorry for something she didn't do. Another indication she had a kind heart.

"Alex, I'm fine. Go back to the game. Our team needs you," I said sternly. Actually, I didn't want her to sit next to me. I was having a hard time controlling myself with her being so close. I didn't want to get used to the comfort she brought me, so I wasn't going to feel guilty for telling this little lie.

"Should I get some ice?"

I needed to calm my tone. "I just need a minute."

"They're taking a break, so I'm going to get some hot cocoa. Do you want one?"

"No, thanks." I was short and to the point.

I was proud of myself for not looking at her ass when she walked away. Now that was good self-control, but it didn't last long. When Dean wrapped his arms around her, like she belonged to him, I stood up. So much for my hurt knees. A few of the other guys tried to get their dirty paws on her too, but when I stood nearby, they scurried away.

"You better now?" Seth laughed.

What was so funny? "Yeah, I'm better." I gave him an evil eye. "Next time, make sure we're all in our starter positions before we continue."

"Looks like you didn't mind your position."

"What? Shut up. I hurt my knees."

"Whatever you say. Just remember, she's your roommate and she's not one of your one-night stands."

"Don't worry. She's seeing someone."

Seth's brows did a quick lift. I'm not sure if he believed me, and I don't know why. I hadn't made a move on her.

I was glad Alex didn't hear our conversation. She was in line with Lexy. When she turned, our eyes locked, but she turned away quickly, flashing a coy smile.

After our little break, we got back into the game. Alex was a trooper. She handled herself very well. I liked that little firecracker inside of her. I could tell she was a competitor and took on challenges well. Lucky for our team, we won the game.

Chapter 10

Alexandria

Whiteboard:
Stocked up the fridge
since you bought last time.
-E

After I had a short talk with mom, I called Emma. It had only been a week, but we could only talk at night since she worked fulltime. Sometimes our schedules didn't match up, so our texts were delayed. Since she was off today, I couldn't wait to hear her voice.

"Emma," I squealed.

"Alex. It's so good to hear your voice. How's everything?"

"School starts on Monday so I'm a bit nervous, but other than that, I'm having fun with my new friends."

"I'm so happy for you. So how's the roommate thing going? Is she nice? You don't like her better than me, do ya?"

I hadn't told Emma about whom Ellie really was and decided to keep it that way for now. "Of course not," I laughed aloud.

Emma told me about the new guy she was dating, and that she would try to visit me soon. After I hung up, tears blurred my vision. When I thought about Emma, I thought about home and my dad.

Feeling my stomach grumble with hunger, I walked into the kitchen. When I opened the refrigerator, I saw how full it was. Elijah had gone grocery shopping this morning. Then I saw the whiteboard and smiled. Sleeping late, I hadn't noticed it until now. I guess he figured that since I stocked it up the last time, he should do it this time around. I was grateful, especially with not having a car.

After I had something to drink, I did laundry, got my backpack ready for my first day of school, and called Liam. He hadn't texted me to let me know what time he would be here. It had been more than a week since I saw him last, and I realized that the less I saw him, the more I thought about just ending it with him. This long distance relationship wasn't working out too well. Though he begged to differ before I left, he knew I was going off to college. I guess time will tell.

Since I had nowhere to go and nothing to do, I decided to read my textbook and get a head start. Next thing I knew, the boring textbook made me fall asleep. I woke up to my phone ringing.

"Liam?" I sounded groggily.

"Hey, Baby. You sound sleepy. Did you just get up from a nap?"

"Kind of. When are you coming? I've been waiting for you all day."

"I'm so sorry. I got tied up, but I'll be there soon. Listen, I'll be bringing a few friends so I don't have room in the car for you. Do you think you could meet me at the Campus Karaoke? I have a reservation under my name at eight. I should be there in couple of hours."

"At eight?" I huffed. "I waited for you all day. You know I don't like going to those things."

"Come on, Baby. Just do this for me. It's my friend's birthday. I'll make it up to you."

What could I say after that? I was just glad I didn't start saying things I would regret. "Fine." My tone became tender. "I know where it is. It's not that far. I'll probably be there first."

"Thanks for understanding. I'll see you there."

I was just about to ask him if he was going to spend the night, but he hung up first. I don't know why I was annoyed, other than the fact that we were supposed to have some quality time together. If I knew ahead of time, I would have told him not to come and I would have gone out with Lexy instead.

I didn't want to be the type of girl that had to have the guy come pick her up, but at the same time, I wondered how much he actually missed me.

Elijah hadn't come home all day. Not that he needed to tell me where he was, I was just curious. All I knew was that he went to the gym on a daily basis, but nothing more. I couldn't help but wonder if he had a job or where he went when he wasn't home. I had to stop being a nosy roommate.

Opening the door, the hostess greeted me, and then took me to the reserved seats. It wasn't a secluded setting as it had been with my dad before, where we had a private room and nobody could hear us sing. This was a restaurant with a bar and a stage in the center.

It didn't look crowded, but after ten minutes, people started walking in, including one particular crowd I hadn't expected—Elijah, Seth, Lexy, and some members of the broom hockey team. Great! I sunk down as low as I could, looking at my watch. It was eight thirty and Liam was already thirty minutes late. He was going to hear it from me.

Thank goodness they headed to the opposite side, but sooner or later, they would notice me. Not that it was a bad thing, but having them see me alone would make Liam look bad. When I sat up, I saw another crowd of girls walk in. Heather and her friends headed toward Elijah's table. I don't know why, but I felt a little sting of jealousy.

"Alex?"

I turned at the calling of my name. "Lexy, hi," I greeted, feeling guilty for trying to dodge her.

"I didn't know you were coming here." She sat down and gave me sideways hug.

"I didn't know, either. Liam told me to meet him here at eight."

"He told you to meet him here? Why didn't he pick you up?" She arched her brows in disapproval, and looked at her watch. "He's late."

My tongue had slipped and I said too much. I didn't mean to make Liam look bad. "It's a long drive and he's bringing his friends," I explained, trying to make it seem like it was no big deal.

"We're sitting on the other side if you want to come join us later. I was passing by to use the restroom and saw you sitting here."

"Thanks, I'm sure he'll be here any minute. When he does, I'll make sure to introduce you to him."

"You better," Lexy smiled and left.

Ten more minutes passed as I stared at my watch. Singers entertained me on the stage. They were calming me down from the anger that was building up toward Liam for being so freakin' late.

How brave that girl was, to sing up there in front of all these strangers. I guess she felt confident since her friend sang with her. Watching them only brought sadness to my heart. My dad and I used to sing together all the time and every time those memories came crashing through, it pained me deeply. I tried to push them away and forget.

Hearing lots of laughter and being curious, I had to peek. Leaning my back against the wall, hoping not to be noticed, I saw Elijah and his friends surrounded by the group of girls that walked in earlier.

"Come on, Elijah. Sing for us. I'll do anything you ask." Heather's tone was flirty and her hand glided on Elijah's biceps, then over his dragon tattoo.

I could see Lexy rolling her eyes. She was sitting in between Seth and Dean. When Heather's hand slithered lower on his chest, I had seen enough. I didn't know what was wrong with me. Sure, Elijah was good-looking, but he was not the type of guy I would go out with or would even be attracted to. Knowing I should go back just in case Liam was here, I was about to turn when I flushed with heat big time, hearing Seth call my name.

"Alex, I didn't know you were coming."

Having no choice, I strode to their table. "Hi," I waved. Without thought, my eyes went straight to Elijah. He didn't even acknowledge me. I thought I saw his lips curl a little, but that was it. Maybe he was annoyed to see his roommate here. Maybe that was the reason I hadn't seen him as often lately. I could understand. He was used to having a place all to himself, and now he had to see me almost every day. Maybe I needed to find another place, preferably with a girl roommate this time.

"Actually, I'm waiting for Liam. He'll be here soon," I said quickly before one of them gave me an invitation to stay.

"You're Alex, Elijah's roommate and Liam is your boyfriend," Heather announced, looking way too happy that I had one.

"He's really not my boyfriend." I wanted to stress that to burst her wicked bubble.

"Oh," she replied, looking slightly baffled.

Not wanting to talk to her any longer, I shifted my attention to Lexy. She rolled her eyes again from Heather's remark, and then looked at her watch, but she didn't say a word. I knew why. Liam was almost an hour late.

"Well," I said, trying to give her a smile, but it wouldn't come. I was not good at faking it. "I should get going. Liam should be here any minute."

"Cool," Seth nodded. "Bring him over."

I shifted my eyes when I saw Elijah sit up straight. He seemed tense.

"He's coming with his friends so…anyway…I better go. Bye." With the last word, I speedily got out of there.

Elijah

Seeing Alex after so many days made my heart thump faster. Not liking the feeling she caused every time I saw her, I tried to ignore her by staying away from our place. The other guys around me sure didn't have that problem. I cringed seeing them undressing her with their eyes.

I couldn't blame them though. She wore a tight short sundress that flared out to show her sexy legs. It clung around her breasts, showing a little bit of cleavage, which the guys were salivating over. And how could anyone resist her sweet voice and the beautiful smile that could make a guy do just about anything for her?

If she asked for a glass of water, the guys would have jumped over the table and each other just to be the first one to hand it to her. She had no idea the effect she had; that was the cutest thing. Trying to stay away wasn't working. Maybe I needed to get used to her. At that moment, I decided to try a different approach. Perhaps I needed to be around her more to get used to her presence.

Heather seemed jealous of Alex and she should be. If Heather were more like Alex, she and I could be a possibility. Who knew?

I don't know what got into me. I hadn't planned to sing, but I wanted to impress Alex, especially since the guy she was seeing was going to be here.

I don't know why everyone kept saying her boyfriend. There is a big distinction between seeing someone and being a couple. Seeing someone meant that she was open. Not that I was going to ask her out. She was off limits. It was one of the reasons why nobody dared to make a move on her.

Knowing Alex would hear me sing, I nudged Heather to scoot over so I could get out of the booth.

"Woohoo, Elijah is going to sing," the girls shouted, clapping.

I turned around and gave them a wink, and then a round of whistling resonated through the room. Our group was loud. Everyone in the restaurant could hear us. At this point, I didn't care. I just wanted Alex to hear me.

I picked up the mic and cleared my throat after punching in the numbers for my song choice. I had the perfect song in mind, Mr. Big, "To Be With You." When the melody started, my friends were screaming. I didn't know why, but my heart pounded so fast against my chest. I was nervous. Hell, I was never nervous. Alex made me nervous. Then I got cocky. It was a way to help me calm my nerves. "Here's to all the ladies in the house," I said into the mic. More screams exploded again.

As I sang my heart out, it suddenly took a flip when I saw Alex. She was watching, but she was trying to hide that she was. Her heavenly big blue eyes were wide, glistening against the light above her. I could tell by the look on her face that she was captivated. Suddenly, my gaze locked on hers, and I was singing to her.

As I continued to sing, I saw a dark gray T-shirt approach her from the corner of my eye. Next thing I knew, she had turned away. My heart twisted, but not in a good way as I watched Liam kiss her on her lips. He introduced her to his group of friends, but I could tell she was not interested. Just before she disappeared out of my sight, she looked over her shoulder and gave me a long, approving smile.

Chapter 11

Alexandria

Wow! What a voice. I was completely blown away. His voice vibrated through every nerve in my body, giving me a sense of pleasure and peace. He not only touched my heart, he touched my soul, if that were even possible. I had chills running through every fiber of my being. I was totally lost, captivated, and I heard nothing but his sexy voice. To top it off, he happened to sing one of my favorite songs.

My heart gave no mercy as it pounded against my chest. I felt dizzy and needed air, but Liam gave me what I needed when he suddenly appeared, wrapping his arms around me, holding me steady. It helped somewhat. What I really needed was a good slap in the face to wake me up and to help me snap out of Elijah's spell. Looking over my shoulder one last time, my eyes caught his and I pretended he was singing only to me.

After apologizing a few times, Liam introduced me to his friends. We sat at the table and ordered dinner. I smiled and laughed

74

on cue, but my mind was somewhere else. When I noted the redhead across from Liam that couldn't keep her eyes off of him, I didn't care. I'd already forgotten her name. Was that normal? Should I care that she was flirting with him in front of me when she knew I was seeing him?

Since dinner was taking so long, everyone kept ordering beer. In order to pass the time, Liam had a stupid idea. He wanted me to sing. The only time he heard me sing was at my father's funeral, but that was it. He kept persisting and dragged me to the stage.

Knowing Liam didn't have a great singing voice, I figured I'd choose a safe, easy song, and it was another of my favorites.

After I punched in the number to "Follow Me" by Uncle Kracker, Liam handed me the mic. The music started and Liam sang. He was unable to follow the speed. Just so he wouldn't make a total fool of himself, I stepped up.

"Way to go, Alex," I heard Lexy shout. I kept looking at the words since I was not at all comfortable seeing strangers watching me sing. I hadn't realized Elijah and his friends had gathered close by. Not only was I embarrassed, I was infused with blistering heat from head to toe. I had no choice but to finish, but when I saw Elijah's huge grin, I couldn't help but smile, too.

Elijah looked cool and collected leaning against the wall. With his arms crossed, he stared back at me, making me shyly turn away. Seeing him looking so dreamy made me forget about Liam. If only Elijah didn't smoke. If only he wasn't my roommate. If only he didn't frighten me, though I didn't know why he did.

"My Baby is awesome," Liam shouted, twirling me around, leading me back to his friends after the song ended. Then the clapping died down.

I'm not sure what happened, but I realized this was the first time I sang karaoke without my dad. Singing in front of my friends was not dreadful. It was actually kinda fun. My dad would have been proud.

As we ate dinner, more people sang. Hearing some oldies that my dad and I used to sing made me teary-eyed. I couldn't help it. I had to excuse myself to the restroom a couple of times. It had only been three months since he passed away. Was this normal?

When I came back, Lexy was standing by the table. She had already been introduced to everyone. She was so sweet and friendly. It was no wonder everyone got along with her. Lexy had a personality that everyone clicked with.

"Alex." Lexy gave me a tight squeeze. "Who knew? You've been hiding your talent. I'm glad Liam dragged you to the stage."

"I'm okay," I said shyly. I wasn't used to the compliments.

"This was nothing. You should've heard her sing at her father's funeral," he gushed.

Lexy looked at me with a questioning look, but she knew better than to ask. I'm sure she saw the surprise and sadness in my eyes. She was good at reading people. I hadn't told any of my new friends about my father's death, but now Liam just opened his mouth. I was pretty sure it was the alcohol that was making him so insensitive.

"Anyway, I was on my way to the restroom so I'll talk to you all later." Lexy didn't look at me before she headed away.

My dad told me many times when I was young that you could never know how another person felt unless you walked in that person's shoes. He was right, of course. Liam never lost anyone he loved. He had no idea what I was feeling right now. It was through his actions and words that I knew this.

Liam started talking and laughing with his friends while he placed his arms around me. It was getting close to midnight. I was not only feeling a little tipsy since I rarely drank, but I was also emotionally tired.

Liam bringing up the funeral and hearing songs my dad and I used to sing together was not agreeing with my stomach. The ache in my heart started to twist deeper and I knew I needed to get out of here. The air suddenly became thick and heavy and I couldn't breathe. I held it together as long as I could, but when I heard the last words my dad sang to me from his hospital bed being sung by one of Elijah's group of friends, I completely lost it. Why did it have to be that song, out of the hundreds of songs on the list?

Excusing myself, I started to run toward the restroom, but since I hadn't seen Lexy come out yet, I ran the other way as tears streamed down my face. I didn't want her to see me like this. Pushing the exit door, I ran outside. I bawled like a baby as I tucked my arms around my waist to hold myself together.

It hadn't been that long since I cried like this. The last time was when I dreamt about my dad. Gasping for air, tears filled my hands and I was unable to stop them from flowing. Feeling my body tremble, I reached for something to lean on, but there was nothing there.

Feeling weak in the knees and unable to control my crying, I sat on the step. The ache was so deep that it felt like someone had ripped my heart out. So much pain poured through my tears that my eyes were puffy and my throat was dry.

As the memories of my dad came crashing through, all I could do was feel sorry for myself as I gasped for more air. Why? Why did it have to be my dad? When I felt a warm body next to mine, I managed to calm down somewhat.

Feeling a strong arm wrap around me, I threw myself on Liam's lap. He had no idea how happy he'd made me feel that he was comforting me. I felt like he really understood my pain for the first time. He had always told me to stop crying, but he didn't tonight. Molding into every space, every curve, every muscle of him, I pressed into him. He felt so good, so strong, so right, and I let myself go.

"I miss him so much," I cried, starting to realize he felt bigger than before.

"Shhh…it's okay. Let it all out," he whispered, caressing my hair. "I know your pain."

I freaked out when I realized it wasn't Liam. I pulled away to see his face. "Elijah?" My lips quivered as tears blurred my vision. I was surprised to see him.

"What happened?" he asked, wiping my tears away. There was so much tenderness and care in his words that it made me speechless.

I was just about to tell him when the door thrashed opened. Liam set his eyes on us and they only grew wide with anger. He was in shock. "What the hell?"

Elijah lifted me up and placed me down. I could see how this would look in Liam's eyes.

"Don't read too much into this. She needed a shoulder to cry on," Elijah explained.

"Whatever. Fuck you," he said angrily. Liam grabbed my arm and yanked me inside.

Chapter 12

Elijah

Seeing Alex rush out of the back exit door like she was on fire, I debated whether to go after her. I had no idea what Liam had said to her or what he had done, but she was crying. Not knowing what to do, I followed her out, but kept my distance. I wasn't sure if I should approach her, but when I heard that gut-wrenching cry coming from her, I had to go to her.

Alex was slumped over crying on the steps, which made my heart sank. I sat next to her and draped my arm around her shoulders to give her comfort, but unexpectedly she wrapped her whole body into mine tightly. Not even a slip of paper could fit between us. I wasn't sure if she knew it was me. She might've thought I was Liam.

I didn't mean for this to happen, but I couldn't help embracing her back. It was the first time we held each other like that. It felt so good, so soothing. Her hug was like my morphine, physically taking away my pain. At that point, I wasn't sure who was actually comforting whom. One thing for sure, a part of me pushed my pain aside for her. Now the smell of her and the feel of her body would be imprinted in my mind. Crap!

When Alex finally realized it was someone else, she backed away somewhat. Her breasts ended up being at my eye level. Shit! It was hard not to take in the view, let alone try to control my urge to stick my tongue between her breasts. She was so fucking beautiful. Thank God we were interrupted before I did something stupid.

Liam practically broke down the door, and seeing us like that, he nearly lost it. I didn't blame him. I would have, too, but fuck! I had to resist the urge to punch the fucker when he grabbed her by the arm like that. It should've been him out here with her to begin with. What the hell did he do? Then I remembered Alex telling me how much she missed him. I wonder who she was talking about?

After I stood up and glared at Liam when he told me to fuck off, he ran inside, slamming the door behind him. I can't wait until he finds out I'm Alex's roommate. I wonder how that will play out? Unless he already knows. Knowing that he would be spending the night, I decided to go home late.

It was around three in the morning when we were sure no one was too wasted to drive before our group parted ways. Seth ended up driving me home. I was perfectly sober until Alex got me all confused again, so I decided to drink more.

Turning the knob to the front door as quietly as I could, I saw that the light was on in the living room. Thinking perhaps Alex wasn't home yet, I thought I'd lay on the sofa since I was so wired. I was shocked to see Alex on the love seat sofa. Holding onto a box of Kleenex, she took up half the space. With her knees bent, she was cradled into a fetus position, fast asleep, and there was no sign of Liam. Did they get into a fight because of what happened?

Plopping down on the other sofa, my heavy eyelids closed as I wondered why Alex was in so much pain. I debated whether or not to place a light blanket on her, but seeing that it wasn't cold at all, I didn't want to disturb her. Just in case she woke up in the middle of the night, I left the light on.

I don't know what time it was or how long I had been asleep, but I was awakened by the sound of a horrendous cry. Groggily I sat up to see Alex bawling like she was when I found her outside the bar. I didn't know what to do. Her eyes were closed and she looked stiff. As her tears continued to fall, she didn't wipe them. That's when I knew for sure she was dreaming.

Taking the Kleenex box out of her hand, I pulled out several tissues from it and wiped her tears. Without thinking clearly, I reached for her. "Alex," I said, running my fingers through her hair. It felt so soft and smooth. When she didn't stop, I debated whether to wake her. I didn't know if that was a good idea. Fuck! What do I do?

I decided to pick her up and put her in her own bed. That way, she would be more comfortable and sleep as long as she needed. As I held her, I had no idea why I sang the words softly against her ear as I tucked her in bed. "You'll find nobody else like me."

Alex rolled over to her side, snuggling against her pillow. I didn't know if she was dreaming or if she knew I'd just carried her to her bed. She mumbled, "Thanks, El...e." A pause. "Love...song." Then I heard the sweetest sigh. A sound I imagined a girl would make as she thinks about the love of her life.

Raking my hair back, I chuckled lightly at her words and watched her lay still. Seeing her chest rise and fall into a peaceful sleep was my cue that I was good to go. Secretly, I wanted that sigh to be for me.

Alexandria

Liam was mad as hell when he dropped me off at the condo. He'd left his friends at the restaurant so he could take me home first. We had our first big fight in months, and it only intensified when he found out Elijah was my roommate. I reassured him nothing was going on between us. After calming his nerves, he apologized and stuck around for a bit. Knowing I wasn't going to give him what he wanted when he tried to take off my clothes, he left. He told me he would come next week without his friends.

Something in the pit of my stomach told me he may be playing the field, but then again, we'd never discussed the seriousness of our relationship. I had no idea what we were besides the fact that he told me many times that we were in a relationship, but not officially, and he wanted to take things slow. I wasn't sure what he meant by taking things slow, but trying to get into my pants didn't seem like going slow. I also knew that doing it after a fight was not how I envisioned giving up my virginity. There was no way I was going to give it to someone who didn't deserve it. I had to be sure. You only lose it once and you sure as hell couldn't take it back.

Elijah seemed to be around more the past couple of days. I don't know if the reason was because school had started, but I enjoyed his company. I didn't feel so alone. We hadn't talked about what happened between us that night. Since he never brought it up, I pretended it never happened. Although I couldn't stop thinking about how sweet he had been, he was definitely a lot sweeter than Liam was these days.

There were three things I couldn't forget about that night: Elijah's voice, how he consoled me when I cried after dreaming about my dad, and how he tucked me into bed. I never mentioned it, nor did I thank him. I didn't want it to be awkward between us. I felt his arms around me that night when I was coming out of my dream and I froze. I was so shocked at the things he was doing that I didn't know what to do, so I pretended to be asleep. I didn't have to pretend much since I really was half-asleep.

I'm sure it was no big deal to him, but it was a huge deal to me. He touched me in ways I never thought possible in this short amount of time. When he sang those words softly in my ear, as if he wasn't sure if he wanted me to hear, it tugged at my heart. The more I got to know him, the more I wanted to know everything about him, and the less dangerous he appeared to be.

Chapter 13

Elijah

Whiteboard:
I have leftover spaghetti.
Help yourself to some.
-Alex

I came in all sweaty with my T-shirt hung around my neck, covering the tattoo by my heart. After my morning class, I went to the gym and then I went for a run. I don't know how long I ran, but it felt good. It always helped me clear my mind. It also distracted me from wanting to smoke. I had tried quitting a while back. I wasn't successful the first time around, but I decided to try again. Not that I smoked like crazy; I only did it to help calm my nerves.

When I stepped into the kitchen to grab a bottle of water, I saw Alex leaning over the counter, reading her textbook and listening to music with her headphones on. She was wiggling her sexy little ass while humming along. The only thing I could focus on was what she was doing with that popsicle stick.

First, she licked and sucked the tip, then opened her mouth, allowing that pop to slowly glide inside. The pop slid in and out several times. Sometimes she twisted it. When she pulled it out, she licked her bottom lip with one long swipe of her tongue. Fuck! I've never been so turned on in my life.

I couldn't look away, wishing that was my dick she had her lips wrapped around. Shit! I had to get that thought out of my mind. Seeing her in short shorts, a form fitted tank top, and the way her hair was down on one side didn't help either. She looked like she was posing for a sexy magazine.

I was just about to walk away when Alex turned, giving me an innocent smile. That sexy smile managed to crawl into my heart without my consent. She had no idea she just seduced me and made me hard.

"Hey, Elijah. How long have you been standing here?" She sounded nervous and her cheeks flushed a pretty pink. I could tell she was trying hard not to stare, as her eyes flashed from the floor to my sweaty chest several times. She didn't give me time to answer. Honestly, I don't even know if I could have since I was still seeing her playing with that ice pop in my mind.

"Do you want a popsicle? It's called a 'Big Stick'. It's my favorite." She showed me hers. "I bought them at the campus market. Did you know there was a mini-mart on campus?"

"No, thanks. And yes, I knew," I smiled, gazing at her lips which were now the same color as the popsicle—reddish orange. If she had offered her lips instead, I would have gladly accepted. I would have sucked them until the color disappeared from her lips and tongue, and then some. I was already doing it in my mind anyway.

"I thought you had a class?" she asked, closing her textbook. Her eyes shifted to my schedule on the fridge.

"I did. How's your schedule?"

"Good. I had a class this morning."

"What's your major?"

84

"I'm undeclared for now."

"That's okay. I was, too, when I was a freshman, but I'm majoring in Economics."

"That's great," she smiled and looked at her watch. "I better get going. I have to work. See you later," she said in a hurry and took off to her room.

Just before she left for work, I told her Seth and Lexy were bringing Chinese takeout for dinner around seven if she wanted to hang out with us. The truth was, I didn't think about inviting her since she lived here, but Lexy told me to ask.

I heard three steady knocks and two short ones following after. "Alex, could you get the door? It's Lexy and Seth," I shouted from my bedroom. Feeling groggy after just waking up from a short nap, I didn't have the strength just yet to get the door. When I heard their voices, I knew Alex heard me.

"Get your sorry ass out here, Ellie. Some of us are starving." I heard Seth laughing.

"Ok, Sally," I scowled, opening my bedroom door.

The white containers and chopsticks were already laid out on the dining table. Lexy and Alex came out of the kitchen with paper plates and drinks. My eyes went straight to Alex and I couldn't look away. With a high ponytail, she wore short shorts and a T-shirt that hugged her perfect shape.

"Hey, sleepy head," Lexy teased, breaking my observation. "You needed to recharge for tonight?"

"I'm not on the list tonight, remember?" I narrowed my eyes at her. I never wanted Alex to know what my other job was. Working part time at the Administration Office paid the bills, but it was boring as hell. Mostly, I input information on the computer and other miscellaneous stuff. Ever since I realized the necessity for a second job, I discovered not only a thrill, but also a hobby. Besides, it was a great way to make fast cash. It was nothing to be ashamed of, but I'd rather not have it announced to the world or to every new friend I meet.

Alex looked at me in confusion. I knew she was hoping I would offer an explanation, but she wasn't getting one.

"I meant our drinking game, silly."

"Oh, then you know the answer. No need to recharge there."

After we filled our plates, we sat around the table and started to chow down.

"Have you heard from Jimmy?" Seth asked, glancing at Alex, and then me. "Did you ask him why he didn't mention that Alex happened to be a girl?" He looked at Alex again. "Not that it matters, Alex."

"He did. He called me to tell me to deal with it." I craned my neck to Alex. "Not that I have anything against you being my roommate. I called to let him know that he should have told us. That's all." I hoped she wasn't getting the wrong idea.

"I understand," Alex said, swallowing. "I left him a message, too. At least you got a call back. He texted me and told me that you're a great guy. He said you would watch out for me." She said that last sentence quickly. "But you don't have to watch over me. I'm not a little girl," she smiled.

She was right. She was not a little girl in any curve of her body, but I did feel the need to watch over her. I wasn't sure if it was because she was Jimmy's cousin or because she was my roommate.

"How are your classes?" Lexy asked, stabbing her fork through the broccoli.

"Great. I got lost a couple of times on campus," Alex snorted. "I just need to get used to the schedule. I love not having to be at school all day."

"How do you like your new job?" Seth asked, shoving chicken in his mouth.

"I love it. I like working with Lexy."

"Don't let her boss you around."

"I don't boss people around," Lexi nudged Seth. "I only boss you around 'cause you act like a child."

"I do not," Seth pouted, and then his eyes sparkled. "Alex, you have an amazing voice."

She did, but I never complimented her. "Thanks," she said shyly, blushing. "But my voice isn't as amazing as Ellie's."

I couldn't believe she'd said that. I didn't like how she was making me feel, so I tried to brush it off. Arrogantly I said, "American Idol thought I was too good for them. There would be no competition if I entered."

We had a good laugh after my comment, but I was still blown away by hers. Seth took a sip of his drink and continued with his endless questions. I was curious about Alex too, but I didn't want to ask. I had Seth for that. He was the nosy one in our group and he wasn't afraid to ask.

"How long have you and Liam been going out?"

"Seth," Lexy scolded.

"It's okay, Lexy," Alex smiled at her. "I don't mind. Liam and I went to the same high school. He was a senior and I was a freshman when we first met, but we didn't hook up until way later. He would come home and visit his family and we ended up getting together at a friend's party. We started dating several months before my father passed away from lung cancer. He died about three months ago. My father smoked all his life, probably like a pack a day." Her eyes became glassy. "Liam was there for me then, but it's difficult when we're in two different schools with two different schedules, not to mention his internship. I don't know what's going to happen."

Shit! I wanted a cigarette, but after what she just said, how could I smoke in front of her? It would be a reminder of her father's death. To make it worse, she told us that it had been only three months. It was no wonder she was crying like that, even in her sleep. He apparently appeared in her dreams. I knew that pain all too well. I've been there, felt it, and done that.

"I know it's difficult when things don't work out," Lexy said. "I'm not trying to be negative or insensitive by saying that it won't, but there are lots of available guys at our school who would love to take you out," Lexy winked.

"Thanks, Lexy. I have to say…." Alex chocked backed her tears. "It's been really difficult since my dad passed away. I didn't know how I was going to make it through the day without crying so much. I was really nervous about coming here when I didn't know anyone, but you guys have been really good to me. You make me feel like I'm part of a family. So, thank you for that. It makes the days bearable." Her last sentence came out fast as she excused herself to make some phone calls, but I knew she went to the bathroom to wipe her tears.

The room was quiet after she left. Feeling my heart dive into that same place she felt, I grabbed another bottle of beer out of the fridge.

"You okay there, Elijah?" Seth asked, knowing why I had to get up. Seth knew about my past and he had always been sensitive about my feelings. He was such a great friend—Lexy and Jimmy, too. I don't know what I would've done without them.

"Yeah, I'm fine," I sighed. I meant it this time. Somehow, I was able to push my pain aside. Alex's wound was raw and fresh. It had been only three months, and yet she was so strong. She was brave to take off on her own like that. I admired her even more after today. Now I understood her a little bit more.

After I asked Lexy to check up on Alex, Seth and I headed to our destination.

Chapter 14

Alexandria

"You ready to go, Alex?" Lexy asked.

"You sure I need a sweater?" I asked without answering.

"The nights are getting colder. Bring one just in case."

Lexy had come into my room after I excused myself. I'd left my door slightly ajar, thinking I would head back out after I looked at myself in the mirror to make sure I was presentable. But when I started reading a text from Emma letting me know how much she missed me, I ended up texting her back.

Emma would occasionally go singing with my dad and me. She let me know that she heard a song that reminded her about the time the three of us sang together; it had me in tears.

After I explained to Lexy, she held me until I stopped crying. I told myself many times that I had to stop crying in front of others. I didn't want their sympathy. They all had their own problems. I didn't want to add mine to theirs.

"I'm ready," I said, standing in front of her in the kitchen. She told me to get ready while she did the dishes. "Where are Seth and Elijah?"

"They're already at the race. We had better hurry. It's not a big deal, but it's a little exciting since it's illegal."

"What?" I questioned as my tone went up a notch.

"Don't worry. I've been there many times." Lexy tugged my arm, shutting the door behind us. "Just don't leave my sight and stay close to me."

On the way there, Lexy explained to me that street racing was illegal, which I knew. So why on earth would anyone go? I soon found out. Following her steps as quickly as I could, I saw how many people were there this late at night.

She was right when she told me how thrilling it was. Excitement filled the air seeing such a grand event, especially since this was all new to me. As I walked down the hill and glanced around, I buttoned my cardigan after I got caught in the sudden brisk breeze. Looking up at the dark sky, not a single star graced us tonight, giving me an eerie feeling. I was almost positive this feeling was because it was against the law and a part of me was worried about being here.

In front of me was a massive empty field. It was nothing but dirt and dead grass, but there were massive circular, florescent markings. I guessed that was where the race would take place. Watching the spectators walking with their warm drinks made me wish I had one, too. Shivering, I cuddled closer to Lexy.

Looking over my shoulder to see where the commotion was coming from, I saw several guys behind a table taking bets from a line of people. Some people were huddled together drinking beer, and others were snacking while lounging on a picnic blanket, conversing with friends around them. I recognized a few of them from my class.

I observed several other people as we continued to walk through the crowds. Though they had jackets on, their tattoos stuck out, clearly visible on their necks and their faces. I saw guys with pierced ears, eyebrows, lips, and even a nose or two. They didn't look friendly at all. Maybe they just didn't like me staring. Was I that obvious?

"Oh, good. We've made it just in time," Lexy said breathlessly as we finally reached the bottom of the hill. "Do you see Seth or Elijah?" She glanced around. I tried to as well, but there were so many people that it was nearly impossible to spot them, not to mention the darkness that complicated matters more.

Just when I wondered how long we had to wait, I heard the engines revving. One black and one silver car, neither looking like typical racecars, were at the starting line. They were just plain solid colors. What was I expecting? This wasn't the Indie 500.

The first driver stepped out of his car, waving to the crowd. He wore jeans and a black sweater. I also noticed his buzzed hair when he took off his helmet. There were loud cheers as well as booing sounds. Since Lexy was clapping and whistling, I did the same. When the next driver stepped out, I heard the same sounds echo around us, but Lexy didn't clap.

"That's Nolan," she said, booing loudly.

"Nolan?" I repeated and stood still. I had no idea. Great. I was here to watch that ass-grabbing jerk. Just as I said his name, he spotted me and winked. I looked away. He had taken off his helmet to greet the crowd. After waving his hand, he blew kisses at the audience. Gross! I turned my head away to spot a girl swaying seductively and standing a distance away from the cars. That got all the males' attention and the wolf whistles sounded from every direction.

She was wearing high heels, a short skirt, and a tight red sweater. Wasn't she cold? When she held up a white scarf, the engines roared louder. I had to cover my ears because of the dreadfully thunderous sound. The crowd was watching and waiting. The air was still and so was my heart. Wondering what she was doing there, I watched intensely. When the scarf came down with a flash, the cars zoomed away. Dirt kicked up, producing clouds of dust that blanketed the area. When it cleared, that's when I realized it was Heather. How could I have missed her? She was almost perfect with that killer body.

The dust from the race started covering over the area where we stood, so Lexy and I headed to higher ground. Everyone was cheering or cursing, since the money they had bet was at stake. You could see the tension in their eyes, their bodies, and their gestures. The crowd seemed possessed with the excitement, the rush, and the desperation for the money they could win or lose.

Watching the cars pass with great speed was exhilarating. I could feel my heart thump faster, wondering who would win. They were neck and neck throughout the race so far.

"Look," Lexy pointed. "See those guys holding the flashing number signs? When they hold up number ten, that's the indication that the race is about to end."

"I see," I nodded. "So they go 10 laps around the track?"

"It depends. Sometimes more."

Standing there watching the racecars zip by and seeing the number cards reaching closer to ten, I was sure I was going to have an anxiety attack. The cards changed again...7...8...9.... Then ten flashed endlessly, like an SOS sign. Everyone started cheering louder. This was it.

I didn't know why I was holding my breath. Maybe it was because I wanted the other guy to win, but it was not going in his favor. It got worse when Nolan skidded to his right, almost hitting his opponent, causing the gap to widen. Damn, Nolan was crazy. There was no doubt now who had won. Nolan's car crossed the finish line first.

"Crap. That means...." Lexy never finished her words. Her eyes grew wide. The cheers that erupted were very short lived. "Shit! The cops."

Before I could say a word or even spot them, Lexy grabbed my arm and pulled me up the hill. "Run, Alex!" she said out loud.

It was chaos. I never heard the sirens, but I saw the crowd. They scrambled like ants on a hill. Everyone was screaming and running as if the place was on fire. Someone bumped my shoulder, almost knocking me over, and then another and another, causing me to stumble. It was as if people suddenly lost their motor coordination when all hell broke loose. What was wrong with these people? We were almost at the top when I had the wind knocked out of me. I lost Lexy's link.

"Alex!" I heard Lexy scream. I was stumbling downhill. Luckily, the hill wasn't steep, but I had to use my hands to break my fall. Burning pain shot out from the cut on my palm. I just hoped it wasn't too deep, but seeing no blood was a good thing. Feeling dazed, I panicked after losing my balance and trying to figure out which way to go as the people around me bumped into me again.

I heard someone call my name, and I was suddenly lifted off the ground. Too busy feeling dizzy, I hadn't realized until a second later that I was slumped over someone's shoulder. I didn't fight the guy who was holding me. I just wanted to be out of there. When I was lowered to the ground, I knew then who it was.

"What the fuck, Lexy? Why did you bring her here?" Elijah was mad. I hadn't seen him mad like this before. Did he not want me here? Why couldn't I be here if it was okay for Lexy?

"I...I—" Lexy started to say, but her words were caught in her throat. She was caught off guard by Elijah's wrath.

"Never mind. Just get her home. I need to find Seth. You made me lose Seth." His tone was accusatory and angry.

When we got home, I thought Lexy would have left, but she stayed. I headed straight for the bathroom to take care of my wound. Lexy followed behind me and leaned against the door.

"Sorry, Alex. I shouldn't have brought you there. I thought it would help get your mind off your dad." Her tone was apologetic at first, and then it became filled with excitement. "But wasn't it fun?"

"I did have fun, Lexy," I confirmed. I didn't want her to feel bad for doing something thoughtful. "I'm glad you took me. I've never been to one of those before. It was exciting. But do the cops come every time?"

"No. Sometimes we get lucky. They change the location every time. The guys who were taking the money are the ones who arrange it all. Either someone ratted the location or the cops played a hunch this time. If you get caught, they'll throw you in jail and let you out the next day."

"How do you know?" I asked, pumping liquid soap in my hands, and then running them under the sink. Thankfully, I only had minor scratches.

Lexy gave me a sly smile and handed the towel to me. "Jimmy got caught once."

"Really?" I said, laughing as I hung the towel back on the rack. Our laughter was cut short when we went to the living room and saw Seth and Elijah walk through the door. Elijah was still huffing mad. His jaw muscles were tight and his lips were pressed in a thin line.

"Out!" Elijah was short and to the point. He made everyone jolt.

Thinking he meant me as well, I started heading to my room. I didn't want to be around him either.

"Alex, where are you going?" he said softly, confusing me.

I stopped when he called my name. Without answering, I went to the kitchen instead and waited for him. I heard harsh whispers as if they were arguing and didn't want me to hear, but it didn't last long.

"Good night, Alex. See you tomorrow at work," Lexy said.

"Good night, Alex," Seth said next. "Go easy on her." I heard him say to Elijah. Why would he say that?

"Bye," I said loudly without a thought to walk them out the door.

Feeling restless, my heart hammered faster as I took out the milk carton and a bag of chocolate chip cookies. It was late at night, but I just felt like having something. After pouring milk into the cup, I took out a cookie as I watched Elijah walk in.

Though his shoulders were relaxed compared to a minute ago, I could see the worried look in his eyes, but not for long. "What are you doing?" he chuckled lightly, apparently finding humor in what he saw.

"Dunking my cookie in my milk. Haven't you ever done that before?"

"No."

"Then you're missing out. Want some?" As I wondered if he would maintain his calmness, I took a bite.

"No, thanks. Not right now. I'm not a big fan of milk." He paused for a second, dragged his hair back with his fingers, and released a short, sharp sigh. "Look. I'm sorry I got angry earlier. It wasn't toward you. It was toward the situation and Lexy. She shouldn't have brought you there."

After I swallowed, I retorted, "Why not? Have you seen the crowd? Why can't I be there?"

"I can't believe you're asking me that question." His face tilted, angling his brows at me as if I should have known better. "Have I seen the crowd? Have *you* seen the crowd?" He blinked rapidly, rattling off his words, but his piercing, beautiful brown eyes and long lashes were distracting me. "There are gang members, gamblers, drug addicts, not to mention the cops."

"I didn't know about the cops, and who put you in charge of me anyway?" I challenged.

"I did."

"I don't need you to take care of me because I'm Jimmy's cousin. I wish everyone would stop doing that." My tone went up a notch.

"That's not the reason."

"Then what is? And I didn't see any gang members or drug addicts. Although I wouldn't know what they look like." I dunked the cookie again and took another bite.

"Exactly. And have you ever been in a jail before?"

"No." Biting my cookie helped me deal with how he continued to distract me. Something about the way he was being so protective and how he was staring at my mouth, he oozed sex appeal.

"Exactly."

"Stop saying 'exactly.' Have you?"

He didn't answer. I'd guessed that was a yes. Before he could walk away from me, I pointed at him with the half-eaten cookie in my hand as I asked another question. "How about the other students and your friends? They were all there, too. Am I not good enough to be there?" I don't know why, but anger boiled inside me.

"No, you're not!" he stammered, startling me. When he took a step toward me, I backed away and bumped into the cabinet.

His words were like a dagger to my heart. Did he really say that to me, making me feel worthless? How dare he!

With his hands planted on either side of the cabinet just inches away from my face, his body was way too close to mine. I couldn't help but stare at the tattoo that curved as his muscles flexed. His broad shoulders and his hard, defined chest were too much for me to handle, especially recalling how he looked without a shirt on.

Blistering, heated energy ignited in the space between us. I was drowning into his smell...into him...into that cage he created around us, and I wanted to dive into his arms. Lowering his head and brushing his lips against my ear, accentuating one word at a time, he murmured. "You. Are. Better." Then he paused. No movement...completely still.

I don't know how long we stood like that. A second seemed like an eternity. I had no control over what I was feeling just then. After a soft intake of breath, he continued. "I don't know what I would have done if something were to happen to you."

His words quickly soothed me, making me melt in awe. I tried not to choke on the cookie still in my mouth. When I felt the warmth of his breath against my neck, I wanted so badly for him to devour me right there. The heated feeling got worse when I saw his lips heading toward mine with a slow hesitation. My heart went into overdrive as the room spun around me. We were now face-to-face as he stared into my eyes with want and need.

Never taking his eyes off me, he rested his hand on my shoulder, and then gingerly slid down my arm, giving me pleasurable tingles...EVERYWHERE. Afraid to move the tiniest of my muscles, I felt locked in place. I was enjoying him far too much. I didn't want it to end. When he finally reached my hand, he pulled it up to his mouth and made the most pleasurable groan I've ever heard.

Looking exhausted and dazed, he shifted his eyes to the cookie in my hand, and mumbled slowly, "I think I'll have that cookie now."

Nothing registered until I saw his lips part and my fingers disappeared into his mouth. Oh. My. GOD! My pulse skyrocketed and I whimpered from the warmth of his tongue and the sensation that shot up my arm. My fingers were very wet sliding out of his mouth. I even felt the feather-light graze of his teeth; and I could swear every single muscle in my body became limp.

His jaw worked quickly, chewing. It was the sexiest thing I'd ever seen. He made eating a cookie so hot. After he swallowed, he turned the other way, picked up my cup of milk, and chugged down whatever was left.

Looking like he couldn't believe he just drank milk, he placed the cup down. "Good night, Alex. Don't ever go racing without me," he ordered, and then he left.

What just happened? Milk and cookies will never be the same for me...EVER.

Chapter 15

Elijah

I was so close to kissing Alex…again. What the hell was I thinking and what the hell was wrong with me? She was my roommate. To top it off, she was in a relationship with someone or whatever the hell was going on between them. I had no clue. All I knew was that Liam was an asshole. He didn't even deserve to be with her.

If Alex were my girl, I would treat her so much better than he does. I would be with her whenever I got the chance. Either he was a dumbass or he was sleeping around. I didn't know which one was better. Why the hell was I even thinking like this? I was not interested in being in a relationship in the first place.

Thank God for that cookie. After using every ounce of my will power to move my lips away from hers, I needed something in my mouth. That cookie saved me. I didn't mean to finish it, but I wanted to stick her fingers in my mouth at the same time. That put me over the edge and I would have taken her right there on the kitchen counter if she'd let me.

I didn't mean to go off on her like that, but what if I wasn't there? What if I hadn't seen them? She might have ended up in jail or worse. I wouldn't be able to handle that. I know she can take care of herself, but I have this need in me. Ever since she moved in, it was as if my body was tuned in to hers. I am always aware of her.

Now that she'd seen what it was like, I guess I could tell her that I was going to be the next one to race against Nolan. I wondered what she would think of me then. Too exhausted to think anymore, I closed my eyes. I went to sleep thinking about my brother.

Whiteboard:
Just a reminder rent is due next week.
-E

Three weeks has passed since school started, but it was the first day of school for me, at least for this boring class. To top it off, it was on a Friday. I only took it to get an easy "A," but now I'm thinking I shouldn't have taken it at all...until I saw Alex.

With her backpack slung over her shoulder, she scurried down the stairs as fast as her legs allowed, and so did that fine ass of hers in those jeans. I watched her take every single step toward the front. She was late to class. I knew the reason why. Liam had visited her last night. He was probably still there.

I didn't know we shared art history class together, but then again, this was the first time I had shown up. I didn't bother to look at what classes she took, even though her schedule was attached to the fridge. Now I had an excuse to study with her. What was I thinking? I had told myself I wasn't even going to look at her that way, but now that I knew she was here, all I could do was zone in on her. The girls that had purposely sat around me to get my attention disappeared just like that.

The class was held in a huge auditorium. That was a good thing. My plan was to sit in the back since she liked to sit toward the front. Maybe she would never find out that I was in the same class. But if she looked at the schedule, she would have known. When she glanced around as if she were looking for someone, she looked straight at me. She knew exactly where I was seated. I'm sure it was a coincidence. When she turned back without acknowledging me, I figured I was wrong. Then she looked at me again and rewarded me with the biggest coy, sexy smile.

My heart skipped a beat, and then it took a nosedive. That smile fucked me over. All I could do was lift my pen up in the air as a way of greeting. Damn! How was I supposed to concentrate after that? I'll be thinking about that smile all day.

Alexandria

I didn't mean to look for Elijah, but I had no self-control. When Lexy confirmed he was taking this class too, I about had a heart attack. I saw it when I looked over his schedule, but since I had never seen him, I thought he dropped the class. A part of me felt so guilty that my heart pounded faster every time I thought of him, but I brushed it off thinking that I was just physically attracted to him. What female wouldn't be?

A part of me knew Liam and I wouldn't last. I was on the verge of breaking up with him, but when he stayed over last night and was really sweet to me, I became soft and gave in. Deep down inside, I knew Liam wasn't going to be the best boyfriend if we ever got to that point, but no one was perfect. No relationship was or ever will be. Maybe I was determined to make it work, especially since my parents' marriage fell apart. Maybe I was holding on, unable to let go of anyone. My heart couldn't take too much pain right now.

While jotting notes down as fast as I could, the girl next to me kept looking at me and whispering something to her friend. Having had enough, I turned to her. Turning red, she gave me a quick smile and asked me a question. "I was wondering, are you Elijah's roommate?"

"Yes," I said hesitantly.

"You're so lucky," she gushed, keeping her voice down. "How do you do it? How do you sleep across from his room and not want to jump into bed with him?"

She had no idea how many times that thought crossed my mind, but seeing someone else did help tremendously. "I'm seeing someone," I whispered back.

"It's a good thing," she giggled. "My name is Cynthia. If you ever have a party, you're welcome to invite me. We're his fans." She pointed to her friend.

A fan? I guess she meant because of his voice. "Okay," I laughed.

"I heard he brings home a different girl every night. Is that true?"

"No." I shook my head recalling seeing Heather the first night, but nobody else since.

Cynthia looked over her shoulder, and then looked back at me in a dream-like state. "He's like a book boyfriend dream come true."

I knew what she meant, but I just smiled. Trying not to make it obvious, I peeked at him over my shoulder. I thought I saw Elijah look my way, but I couldn't tell. Surrounded by beautiful girls, why would he even bother? I'm sure he was distracted.

Cynthia tapped my shoulder while I continued to jot down lecture notes. "Yes," I smiled, even though I was slightly annoyed.

"I heard he gets all the girls he sleeps with to orgasm." Cynthia couldn't stop giggling. "I heard even girls that have boyfriends want to sleep with him. You know, a one night-stand, just so they know what it would feel like to have one."

I had heard enough. I didn't want her to spread rumors; at least I thought they were rumors. "The girls he slept with were probably so in love with him, that just having him inside them would be enough to make them explode." I couldn't believe the words that came out of my mouth. What the hell was I saying anyway? Just the thought alone made me tingly and warm. Hearing Cynthia's words, whether true or not, made me turn to face Elijah.

Giving him my warmest smile since I didn't know what else to do when he caught me looking at him, he held up his pen and waved a greeting with that sexy grin he wore so well. Shrinking into my seat, my face felt flushed. How was I going to concentrate after that?

Elijah

Whiteboard:
Thanks for the delicious meatloaf!
I'll have to keep you as my roommate forever.
-E

Knowing I couldn't stay away forever, I decided to head home after dinner. I wondered if Liam was still there. Hearing two distinct voices coming from Alex's room answered my question.

I don't know what the hell was wrong with me, but something in the pit of my stomach made me want to vomit at the thought of Liam. The main reason was, that asshole didn't deserve her. Why was she still with him when I knew how many times he made her cry? I had no fuckin' clue.

Before I headed to my room, I wanted to get a snack. For some reason, I wanted a Big Stick popsicle. When I heard their voices getting louder, I knew they were having a disagreement. Since Alex's room was next to the kitchen, you could hear their voices through the thin walls.

Being nosy, I leaned in closer to her door. I could only hear Liam cursing and yelling. I wanted to go in there and throw his sorry ass out. Alex didn't deserve to be yelled at like that. My fists got tight, my muscles tensed, and I was really close to thrashing the door open and introducing Liam to my right hook when I heard his voice get even louder.

Before I could decide what to do, Liam stopped shouting. Not wanting to get caught, I went back to the kitchen—just in time. Liam stormed out of the room. He was exactly how I remembered him from Campus Karaoke. He was stomping around like he had a stick up his ass. When he saw me, he scowled and sized me up. That did it! He pissed me off. I wanted to glare back, but in a different way.

Holding my guarded stance, I slowly curled my lips into a smirk, and hid the popsicle behind my back. "Alex, do you want…." I started to say aloud to his face, darting my eyes at him, and then softening my tone so Alex couldn't hear the rest, "my big dick?"

Yup, that did it. His glare intensified even more, and his face became blood red. The veins in his neck bulged out and his eyes were filled with venom. Thank goodness Alex came out, or I would have broken his nose.

"What did you say, Elijah?" Halting at a dead stop when she saw Liam, she timidly stood behind him.

Holding up a popsicle with the most innocent smile I could give, I asked, "Do you want a Big Stick popsicle? I don't know if you saw them. I bought some yesterday."

"My favorite. Sure, I could eat one to cool down." She weaved around Liam and took it out of my hand. Heading back to her room, Liam followed.

I'm not sure if I made things worse, but a couple of minutes later, Liam walked out the front door. I couldn't help what I felt. I was glad that prick was gone.

Chapter 16

Alexandria

Liam stormed out. He wanted me to find another place to live. I didn't have time to look for one. School had started and I was pretty sure everyone was set with their living arrangements. When I told him I didn't want to, he blamed it on Elijah. He accused me of wanting to stay because of him. I could understand why. He had seen me in his arms that night, but I had thought it was Liam at first. It was his fault for not being there for me.

Besides, I didn't want to move out. Elijah was a perfect roommate. He even bought me my favorite cookies and Big Stick popsicles. I didn't understand why Lexy told me that I could stay at her place if parties or girls got out of hand here because I hadn't seen anything like that. And seeing Lexy and Seth on a regular basis was an added bonus not to move out.

"Everything okay?" Elijah asked as I walked out of my room. He was flipping through the channels. Sitting lazily on the sofa, his legs were spread out with one hand on the armrest while the other hand held the remote control.

"He's just mad, but he'll get over it." I sat on the sofa across from him after I threw away the stick in the trashcan.

"It seems like he's mad all the time."

"He's just frustrated with the situation. I live three hours away from him and I don't have a car, but I'm very close to having one."

"What do you mean?"

I could have sworn I had mentioned it to him before. Maybe he forgot. "I've been saving my money for a down payment."

Elijah turned his attention away from the television, shifting his body toward me. "You surprise me all the time." Then he started to flip through channels again.

"Thanks," I smiled, hoping what he said was a good thing. "Oh, stop. That's my favorite movie." I pointed at the television screen.

"Grease?" he chuckled lightly. Twisting his head to me, his eyes twinkled like he wanted to share a dirty secret. "Don't tell anyone, but I like it too," he winked, biting his bottom lip, possibly thinking what I would say next. "I had a major crush on Olivia Newton-John."

Oh God! That wink made my stomach flutter.

"What's your favorite song?" he continued.

"I guess I'd have to say, 'You're The One That I Want.' I had a major crush on John Travolta. My dad and I used to sing that together. Actually, I made him," I said somberly. "I know it sounds strange, but my dad and I were very close. Most daughters are closer to their moms, but it was the other way for me."

Elijah nodded, giving me his complete attention. His eyes said he was yearning to know more.

"We used to sing a lot together. My dad had a great voice," I continued as my lips quivered. I purposely took a few deep breaths to hold myself together. There was no way I was going to break down in front of him again. "He would let me bring some of my friends. My best friend back home, Emma, would come with us a lot. Those were the good old days," I smiled. "You know, that night at Campus Karaoke was the first time I sang in public since his funeral. It was difficult for me before, but I think I'm slowly starting to let him go."

"Alex, it's only been a few months. It's okay to grieve. It's okay to cry. Some people take years to grieve for their loved ones, but you're so strong. I would have never known. Is that the reason why you ran out the door that night?"

"Yes, but it got worse when I heard the song my dad used to sing to me when I was little, 'You are my sunshine.'"

"Oh, shit! I didn't know."

"It's okay. It's not your fault."

"It was one of the songs our fraternity big brothers made us sing to the sorority pledges. But you know what? The more you hear it and get used to it, it will make it easier."

"You think so?"

"I know so. And you know what else?" He slightly leaned toward me, as if what he was about to say was something important, something he really wanted to stress, and I could see the sincerity flashing in his eyes. "Your dad is smiling at you right now. And he's proud of you for being so strong."

"You really think so?" I questioned, but I only said that to distract him. It was more of a rhetorical question. "Thanks." My eyes started to blur with tears. The truth was, besides Emma, Elijah was the only one who seemed to truly understand how I felt. He didn't tell me to stop thinking about my father like Liam did. Elijah's words gave me comfort, and I didn't feel so alone.

After having this conversation, I felt like our friendship grew to another level. I'd judged him because he smoked, his tattoos, being standoffish toward me when we first met, and other things, but what I missed in the beginning was his genuine heart. He wasn't the bad boy other girls made him out to be, and if he was…well…he was a bad boy with a beautiful heart, and that alone made him more attractive.

"What's your favorite part of the movie?" His question helped stop the tears from falling.

I quickly dabbed a drop that was about to fall. "I like everything about the movie. I think it was so cute at the end how they tried to change their appearance for each other. You know how Sandy dressed all hot and sexy and Danny dressed all preppy? And

106

how could you not love the ending? How they drove off into the sunset together. That was sweet."

Elijah nodded in understanding with a grin, and then changed the subject. "Since Liam left, I invited Lexy and Seth to come over. You don't mind do you?"

"Nope, I don't mind at all."

"I hope you like to watch scary movies. We're going to watch "The Ring."

I gulped in fright. "Um…Sure."

Lexy and I made the popcorn while the boys set up the movie. It had been a while since I'd seen a scary movie. I have nightmares when I watch them, but I figured I'd be ok with my friends there. How wrong I was!

Lexy sat next to Seth, which meant I had no choice but to sit next to Elijah. I could tell they were enjoying the movie, but while I, on the other hand held onto the sofa pillow and bit my lower lip.

Occasionally, when I would cover my eyes with my hands, Elijah would chuckle and nudge me to watch. Sometimes his knee would touch mine by accident, but he would quickly shift away. One time, his arms went around my shoulder as if we were a couple, but he apologized and folded his arms in front of him again. I knew his actions were not intentional, but I didn't mind his soft touches. In a way, the physical contact gave me comfort through this dreadful scary movie.

Most of the time, I had my eyes closed throughout the movie. Looked like I wasn't getting any sleep tonight. It was past midnight when Lexy and Seth left. Turning on all the lights in my room, I plopped into bed after I washed up.

Unable to sleep, I decided to check my phone. I had missed a call and a text from Liam. Watching the movie with my friends helped me forget about the fight we'd had, but seeing his text brought it all back; and I didn't know what I was feeling at this moment.

I'm sorry I took off like that. I didn't have the right to tell you what to do. I miss you. I'll come by next weekend.

I texted him back. *See you next Saturday.* The best part of texting was that even though I was still mad, he didn't know it. I would cool off by the time we saw each other again anyway. What was the point of arguing when I knew I couldn't make Liam see my point?

The next text was from Emma. *What are you doing? Hope you're not having too much fun with Ellie. Just kidding. Miss you.*

Miss you, too. Just saw a scary movie. I know. I'm crazy, but I did. Now I can't go to sleep. Are you up?

With no response from her, I tried falling asleep while listening to music, but all I could picture in my mind was that girl in a white long dress. With long, black hair and dark evil eyes, she was all I could see when I closed my eyes. Popping my eyes open, I thought about sleeping in the living room. Maybe knowing Elijah was closer, I could fall asleep.

Taking my blanket and my pillow, I laid down on the sofa, but that didn't make it any better. The humming from the fridge and noises I never noticed during the daytime were very evident now. A shadow that was most likely cast from the tree outside didn't help the situation either. Looking at the clock on the microwave, I saw it was after three in the morning, so I resorted to my last option. I knocked on Elijah's door with my pillow and blanket.

"Al...ex?" My name was drawn out in a question.

"Elijah, are you sleeping?" I asked timidly.

"Would I be answering if I was sleeping?" he asked, slightly chuckling.

Duh! "Umm...do you think you could sleep on the sofa? I mean...I can't sleep."

"Are you scared?"

I didn't know how to answer. I sounded like a little girl. "Yes."

"I'm not sleeping on the sofa. You can come in here."

I pushed the door open and stepped inside his room for the first time. Elijah was laying on his bed, but his eyes were wide open.

Though it was dark, the open blinds allowed the light from streetlight to penetrate through.

Elijah's room was about the same size as mine. It looked pretty much the same, except for different type of furniture. He had a desk and a dresser, and it was simple and clean for a guy's room. There was nothing hanging on the walls—no posters, no paintings—just like mine. I assumed all of his clothes were hung up since there were none on the floor. He had some photos on top of his dresser, leaning against the wall without any picture frames. I'd planned to look at them in the morning.

"I didn't know you were this scared," he said, placing his arms behind his head. I could tell this was a mistake. He was giving me funny tingles just by the sight of his biceps flexing, and he was looking all dreamy.

"I'm sorry to bother you, but I keep seeing that girl in my mind," I said with a snort, as if it was the silliest thing to be said by a grown person. "Is it okay if I sleep on the floor?"

"Don't be ridiculous. I have a king-sized bed." He patted the bed, gesturing me to come. "It's large enough for the two of us."

"A king-sized bed?!" I said a bit too loud. "Mine is only a full. You're only one person. Why do you need a king-sized bed?"

"You really want an answer, Alex? You may end up dreaming about it."

His naughty tone already told me I didn't need to know. "Nope. No thanks," I said quickly.

"Don't worry, I won't bite. Place your blanket on the edge of my bed and use mine. It's not that cold tonight. You can use your pillow if you'd like."

"O-kay." I was hesitant, fidgeting, wondering if I should take up on his offer. "Thank you. I promise I don't snore," I giggled, trying to make this awkward situation better as I lifted my side of the blanket.

"I can't promise you I won't," he said playfully. "If I do, just shift my head to the side."

"Good night, and thank you," I said softly.

"Good night, Alex. Think happy thoughts."

109

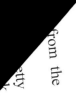

Chapter 17

Elijah

I don't know why I couldn't fall asleep, but when I heard noises in the living room, I knew Alex was having a difficult time falling asleep, too. I was just about to go out there and ask her if everything was all right when I heard a soft knock at the door.

When Alex came in, she looked like a lost little girl. I wanted to comfort her. When she wanted to sleep on the floor, I'd offered her my bed. Big mistake. Now I wouldn't be able to fall asleep for sure.

Closing my eyes, I tried to pretend she wasn't here, but it was impossible when I felt her body shift from side to side. Turning to her, I could see her shuffling in and out of the blanket, trying to decide if she needed it.

"Alex. Are you asleep?" I whispered, trying not to wake her up just in case she was on the verge of falling asleep when she was finally laying still.

Alex turned to me, peering up to catch my eyes. "I can't sleep. Do you think you could sing me a song?"

That was an odd request, but she got a laugh out of me. "Are you serious?"

Alex laughed. "Please. It will help." Her cheeks were pinched and her lips perked out. It was the sexiest pout I'd ever seen. Hot damn! I wanted to suck those pretty sweet lips of hers. How could I say no after that?

Gazing into her eyes, I sang to her. Sure enough, her eyelids started to flutter. She gave me a warm smile and slowly drifted off to sleep, and so did I. I don't know how long I had been sleeping, but I woke up when Alex started bawling and talking in her sleep. "Don't go daddy. Don't leave me. Please stay."

She hadn't woken up like the last time. Seeing her like this was killing me. I scooted to her side, slipped my hand underneath her, and pulled her to my chest. With the other hand, I rubbed her back while telling her it would be okay.

I wasn't sure if she was aware of what she was doing when she crushed into my chest, wrapping her arms around my neck tightly. Her body shook as she continued to cry and I knew the reason why. I had cried like that many times before, but alone. I felt her pain as if it were my own. All I wanted to do was comfort her, to take it away, but having her this close to me was driving me insane.

Allowing her tears to soak into my shirt, we both fell asleep again, but this time with our bodies entangled.

Alexandria

Feeling the body heat woke me up. Though somewhat groggy, I'd had enough sleep and blinked my eyes to open. I was surprised to find my hand on Liam's chest, but his wasn't that firm. Panicking and worried about where I was, I jerked back to see the sexy stubble and strong jaw line. I pulled back even further to see a dragon tattoo. My body was practically on top of Elijah's. Crap!

Thinking of last night, I knew nothing happened. We were both fully clothed, but why was I on top of him? Oh, please don't be awake. Feeling hot flashes rush to my cheeks, I peered up further and released a breath when I saw that his eyes were closed. Thank God!

Pulling away ever so slowly, I managed to get off the bed without disturbing him. After I picked up my pillow and my blanket, I started to tiptoe out of his room. Just before I left, I snuck a peek at his photos. I was assuming they were pictures of his family—his mom, his brother, but where was his dad?

Elijah got his dark hair from his mom, but I figured he looked more like his father since his brother's facial features resembled his mom. They were a good-looking family. Hearing a snort sound, I snapped my vision to Elijah. Thank goodness he hadn't awakened yet, but I panicked when I saw the clock on his nightstand. I had work in one hour. Working on Saturdays sucked.

Elijah

I was very much aware of Alex's every move last night. How could I sleep with her body wrapped around mine? It was difficult when all I wanted to do was give in to my temptation and devour her.

Knowing how she would react, I pretended to be asleep. When I saw her staring at a photo of my family, it made me uneasy. I made a sound to get her attention. Yup, that worked.

Maybe I should have slept on the sofa last night. Now, I'd never be able to get her off my mind: the way she smelled like flowers, the way her body molded perfectly to mine, the way her hair tickled my face and arm, the way her hand ran over my chest. I was totally screwed. What was I thinking? That was the problem. I couldn't think clearly around her.

Alexandria

One good thing about working on Saturdays was Lexy. Last week, I only got to see her a couple of times since our schedules were different. Working together would not only make the time go by faster, but we would also have the chance to catch up on our gossip.

"Hey, Alex." Lexy slipped her clear plastic gloves on.

I waved at her from the cash register, ringing up a customer.

"What are you doing tonight?" she mouthed, making a burrito that someone had ordered.

"Not sure," I said, and then froze. Elijah strutted toward Lexy and ordered his lunch.

He looked tired, so that made me question if he was able to get any sleep last night. I wondered if he knew I was practically sleeping on top of him. Being the kind of sleeper that didn't move around much, I had no idea how I got into that position.

"Why?" Lexy said to Elijah angrily. I had no idea what they were talking about. Elijah kept whispering in her ear while Lexy kept asking why. Finally with a huff, she threw him his plate, and he almost dropped it.

"Alex," Elijah said, shifting his baseball cap. He was hiding his expression under it. "You sleep okay?"

"Yes, thank you." It was all I could say as I tried not to look him in the eyes. I was afraid my eyes would deceive me, and he would know that a part of me enjoyed our bodies being entwined like that. After he gave me a twenty and took his change, he headed to his usual spot, turning girls' heads along the way. They were checking him out. Since there were no other customers, I walked around the tables to pick up trash.

"Hey, Alexandria."

Great! I knew that voice. I rolled my eyes, turned to him, and gave him a fake smile. If he weren't such a jerk, he would actually be sort of attractive. He had a nice toned body, smooth face, and beautiful green eyes. I don't know why, but my eyes went straight to Elijah, who was honing in on our conversation, then it shifted to Lexy who looked annoyed.

"What are you doing tonight?"

"Studying," I said quickly. "Do you know what that is?" I don't know why I was being rude to him. He didn't grab my ass this time. Trying to brush him off, I went to the next unoccupied table, but I heard footsteps behind me.

"Yes, I know what that is. I could study you if you'd like," he said smoothly.

Ignoring him, I went to another table and placed the cups onto the tray I was holding, but Nolan kept following me.

"I saw you at the racetrack. Why don't you come tonight and be my lucky star."

"No, thanks. I'm sure you have plenty of lucky stars you can choose from. Now if you'll excuse me, I have work to do."

When Nolan grabbed my wrist, I heard Elijah's chair slide out, echoing across the room.

I was assuming Nolan had no idea Elijah was headed toward us since his back was to him. Still holding onto my wrist, he spoke. "You can even be the starter girl. You can be right where the action is."

I don't know why, but I got a thrill from the idea, but it was broken by Elijah's presence.

"Get your hands off her," Elijah gritted through her teeth.

"What did you say to me?" Nolan let go of my wrist and leaned his body into Elijah's chest, a way of challenging him. Neither of them gave a damn about the people around them. In fact, some of them picked up their lunch and left.

"I said...get...your...fucking...hands...off...her." Elijah's words were slow, but they were very clear.

Nolan backed away as if to submit, but his words clearly showed he hadn't. "What the fuck for? She's not your girl. In fact, she's going to be the starter girl tonight."

Thank goodness most of the customers left and the manager just walked in.

"No, she's not. And don't ever ask her again." Elijah's tone was cool and steady, but it was the look of death in his eyes that scared me the most.

Nolan looked confused and I was pretty sure I gave Elijah the same look. What was the matter with him? He had no right to make decisions for me. Piercing my eyes at him, my tone was not friendly. "I'm going tonight and you can't stop me."

Nolan looked so proud and pleased that I had spoken up to Elijah. There was too much testosterone in the space between them as they now stood face to face, their eyes full of arrogance and rage. "He's just scared I'll beat his sorry ass and he'll look like a fool." Nolan added to the blistering fire.

Elijah flashed his eyes at me at the same time I did his, as if he just got caught hiding a secret. Now I knew why he didn't want me there. He was racing tonight. Holy shit! I didn't know Elijah raced. Was he ashamed to tell me? Now I really wanted to be the starter girl.

"I'm going," I said as if matter of fact.

"No, you're not," Elijah said as if his words were final.

"Yes, she is. She will stand on my team," Nolan cut in.

That got Elijah's attention big time. With his fist tight and the muscles on his arms flexing, he bore his eyes into Nolan with anger that slowly seethed. "No…fucking…way."

I knew that would set Nolan off. I could tell he was in motion, about to take a swing at Elijah. Before he could, I threw half a cup of water on Nolan's face. Nolan shot his eyes at me as if he couldn't believe I had done that. Elijah, on the other hand, let out a hearty laugh, giving me an approving look. He had no idea how pissed off I was at him, so I dumped the remaining water on his T-shirt. Yup, that smirk came right off his face, replaced with a look of shock. He was lucky I was easy on him. Heading toward Lexy, I saw that her eyes were wide and her lower lip dropped. Her laugh was so contagious.

Chapter 18

Alexandria

I didn't see Elijah the rest of the day after what happened in the dining hall. I didn't care if he was mad at me because I was angry enough to carry over to next week and then some. After Lexy picked me up, we headed to the race, but on the way there, I asked her a lot of questions.

"Why is Elijah against me going to the race? I don't understand."

"It's dangerous. There are the cops, for one thing, and it's not the safest environment. There was one time when a driver lost control and his car flipped into the audience. You can just imagine what that was like."

"That's terrible. I never even thought of the possibility. Were you there?"

"Yes, but I was lucky. I was on the other side of the track." Lexy looked at her side view mirror, and then turned left. "It's just as dangerous for him, too."

"I know, but he needs this." She flashed a look at me, as if she had said too much.

"What do you mean?"

"I'm not supposed to tell you, so please don't say anything. I'm only telling you so that you can understand him and why he does it in the first place. I don't want you to think badly of him. It's just that life sucks sometimes and you gotta do what you have to do to make ends meet. It's not like he's selling drugs or hurting anyone."

"Okay, Lexy. I'll pretend you never told me." I was all ears.

"Elijah started racing when his younger brother got really sick. He did it to help pay the medical bills, but mostly to pay the household bills for his family. When his brother passed away, his mother committed suicide shortly after. That's why he took off a year from school. It's the reason why he didn't graduate with Jimmy."

"Oh My God," I whispered, covering my mouth. I recalled seeing the photo of his family and another one of his brother and him. Lexy looked over her shoulder, and then turned left. "What about his father?"

"His father was a big time gambler. His parents got divorced a while back. His father stopped paying child support. It was difficult since his mom was a housewife and never held a job in her life. He started racing to help his family. It's sad that he doesn't know where his father is, but on the other hand, he doesn't care. He says his father is dead to him anyway."

"How long ago did his brother pass away?"

"Just a year ago."

"A year ago?" My tone went up a notch as my stomach sank. I had just told him about my loss, yet he was in pain, too. Now I felt horrible. "How did his brother die?"

"Cancer," she said quickly and changed the subject. "We're here. Make sure to stay close to me. If I lose you, I'm in big trouble."

"Lexy." I placed my hand on her shoulder before she could get out of the car. "I appreciate you telling me about Elijah. I won't let on that I know."

"Thanks," she said. "We tried to be there for him, you know. People grieve in different ways. Elijah is genuinely a great guy. I think he blames himself for not being able to save his brother and his mother. We're just glad he came back to school and is doing his best to get that college degree and start living again."

"One more thing." I reached for her again. "You don't have to feel like you have to watch over me."

"We all watch out for each other, Alex, but it's not because of the reasons you think."

"Then why?"

"First of all, you're my friend and you had no idea about the races. Second, Elijah asked me to. You're not to be out of my sight. Now that Nolan showed an interest in you, he doesn't want you hanging out with that crowd."

"I don't plan on it."

"It doesn't matter. Nolan will go after what he wants, just like Elijah."

I could understand what Lexy was talking about. Nolan could be aggressive if he wanted to be. Lexy got out of the car and I followed, adjusting my scarf.

"So what's going on with Liam?" she asked out of the blue.

"I don't know. He's changed or maybe I've changed. He was good to me at the beginning, but I think this long distance relationship isn't helping. Sometimes I think I should break it off. I don't feel the same about him as I did back then. He's always mad at me or maybe I'm mad at him. I don't know how I feel anymore."

"Long distance relationships can do that to you, but if you don't love him, then cut him off. Why waste your time and energy?"

"I know. It's just that I'm not sure. It's easier to see what happens than doing something about it. Once we're broken, I know there's no going back. It's hard to let go."

"I understand," she sighed. "It was difficult for me to break it off with Jimmy."

It was my turn to ask questions. "Did Heather and Elijah break up?"

"Who knows? They're on and off. They've never really been officially together. Elijah won't commit because he swore off relationships after the last disaster."

"Last disaster?" I asked, hoping to hear more.

Lexy stopped and held a serious look. "Don't tell him I told you about her. She was a manipulative, selfish, gold digger, and a slut."

"A slut? Really?"

"I have no proof, but I'm pretty sure Nolan paid her to get any information on Elijah. Who knows what else she did with him."

"Is that why Nolan and Elijah don't get along?"

"Partially. They've always been the top two racers and they both have massive egos they can't control."

I laughed and changed the subject as we proceeded ahead. "Is Heather going to be there?"

"It depends on her mood. She's probably upset she's not the starter girl, so knowing her, she won't be there."

Our conversation stopped after that. Hugging my jacket closer to my body, we walked the rest of the way in silence. It was dark as we trudged across grass, then gravel. I didn't see many cars, but I knew people parked farther away, so as not to draw any attention. After entering a private door, my question about how many people would be attending was answered.

It was more crowded than last time. Shoulder to shoulder, we bumped into people walking in. People betting, music blasting, and alcohol was everywhere. My body tingled with exhilaration and I couldn't fight the butterflies dancing in my stomach. Looking around, though I wasn't positive, it looked like an abandoned racehorse track. As I looked further up, I saw rows and rows of stadium seats. This felt like the real thing and not something illegal. I couldn't help feeling both nervous and excited for Elijah.

"Come on. Elijah told me you're the starter girl today." Her words were lost to the crowd as she pulled me along. We had just passed in front of the loud speakers.

Did I hear her right? "Elijah didn't want me to be the starter girl," I hollered at Lexy. It was getting hard to hear as I dragged my feet through the dirt, trying to keep up with her.

119

"He told me to bring you to the starting position."

"He did?" I mumbled under my breath. Suddenly, I was jolted by the same rush and joy that illuminated from the jovial crowd.

Two cars were approaching, indicating it was about to start. I recognized the silver car from the last race so the black one had to be Elijah's. Feeling every fiber of my being tense with nervousness, my heart drummed with the roaring sound from the racecars.

"I'll be right there," Lexy pointed. "When the cars pass you, run to me."

Giving her a thumbs up, I stood there thinking what the heck was I doing here. When I heard the wolf whistles from the crowd, I knew it was for me. Unlike Heather, I wore jeans and a jacket to bundle up.

Standing there as I waited for the race to begin, a huge part of me felt alive and exhilarated. Excitement filled my body and I felt it tickling to my very core. When Nolan's name was announced, he came out of his car. The crowd cheered and booed. Then he looked at me and blew a kiss.

Rolling my eyes at Nolan, I waited for Elijah to step out of his car. When he did, all geared up, he stole my breath away. Damn, he looked hot! His jeans and black T-shirt hugged every muscle on his body. There was no imperfection about him. When he slipped on his leather jacket, fuck! All the ladies were screaming his name.

After he raked his hair back with one long slow stroke, he placed his helmet on his head. When he caught my eyes, he gave me a wink and a shy smile that I just died for. He pointed to where Lexy stood. I understood what he meant. He wanted me go there afterward. I let him know I understood by giving him a thumbs up.

"We love you, Elijah," a group of girls cheered loudly from the stands.

I watched him wave at them and I don't know why, but jealousy coursed through me.

After they got in the cars, I looked at Lexy for direction. "Your scarf!"

I took off my white scarf and held it up. It ruffled against the soft wind. Hearing the thunderous and unpleasant sound from the car engines, I held my breath and brought the scarf down. It happened so fast; I felt the tunnel of wind whip by. The dirt kicked up, making me cough. After the dust died down, leaving me a better view, I ran to Lexy.

"Lexy, that was awesome," I squealed, keeping my eyes on the cars.

"We have to get to higher ground. Elijah will have my ass if we're down here. Remember what I told you about what happened when the car lost control?"

I agreed and we headed higher to find Seth. Holding on to Lexy, I kept my eyes rooted on the cars as we climbed the stairs to our seats.

The tension in my stomach would not settle no matter how many deep breaths I took. My grip on Lexy got tighter, and my teeth were clenched so tight I thought my jaw was going to break.

On the fifth turn, Elijah was in the lead. "Come on," Lexy muttered under her breath. The crowd around me got louder, but practically went silent when Elijah's car suddenly skidded to the left. Nolan had slammed into the side of Elijah's car. I didn't know if it was an accident, but I hoped it was. Once Elijah got back on track, I was able to relax again.

The cheers erupted again. As much as I wanted Elijah to win, the chances seemed slim, seeing Nolan was now in the lead. Even after a few more rounds, Elijah was still behind. I felt bad that he might lose this race, more so because I knew he needed the money. He never had a father who saved up college funds for him like mine.

Looking down at my feet, so I wouldn't see Nolan pass the finish line first, I held my breath waiting for the crowd to make more noise. Suddenly, Lexy broke our link, jumping and screaming. I looked up to hear and see everyone doing the same, but I didn't know what had happened. I couldn't see a thing over all these heads, even though I was standing up on my tippy toes. Who won? I was so confused. The screams and clapping got louder. Right as I was about to grab onto Lexy to find out what was going on, I felt two arms embrace me. I was lifted off the ground. My body was being swung around.

"Alex." I heard a deep voice. "I won!" It happened so fast it took me a minute to register who it was. Elijah placed me down and kissed me on my lips. It was quick, but it was enough to shoot fireworks through every vein, bone, and muscle in me. That kiss had my head spinning. I was in shock and couldn't move. I couldn't process anything that was going on around me. Elijah won?

Elijah was out of my sight after that. His friends dragged him away from me and what I heard next touched my heart. They started to sing and sway together with their arms on their shoulders to an old song called, "We are the Champions" by Queen.

"Campus Karaoke," Jonathan shouted.

"Last one there pays," another hollered.

"Come on, Alex. Let's go." Lexy tugged my arm. "It's going to be hell getting out of here."

Chapter 19

Elijah

What a rush! When that motherfucker hit my car, I thought I was out of the race, but I knew my brother was watching over me. Driving as fast as I could, I concentrated not just on the road, but also on what was motivating me to win. Faces flashed through my mind, but the face that stayed with me was Alex.

I saw her beautiful smile and her pouting lips. I could still faintly smell her floral perfume from when her body fit perfectly with mine, making me feel alive. She was my incentive to get to the finish line.

When I got out of the car, the first person I looked for was Alex. I already knew where she was standing. The crowd was cheering like mad. The women were screaming as I ran up to Alex. Along the way, I gave high fives to people that held out their hands.

The rush of winning took over and I was acting purely on adrenalin. Alex looked so damn cute standing there all confused. I couldn't control myself and what I did next was out of my own selfish need. After I swung her around and placed her down, I took her lips on mine. It was short and quick, but man, she tasted so good. I wanted more. Lexy gave me a strange look. I shrugged my shoulders and a group of fans whisked me away before Alex knew what had happened to her.

After the crowd died down, I went to James, the guy who arranged the race tonight. I got my money and got out of there as fast as I could. Thank God the cops didn't show this time. I'm sure it was a result of Seth spreading the wrong location around, while at the same time letting others know where it was really being held.

Seth texted to let me know they were heading to Campus Karaoke and that's where I was headed next, after I dropped off Seth's dad's racecar at his shop.

Alexandria

I didn't know what to make of Elijah's kiss, but I couldn't stop thinking about his lips on mine, or how he made me feel. If I felt like that from a small peck, I wondered how I would feel from a real kiss. It made me think about my feelings toward Liam.

The clapping when Elijah entered broke me out of my trance. Sliding into our booth after he waved, he quickly looked my way, but that was it. Suddenly I was shy and didn't know how to act around him. After we all ordered the drinks, his group of friends took turns singing.

"What the hell happened?" Seth asked.

"I'm sorry about your car. I don't know, but I'm going to make that fucker pay for the damages. That was way out of line," Elijah replied.

The racecar belonged to Seth?

Seth seethed in anger. "Forget about it. That asshole is not going to give me a penny. I can help my dad fix it. Don't worry about it. I'm just happy you won. You should have seen the look on Nolan's face. I wish I would've taken a video of it and put it on You Tube. Now that would have been epic."

124

"Don't do anything to stir him up," Lexy intervened. "If he's crazy enough to pull that stunt, who's to say what he will try next? Don't add more fuel to the fire. Well...anyways...." Lexy looked at her watch. "It's midnight. Happy Birthday, Elijah!" Lexy shouted.

His group of friends were already on stage. The music came on and everyone started to sing "Happy Birthday." Right on cue, the waitress brought out the cake. I didn't know it was his birthday. There was nothing I could do at this point, except sing along and get him something tomorrow.

Elijah had his face in his hands while he shook his head, and then looked up. "It's not a big deal, but thank you." He lit that shy sexy grin I loved so much.

After the song was finished, Elijah flashed a quick glance at me, and then blew out all the candles. Someone from the stage spoke into the mic. "Come on, birthday boy, you're on next."

Elijah gave a wicked grin. "I'm not going up there alone." He tugged Seth, and Lexy, and since I gave him the biggest struggle, he picked me up.

"Elijah, put me down." That is what he did, right onto the stage.

Holding on to me so I couldn't break free, he punched in the numbers and the music came on. The excitement grew when I realized which song he chose. I was trembling, but I couldn't help myself. I wanted to sing and having Lexy with me helped big time. Shaking our asses to the rhythm, we started to act crazy.

Elijah and Seth sang first. Then Lexy and I sang the female parts. It was "Summer Nights" from Grease, and I was having the time of my life. I looked at Lexy, who was looking back at me, smiling and laughing as we took turns singing. The song ended and just as I was about to get off the stage, Elijah held me back. "Not so fast."

I found myself being dragged back on the stage and another song began to play. Elijah started singing the song. I realized it was a duet from Grease again, "You're The One That I Want." My favorite song. He remembered.

Elijah started singing Danny's part. Holy shit! Could he have made singing that song any hotter? I'm pretty sure every girl in the room was drooling. That boy was sexy as all fuck.

When Sandy's part came on, I sang.

As we both sang together, we couldn't help but stare into each other's eyes, smiling and dancing. I was really having fun. It was as if it was just the two of us in this room singing that song to each other. It was electrifying and just then I knew my heart was set on him.

I gave Elijah the biggest smile when the song ended. He knew how much that song meant to me. Somehow, Elijah took that sad memory and replaced it with a happy one.

"Happy Birthday to me," he said, draping his arm around my shoulders and planting a kiss on my forehead. "That was the best present ever. Thanks, Alex."

I had no idea why he thanked me, but I didn't want to read too much into it. He was on a high from his win and his birthday.

Chapter 20

Alexandria

Whiteboard:
Sorry! Didn't have time to take laundry
out of the dryer. Will tonight.
-E

"Liam? What are you doing here?" I asked, seeing Liam at the door, huddling from the cold with his arms crossed.

"Didn't you get any of my messages?" His tone was cold, gazing first at Lexy, then Seth. Elijah dropped the arm that was lazily draped on my back. Liam didn't bother to say hello to my friends. He just looked at them as if they were nothing.

"How long were you waiting?" I was in shock to see him unexpectedly. Not knowing what to do, I just stood there. Elijah opened the door. Lexy and Seth followed him inside.

Liam didn't answer my question. "Looks like you were having too much fun to check your messages." He sounded upset, but I dismissed it.

"Do you want to come in?"

"Not really, but I don't want to talk out here. I guess we need to go inside."

Liam followed me to my bedroom and closed the door behind him. Sitting on my bed, he stared at me as if he was waiting for me to say something. Not wanting to sit too close to him, I sat on the edge of the bed.

"You know you have this all wrong. Elijah and I are just friends," I said, trying to break the ice. I had no idea why those words came out of my mouth first. He didn't ask me a question, but seeing Liam made me feel guilty for the way I felt when Elijah kissed me.

"Did you find a new place? When you meet my parents during Christmas vacation, I don't want to tell them that your roommate is a guy. My parents are traditional. They won't approve."

"You want me to meet your parents?" I asked, surprised. "But you said when we meet each other's parents it would mean we were taking the next step. Is that what you want?"

"Yes, I do. I thought you could visit my parents with me during your break."

"How long would we be gone for? I need to visit my mom, too."

Liam started to relax. I flinched when he moved closer to me. "Come here." He patted the space on the bed beside him. "I missed you."

I couldn't reply. I was still upset with the way he ran out the door when I told him I wasn't going to find another place to stay. Since I wasn't moving, he pulled me into him. Like always, I gave in and let him embrace me. "How about we look at the apartments I talked about last time?" he asked sweetly, kissing my neck and running his hand up my sweater.

His hand tenderly glided up my back, unhooking my bra while the other hand cupped one of my breasts. His lips outlined my jaw and his tongue entered my mouth. As he hungrily kissed me, he started to pull up my sweater and that's when I pushed his hands away.

Every time he was here, it felt like sex was the only thing on his mind. He knew I wanted to wait until we were in a steady relationship, especially since I was a virgin, but he always tried. Being away from him gave me a chance to think about what I wanted and needed. The fact that I was so comfortable around my new friends, I was beginning to see him in a new light. I wasn't sure I wanted to be around him anymore.

Breaking out of his hold, anger boiled inside me. Ever since we started dating, I'd always given in to his demands. Breaking my plans with Emma, changing my clothes to look the way he wanted, even growing out my hair for him. I was hanging out with his group of friends, even though I didn't really like them, and I had to stop talking about my dad because it would upset him. Enough was enough. Piercing my eyes at him, I gritted my teeth. "I'm not looking for another place to live."

He narrowed his eyes on me. "I told you I'd pay for it."

"I don't want you to pay for it." I moved as far away from him as I could.

"You're going to have to get used to that when we live together after I graduate."

"What if I don't want to live with you? You never asked me what I wanted."

"Of course you do. Why wouldn't you?"

What did he just say? I let out a sharp breath.

"Are you going to live here with Elijah the rest of your life?"

I was just about to say yes to aggravate him, but then thought better of it. "What do you have against him? You don't even know him. He's...he's...." I stopped.

"I don't like the way he looks at you. I don't like the way he thinks you're his."

"He does not. You can read minds now? How do you know what he thinks?"

"I'm a guy. I know."

"You know nothing," I stammered.

Liam stood up looking pissed off. "What did you just say to me?"

I don't know why, but for the first time, he frightened me. It was the evil, dangerous look in his eyes and his domineering tone, but I didn't care. I had enough.

"You heard me." I matched his tone. "You have no clue what's going on between us. Everything is about you. What you want. What you need."

"That's not true. I can't believe you're acting so ungrateful right now. I drove three fucking hours to see you." His tone went up again, taking a few steps towards me.

"It's true. You just don't see it. I don't think this is going to work out between us. Every time we see each other, we're fighting."

Liam looked at me as if I said the strangest thing. Then his eyes grew angry. "We keep on fighting because of him. You need to move out. I'm not going to ask again."

I couldn't believe his demand. That pissed me off even more. "What we need is time apart. It—"

Liam didn't let me finish. His whole face flushed and his brows lifted. "What you need is to move out."

"You're not listening to me," I hollered. "You never do." Liam was coming toward me. I didn't want to find out what he would say or do. He had never shown me that he could be the violent type, but I didn't want to stay to find out. I ran out of my bedroom and out the front door.

I had nothing with me. I didn't even know if Elijah was still home or if Seth and Lexy were still there. All I knew was that I wanted to be far away from Liam. I heard my name and then a car door slam, but I kept running, never looking back. The cold fall breeze whipped my face, but it felt good. My heart thumped and my lungs were working in overdrive. I hadn't run this fast in a long time.

Looking around, I rested my hands on my knees. My body was slumped over as I gasped for breath. I had no idea where I was. I had never ventured off this way before since it was not heading toward the campus. Looking around, I could hear music coming from one of the condos. I knew someone was having a party. I was just about to leave when I heard my name.

"Alex?"

I knew that voice. "Elijah?" He appeared out of the shadows.

"What are you doing here?" He dropped his cigarette and crushed it with his shoe. That action brought back the bad memories of my dad. Peering around him was Heather. For some reason, that really bothered me. My heart was playing tug a war with my feelings. Sometimes I wondered what it would be like if Elijah and I were going out and other times, I didn't care.

"I…were you at the condo? I mean…." I started to say and lost my words.

"We got a text from Dean. They're having the after party at his place. I thought you were with Liam." When he strode toward me, I saw Heather throw up her hands. Without a word, she went back inside.

"I was, but we got into a fight." I wanted to tell him that I had broken up with him, but decided not to. What was the point?

"What's he mad about this time? Sorry." Elijah slipped his hands into the pockets of his jeans. "It's none of my business."

"That's okay. Enjoy your party. Looks like your date went back inside. She didn't look too happy. I'm going back home now."

"Hold on." Elijah took out his cell and started texting. "I'll walk you home."

"No, it's okay. Your friend is waiting for you."

"You can stay if you like."

"Thank you, but I'm tired. It's been a long day."

Elijah didn't listen. He started to walk ahead of me. "Are you coming, or do I have to walk home alone?"

Shrugging my shoulders, I joined him.

"It's a beautiful night, isn't it?" he asked, peering up at the dark sky.

There weren't many stars out and I wondered what he was talking about. "Might be better if there were more stars."

"Now, that's where you're wrong. You're looking for something you don't see, what you wish you could see, instead of focusing on what you can see."

I never looked at it that way. Elijah just opened my eyes. "You're right. It is beautiful."

Elijah halted beneath a streetlight and turned to me. "Sometimes you see the most beauty in the fewest things." Unexpectedly, his finger came toward my face and lightly brushed the tip of my nose. "Kind of like the freckles on your nose."

"What?" I shivered, unnerved by his words. "My freckles? Yuck. I don't like them."

"I think they're cute. They're very faint, so most people wouldn't notice, but I've seen you up close many times."

Elijah made me flush with warmth. "Thank you." It was all I could say. Did Liam even know I had freckles on my nose?

"So, Freckles, tell me about your dad," he said out of the blue, walking forward again.

"Did you just call me Freckles?" I giggled.

"I sure did. It's your new nickname. We all have a nickname, except for you. I even call Lexy, Lexus, sometimes."

I laughed lightly, dismissing what he had said, then got back to his question. "I'm not sure what to tell you or where to begin. You already know enough about him. How about you tell me about your brother?" As soon as I said the words, I regretted them. It was a slip of the tongue.

Elijah stopped and turned to me. "My brother? Who told you I had a brother?" He sounded upset.

Not wanting to point the finger at Lexy, I had to think fast. "I saw your photos that night when I slept in your bed." I gulped when I said those words. It sounded so naughty and intimate.

Elijah started walking faster, leaving me behind and ignoring my question.

"Elijah, I'm sorry," I said out loud, jogging, trying to catch up to him. Then…THUMP! I fell flat on my face. Thank God it was on the grass. My foot dipped into a hole.

"Alex, are you hurt?" Elijah reached for me, helping me dust off the new cut grass residue.

"I'm okay," I mumbled, slapping off the areas he shouldn't touch. Standing there, our eyes locked in place. I saw so much pain in them as he searched for words.

My body quivered when his hand reached for my face. He moved his hand tenderly, as if he was touching the most delicate, precious thing. He glided his thumb around my cheek. At first, I thought my face was full of grass, but I was wrong…very wrong.

It seemed like time had stopped as we stood there. Though we were engulfed in almost complete darkness, the streetlights gave enough light for me to see his glistening eyes. I couldn't tell if they were tears or just the light that made his eyes twinkle like the stars.

"Alex," Elijah whispered softly, continuing to caress my cheek tenderly. His lips parted to speak, but then he closed them. His eyes blinked slowly before drilling into mine. "My brother…." He paused. "He died from Leukemia. He was only thirteen years old. I couldn't save him. I wasn't a donor match. They couldn't find one in time. I wish I could've saved him." Every word he spoke, I felt his ache gripping my heart.

"Elijah," I swallowed. I could see so much pain in those beautiful, somber eyes. As he continued, they glistened brighter. Now I was certain they were tears. "It's not your fault. You shouldn't blame yourself for something you had no control over. I know that if it were possible you would've switched places with him. You're an amazing person. Your brother would be very proud of you right now."

Elijah's upper lip curled just enough for me to assume he may have agreed with me or he'd like what he heard. "You think so?" he asked softly as his fingertip glided over my bottom lip.

Oh God! What was he doing to me? He was making my pulse race, making me lose my mind. I had forgotten what we were talking about.

"Yes," I whimpered, seeing his lips reaching for mine. Closer…closer…almost touching…and why was I not stopping this?

Next thing I knew, something wet slapped my face, then other parts of my body. We stood there dumbfound, looking at each other in shock and getting wetter by the second.

"We're getting wet!" I yelled.

"What the hell? Don't they water the grass during the daytime? Run," Elijah shouted. Seizing my hand, we ran across the lawn as he led the way.

By the time we got to our place, we were soaking wet. We were laughing and enjoying this unexpected moment. It looked like we took a shower with our clothes on. Wrapping my arms around myself, I shivered like crazy. Elijah cuddled me into him, warming me up with one hand while the other reached inside his pocket for the keys.

I didn't feel guilty that I was enjoying being in his arms. He was just being sweet, the way a friend would be. He touched my heart with his pain tonight, and somehow my pain was pushed aside. I wanted to comfort him as he had done so many times for me.

"I'll make some hot chocolate," he said as we entered our place.

"With cookies?" I asked excitedly.

Elijah chuckled, heading to his room. "Whatever you want, Babe."

I don't think he even realized he'd called me, Babe. I'm sure it was a slip of the tongue, but it made me feel uneasy and exhilarated at the same time.

Chapter 21

Elijah

Whiteboard:
Rent is due soon
-E

If those sprinklers hadn't turned on, I would've kissed her. I don't know what I was thinking when my lips headed toward hers. I brushed it off, thinking it was partially due to the alcohol, but I didn't drink that much. I never really did. So I blamed it on my high from winning the race.

Entering our condo, I turned on the heater and told Alex to take a shower first. After I took mine, I made some hot chocolate and put some cookies on a plate for her.

"Don't tell me you're going to dip that cookie in there," I grimaced.

"Why not? It tastes delicious," Alex replied, carefully maneuvering her cookie with the tips of her fingers, so she wouldn't drop it. "It's the same concept, only it's warmer and it melts faster." She opened her mouth, letting a piece fall in. With one swipe of her tongue, she licked the crumbs from her bottom lip. I had to take a deep breath. That was way too much after seeing her drenched in the rain and what almost happened. Not to mention, remembering that episode when I ate the cookie from her hand to stop myself from kissing her.

"Don't you need to go back to the party?" Alex asked, taking another bite. She made eating a cookie look so tempting. It seemed like I was missing out. Maybe I should take a bite.

"Do you want to come with me? Lexy and Seth are there." I ran my finger around the rim, gazing inside the mug.

"No. I'm kind of tired."

"I'm kinda tired, too. Drinking hot chocolate does that to me." I was going to head back to the party after I dropped her off, but I couldn't leave her here alone, especially after Liam left her.

"Elijah, can I ask you a question and you don't have to answer if you don't want to," she asked timidly, wringing a strand of her hair behind her ear.

"Sure."

"Why did you get that dragon tattoo? I think it's beautiful."

I stared at my drink for a second, and then looked up. "My brother loved dragons. I got that tattoo so I could show him that I'd always have him with me, forever printed on me." I swallowed back my tears and blinked several times before I continued. "He fell asleep smiling with his hand on the tattoo and never woke up."

"I'm sorry," she said. "That's beautiful, Elijah. I wish I could've done something like that for my dad."

"It's never too late."

"I guess, but I'm also a big chicken."

"I've noticed." I rolled my eyes playfully, trying to lighten the mood.

"Hey, I can't help it."

"Next time you're scared, don't knock and ask me if I'm sleeping. You can just walk in. However, I might be naked in bed. You've been warned."

"Elijah," she squealed, turning red. "Make sure you close the door if you are, and if not, just leave the door open. That will be your sign," she snorted, then turned away as if she had said something she shouldn't have said.

Though the thought of her coming to my bed was thrilling, I knew it would never happen again.

"Before I forget, Seth's fraternity is hosting a Halloween party. Want to come? Lexy will be there. I'm sure she'll mention it to you."

"Oh yeah, she did. She's going to take me costume shopping after work sometime this week. Do you have a costume?"

I raised my brows. "Do *I* have a costume? I go as myself."

"You're no fun." Alex scowled at me.

"Are you going to invite Liam?"

Alex's eyes shifted to the television. "I don't think he'll come. He's too involved with his friends. He'll probably want me to go to his, but I don't want to hang out with his snobby, rich friends. And besides, we got into another fight, so I don't know what's going on."

"Oh." It was all I could say. I was just about to say good night when she headed to the kitchen, then came back.

"You have another tattoo, don't you?"

I flashed my eyes to her. "How did you know?"

"I...um...saw it when you had your shirt off," she said slowly, hesitantly. "I saw the letters C-L-A-R, but I didn't see the rest."

I dragged my hair back. "This is when I tell you it's none of your business." I winked so she didn't think I was upset with her.

Alex nodded and parted her lips to reply, probably wanting to ask another question, but she was apparently unsure. I could guess what her next question would be. Before she could ask, I intervened. "Let's talk about something else," I said sternly.

"Sorry," she muttered.

Maybe I should've gone to the party. She was full of questions tonight. "How do you know when you really love someone? How do you know if a guy really loves you? I'm asking because you seemed to have lot more experience with relationships."

I thought about it for a moment. No one had ever asked me this question before. "Did Liam make you walk on air? That's how girls usually describe it when they fall in love."

"Not lately," she said under her breath.

I headed to the kitchen and Alex trailed behind me. After placing my mug in the sink, she did the same. "Have you ever heard the song called 'To Love A Woman,' by E.C.?"

"Maybe. How does it go?" She gazed into my eyes, begging. "Can you sing it to me?"

"No way," I blurted.

"Why not? You have such a great voice. I love to hear you sing, please." Alex grabbed my sweater and wouldn't let go.

With that smile and those innocent, bedroom eyes looking back at me, how could I deny her request? "Okay, just a snippet of it." I cleared my throat and focused my eyes onto hers. "You see her across the room, every other face disappears...the earth shakes inside of you, her smile crawls into your skin...touching your heart, your soul...you can do nothing, but dream of her...all you want to do is hold her in your arms."

Before I knew it, I had pinned her against the cabinet—lost in the moment, lost in the song, lost in her. My arms were planted around her. She was my prisoner, locked and mesmerized as I continued to sing. My voice became softer as I sang to her by the side of her neck. "You want to breathe her in and taste every word on her lips...touch her...taste her...make love to her until you can feel her in your blood...."

I backed away, needing a moment to clear my head. At the same time, I heard a long intake of breath from her. She looked like she was going to faint, and my ego went up a notch knowing that I could make her feel that way. I continued again, gazing into her eyes. This time I ran my hands on her cheeks, then through her hair. "...with every kiss, and every touch, she takes away pieces of you...till there's nothing left...but you need her so you let her...cause you love her...and you cannot breathe without her."

I had sung the whole song and I only meant to sing a section of it. I was caught in the moment, caught in this feeling I wanted to ignore, but it felt so good. I couldn't stop. "Alex," I whispered her name when I realized my hands were wrapped around her waist, though they weren't meant to be there.

My body was lightly pressed on hers. Dazed, I murmured, "Now that's how a man should really love his woman." Not knowing if I'd answered her question, I said goodnight and walked away without looking back.

I couldn't look at her. I was afraid of what I would do if her eyes gave me permission to do what I wanted to do at that very moment. Walking away was the only way I could maintain control, but she stopped me.

"Elijah, did you ever love anyone like that before?" she asked softly, still looking overcome, still planted against the cabinet as if she was stuck there.

"No. Goodnight, Freckles," I said and went to my room.

Alex's questions brought up the memories of my mom and my brother. As I lay in bed, I could clearly remember that dreadful day, as if it happened yesterday.

I didn't know what else to do. All I could do was be strong for my little brother and pretend everything was going to be all right. But it wasn't and he knew it wasn't. As he lay there helplessly in bed, I thought about all the good times we had shared, playing catch, watching movies, playing videos games, and tackling each other. I was eight years older than he was, but the age didn't matter. We were close.

How could a healthy, thirteen-year-old kid all of a sudden become so sick? His life had just begun. It wasn't fair for him and it wasn't fair for those of us who would be left with nothing but heartache and the memories of him. Life was cruel. I knew this all too well. It just sucked, and sometimes you couldn't do anything about it.

"Hi," Evan said softly, looking pale and weak.

"Hey," I said as cheerfully as I could. "You're never going to believe what I did."

"What?" His eyes grew wide with excitement, just like they always did whenever I said those words to him.

"Don't tell Mom, okay? I got it done today, so I'm a little sore. Don't you dare punch me there, got it?" I narrowed my eyes at him playfully so he knew I was messing with him.

A soft chuckled escaped his mouth. "Hurry. You talk too much. After I see it, then I'll decide. Where's Mom?" I could tell it took a lot more of his energy to speak today than yesterday, but his eyes twinkled with excitement.

"Mom's right outside. I told her I wanted to be alone with you." I took off my long-sleeved plaid shirt, lifted the sleeve, and showed it to him.

He gave me the happiest smile I'd ever seen. I wished I could've framed that look. I did in my mind so that I would never forget. Then his lips dropped, quivering, blinking his eyes to hold back the tears. "You did that for me? You got that cool looking dragon tattoo for me?"

"I sure did, buddy. I know how much you love dragons."

He looked away to wipe the tears, and then turned back to me. "So you could always remember me. Is that why you did it?"

My cool composure flew out the door. I couldn't look him in the eyes, knowing death was just around the corner. Unable to say a word, in fear I may lose it, I nodded instead.

"Can you give me a hug, Elijah? I can't jump on you anymore."

"Of course." I reached down and wrapped my arms around him. He was a lot weaker than yesterday and his words were slow in coming.

"When people go to Heaven do they remember the family they left behind?"

I released him. "I'm not sure."

"When it's your turn to go to Heaven, do you think we'll know each other?"

He was asking me a lot of questions that I didn't have answers to. My heart was breaking and the only thing I could do was to try to lighten the mood with some humor. Pointing to the tattoo on my arm I said, "How could you ever miss this? You'll remember me."

Evan snorted lightly. "Yeah, you're right." He paused. "Will you promise me something?"

"Of course."

"Will you stop smoking?"

"How did you know?" I was surprised. I had never smoked in front of him before.

"I peeked out the window one night and saw you with that girl you were dating. Both of you were smoking."

"You saw me with Clara? I didn't mean for you to see that. I don't smoke much so don't worry."

"I want you to stop. If you don't, when I get to Heaven, I'm gonna ask God to send you the hottest girl so she'll make you stop. You know, the kind of girl you can't live without. You'll do it for her." He started to laugh again, but it was very faint and short-lived.

"If you're planning on sending me the hottest girl, I'm going to wait. Anyway, I want the girl to love me for who I am and not what she wants me to be. And why am I talking about relationships with you?" I lightly rubbed his arm.

He managed to give me a smile and asked, "Do you think Dad knows I'm sick?"

"Evan. I don't want you to think about Dad right now." My tone was not pleasant. The word "dad" always made me react with anger. He left us three years ago when he became addicted to gambling, and we hadn't heard a word from him since. I had to calm down for Evan's sake. "If Dad knew you were sick. I'm sure he would've been here." It was a lie, but I knew he needed to hear that.

"Okay," he said. He rubbed his eyes, trying to hide his pain. Then he focused on me again. "How are you going to explain to Mom about your tattoo?"

"Don't worry so much, buddy. Just think happy thoughts."

Evan suddenly gazed to his right. "Do you see the light? Do you see her?" He tried to point to the window, but his arm dropped before he could.

I turned to his line of vision. What the heck was he talking about? "See what?"

Evan gingerly placed his hand on my tattoo without a reply. "I'll never forget you did this for me. Elijah...you're the best brother anyone could have." His voice was very faint, but it was very clear, piercing loudly through my heart.

Evan looked to his right again with a smile. I turned in that direction again, but I saw nothing. When his arm slid off my tattoo, I shot my eyes to his. His eyes were closed, and there was no more movement from his chest. That's when I knew.

It felt like someone punched my gut. The pain I felt was nothing I'd ever felt before. Sounds I didn't recognize escaped my mouth. As I held my little brother's hand for the last time, I let out a loud cry. My chest hurt, my hands trembled, and I shook so much it felt like any minute a bomb would explode inside of me. That's when my mother and the nurses rushed in.

Seeing my mom drop to the floor screaming, slapped me back into reality. For a second there, I had thought this was all a dream, but it wasn't. Suddenly, my focus returned and the pain ebbed just long enough for me to reach my mom.

I dropped to the floor beside her and hugged her. That was all I could do to comfort her. I couldn't take the pain away. Her cry was loud enough for the both of us. One of mom's hands pressed on the tattoo so tightly, pain ripped through me, but I didn't care. It was nothing compared to the pain I felt in my heart. Death had punctured a hole that couldn't be mended. How do you get past this?

Chapter 22

Alexandria

Lexy took me to the biggest Halloween shop I'd ever seen. There were rows and rows of costumes and it frazzled me. It didn't help that there were scary, disgusting looking figures everywhere I turned. Even seeing Jason's mask on display gave me the shivers, sending goose bumps down my back. I was happy when we headed to the women's section.

"Do you know what you want to be?" Lexy asked, struggling with a long blonde wig on her head. "I think I want to be something totally different. How about this one?"

"Lexy, you look hot in that wig," I exclaimed.

She laughed, taking if off. "Maybe I'll be a sexy pirate or a devil."

"How about this one?" I held up an angel costume.

"Hell no. I want to get the guys attention, Alex. I want to look like someone you want to sleep with, not someone you want to pray with," she laughed, turning to the other rack.

"Do you know what Seth and Elijah are going to be?" Even though Elijah had told me he wasn't dressing up, I thought there was a chance he was joking.

"Seth always dresses up as something really scary, and as for Elijah, he thinks he's too cool to dress up. I've been trying to get him to dress up for the past I-don't-know-how-many years. I just gave up. He'll come as his boring self."

"How about these?" I held up two costumes. "Why not be a superhero? Wonder Woman or Batwoman?

"Oh."

That got her attention big time.

"Batwoman. I'll try that on. Did you find something for yourself?"

"Yes, what do you think of this? I just need a curly blonde wig. Or I guess I could just curl my hair but it will be too long."

"You're going to look so hot. With your figure, you'll look just like her."

"You think so?"

"Come on, let's try it."

After grabbing a few costumes, we headed to the dressing room. I knew what I wanted, but Lexy tried on one after another, unable to decide.

"What do you think about this one?" she asked, spotting my phone in my hand. "Everything okay?"

"I don't know. Liam hasn't called. I told him that we needed a break, but all he cared about was that he wanted me to move out. He doesn't get it. It's like whatever I say means nothing to him. I was hoping he'd at least call to apologize, but it doesn't matter anyway. I'm breaking up with him. I just need to do it face to face."

"Oh." Her tone took a dip. "Forget about him. He's playing games with you. He's probably waiting for you to grovel at his feet first. There's going to be tons of guys at the party tonight, and with your outfit, you won't have any problems."

"Thanks," I said checking again for messages.

"Okay, I've decided. I'll be the sexy devil. Halloween is tomorrow and I don't want to come back again. I'm starving. Let's go."

We quickly cleaned up, paid, and left.

Whiteboard:
Thanks for the left over spaghetti.
Wondering what you'll be dressed as tonight.
-E

Lexy and I had to work the evening shift, so we went back to my place to get dressed. Elijah was helping Seth and his fraternity brothers. I was glad he was already there. Instead of eating out, I invited Lexy to eat the leftover spaghetti.

"That is so cute," Lexy gushed, directing her eyes on the whiteboard.

"Oh, that," I smiled, taking a heated plate out of the microwave oven and handing it to her. "It's how Elijah and I communicate sometimes."

"I've seen it before, but I didn't say anything." Lexy headed to the dining area.

"I have to say, Alex. You make the best spaghetti," she complimented, placing a fork full in her mouth.

"Thank you. It was my dad's special recipe."

"Sorry about your dad," she shrugged sheepishly.

"That's okay, Lexy. Elijah is right. The more I talk about him, the more the pain becomes bearable."

"I'm here for you," Lexy managed to say, taking another bite. "I'm lucky that I still have both my parents. Elijah on the other hand…." she stopped.

The chunk of spaghetti I just swallowed didn't go down smoothly when Lexy spoke about Elijah and what he had gone through. Life sucks sometimes, but having good friends to ease the grief can make up for not having any family for support.

"How about your mom?" Lexy asked, changing the subject.

145

"She's fine. My parents were divorced. I'm sure she grieves for my dad in her own way, but not in the same way as me. At least that's what I think."

After we ate and got dressed, we took pictures and sent them to Emma. Then we were on our way. I had a million butterflies dancing in my stomach, but I didn't know why.

I thought we were going to someone's house but it was actually at a restaurant. There were tons of people dressed up, looking stress-free and enjoying themselves. It was great to be surrounded by this contagious euphoric atmosphere.

"Tickets," the guy at the door said.

"What ticket?" I asked Lexy. She was digging through her purse. "Lexy, I didn't get a ticket," I panicked.

"Relax. I have yours." She handed him two tickets. When I got a glimpse of it, I saw how much they cost. They were fifty dollars each.

"Next!" the guy said out loud. That was our cue to move out of the way.

"Let me pay you back. I'm sorry. I didn't know I had to buy a ticket," I sighed, feeling like a dork. I had to raise my voice when Lexy led us further in. The music blasted in my ears.

"Don't worry about it. I didn't pay for them. You weren't supposed to see how much they cost."

"Who paid for mine?"

"Compliments of your roommate. Don't say anything to him, he'll get mad at me. Promise?"

The only thing I could do was nod. Thinking about how Elijah had paid for my ticket was running around in my head; I couldn't help but zone out. I was distracted, deep in my thoughts when I heard the whistles and noticed stares from the guys that hung out with Elijah. Dean was in that crowd. He waved us over.

"It's the hot devil and the hooker." Dean placed his arms around our shoulders, guiding us to where his group was sitting.

Hooker? He didn't get my costume, but that was fine. Maybe not a lot of people would, but I didn't care.

"Why, Elvis," Lexy flirted at Dean. "Aren't you a sexy thang? Love that wig." She touched it.

"Here we are," Dean grinned.

There were no chairs available around the table so we stood instead.

"Where are Seth and Elijah?" Lexy asked.

"Around here somewhere." Dean reached over and handed us each a drink.

"Thanks." I took a small sip, checking to see if I'd like the taste. I was so thirsty and nervous that I gulped the whole thing down.

Lexy blinked her eyes and dropped her jaw, looking shocked. "That thirsty or that nervous?"

I shrugged my shoulders and gave a "whatever" look.

"Alex?" I heard my name and turned.

"Cynthia?" I recognized her from Art History class. She and I sat together once.

Cynthia's eyes racked down my body. "It's good to see you here. You look fabulous. I love that movie."

"Thanks. You look great, too," I said, waving to her group of friends. Cynthia was dressed in a Little Red Riding Hood outfit— cute, but a little slutty.

After I introduced Cynthia and her friends to my group of friends, I turned to adjust my wig. When I turned back around, I could see their eyes bugging out of their heads and their jaws on the floor. You could practically see them drooling. When I looked up to where they were staring, I was pretty sure my facial expression matched theirs. I could not believe what I was seeing.

Oh My God! It was Danny. I mean…it was Elijah. That guy was the sexiest thing I had ever seen. He was wearing a black leather jacket, slightly off his shoulders. The form fitted T-shirt that curved every part of his toned chest was absolutely delectable, and his hair was slicked back. He strutted like the stud that he was. I was sure all the girls in this place wanted to drop their panties for him. I was completely mesmerized and I couldn't believe he dressed up like Danny. Now it was his turn to be surprised.

Elijah

The ladies drooled as soon as they saw me. It was awesome how they parted like the red sea as I walked through a group of them. I strolled up to my group of friends and came to a dead stop when I saw Alex. I was in complete shock. Dressed in black leather pants, a black top that clung to her breasts, red killer heels, and a blonde, short curly wig, she was my Sandy.

With a flash of her smile, the one that always left me undone, she waved shyly. I knew she liked what she saw from the look in her eyes. It was the same look all the ladies gave me, but the only one that mattered was hers.

"Danny?" she asked hesitantly with an awed expression on her face. "I thought you didn't dress up?"

"Yeah, Danny boy. When did you change your mind?" Lexy gave me a good smack. I hated when she did that.

"Did you both plan this?" Seth chuckled, eyeing Alex in a way I didn't like, but I couldn't blame him. So were the other guys. I wanted to cover up that gorgeous body of hers with my jacket.

"I'm not dressed up. I always look like this." I flicked my jacket and acted tough, just like Danny does in Grease.

"Yeah, whatever." Lexy slapped me again, and then turned to Seth. "Really? Jason again?"

"I had no time to shop. It was the easiest thing to put on."

"Gonna race tomorrow night?" Dean asked me. Why in the hell would he bring up a subject like that in front of everyone? I guess it was okay since it was so loud in here; it was difficult to hear the person standing next to you.

"Don't announce it to the world," I said sternly.

Dean gazed around. "Sorry. I thought it was okay since we were among friends."

"You just never know."

"You're racing again?" Alex asked. I could hear the disapproving tone in her words.

148

"It pays the bills, Alex," I said sharply. I wanted to say that I didn't have a dad who saved up a college fund like hers, but I knew better. I didn't have to say anything after that. Either she understood or didn't care. I hoped it was the first.

Alex and Lexy took off for the dance floor with some others while I grabbed a beer and sat between Seth and Dean.

"So, how's it going with Alex? Is she a good roommate?" Seth asked.

"She's great. I thought she was going to be a pain at the beginning. You know what I mean? But somehow, without even talking about it, we take turns...like getting the groceries, and knowing the other person's schedule so we don't hog up the bathroom."

"I'm not sure about you, but I would have a difficult time sleeping at night knowing a fine piece of ass was sleeping in the other room," Dean added, taking a sip of his beer.

Little did he know that thought crossed my mind many times. Unexpectedly, an arm slithered up my chest. "Heather," I greeted. I did a double take when I saw her dressed up like a Playboy Bunny. She looked hot, but I was surprised that I had no interest.

"Elijah, I've been looking all over for you, baby," she whispered in my ear. I could tell she was horny. If I gave her that look, she would have followed me anywhere if I wanted to fuck her, but I wasn't interested at all. I was hoping if I ignored her, she would go away, but she kept running her hands all over me, even down to my crotch. That's when I jumped out of my seat and turned to look for Alex.

Jealousy crept over me when I saw her dancing with a few of the frat boys surrounding her. It was difficult not to watch her dance. The way her body swayed to the music was hypnotic. I wasn't really upset until I saw Nolan approaching her. Seth placed his hand on my chest to calm me down.

"Don't go over just yet. Let's see what happens."

Sure enough, he was making his move. But unlike before, she didn't push him away and that kind of ticked me off. What was she thinking?

Chapter 23

Alexandria

Wiping drops of sweat with the back of my hand, I laughed and smiled at Lexy and my new friends as we danced away. The wig was itchy, but I ignored it. I even wanted to scratch my ass. These leather pants were making me feel hot and sweaty. What could I say? That's what I got for buying a cheap costume.

Suddenly, I felt the room spin a little and I flushed with heat. Floating off the ground, I was in a blissful state. Yup, I was buzzed. Dean's drink had tasted like punch but definitely had a lot of alcohol in it. I knew better than to take a drink from a stranger, but since it was from someone I knew, I gulped it down. Not a good idea. I made a mental note to never do *that* again. My dad would have been...I stopped thinking.

Dancing with my friends helped me forget about everything else, including Liam, Elijah, my dad, and just life in general. I was in the moment with no worries, just having a great time. The world had shut down around me until I turned to smile at Lexy, but she had moved on to someone else and I saw Elijah instead.

I gave him a smile, but instead of getting a smile back, I saw the disapproving look on his face. Great! Or was I wrong? Was he upset about something they were discussing, or about the guys I was dancing with? Was he jealous? Surely, he wasn't, but when I saw Nolan standing in front of me, I knew exactly what it was about. That one-second of satisfaction I had from the possibility he was jealous was gone when I saw Heather.

"My starter girl." Nolan's brows twitched flirtatiously. His body was too close for comfort. Next thing I knew, his hands were on my hips, swaying with me. I didn't care much for him, but now I had a dance partner and he was good.

The bass pumped through my ears and to my heart. I could feel it through my body, down to my toes as Nolan moved with mine in perfect harmony. The song, the beat, the moment, I was lost until the asshole started to run his hand down my back to my ass and grinded my body into his.

"What the hell, Nolan! Get off me," I stammered.

Nolan laughed in my face, still holding on to me. "You know you like it."

"I'm serious. Stop!" I shoved, but to no avail.

I didn't have to fight him again after that. When his body flew off mine, I stumbled sideways but didn't fall as expected. My breathing was heavy and ragged from dancing and anger. I knew the figure with his back toward me, blocking my view. Elijah held a guarded stance. With tight fists by his side, he was ready to give Nolan another blow.

"I've already warned you once. Don't you ever fuckin' touch her again. I'll break both of your wrists. Let's see if you can drive like that."

Nolan's friends were ready to fight, but so were Elijah's. When Nolan got in Elijah's face, I heard a whack.

I thought he punched Elijah in the face, but it was actually his hand blocking Nolan's fist. Elijah threw one right back, smack on

Nolan's jaw, causing him to hit the ground. Getting right back up, Nolan swung, but missed.

Just as Elijah was about to hit him again, Seth and Jonathan held him back, while Nolan was held back by a few of his friends. They were separated as their eyes burned into each other with hatred. Nolan and his friends left the party, acting like assholes the whole time.

I was just about to thank Elijah when he grabbed my arm. "Come with me," he ordered. He didn't wait for me to reply and tugged me out of the restaurant. I was pretty annoyed that Elijah was mad at me. It's not like it was my fault that he got into a fight with Nolan.

"What the hell were you thinking, dancing with him like that? And to top it off, you're wasted," he scolded.

I was so surprised by his tone, that all I could do at first was blink and soak in his words. Then it all came pouring out. "You have no right to tell me who I can dance with. I was just having fun. I had it under control and I'm not wasted." My tone was just as angry as his was.

"Under control?" he huffed. "He had his hand on your ass and he was practically fucking you on the dance floor. Is that what you call fun?"

"Who I dance with or who I fuck on the dance floor is my business. Who made you my babysitter?"

Elijah's eyes grew. His jaw was tight. He ran his hands through his hair and exhaled a deep breath. "You're right, I have no right. Don't play with fire; you'll get burned. Nolan is not your type. And aren't you still with Liam?" His tone was accusatory.

"I'm not sure," I spit out the words. Though I had planned to break up with Liam, I didn't want to tell Elijah. This topic had nothing to do with what we were arguing about. At least I didn't think it did.

"Don't you have a girlfriend? You're such a hypocrite. Aren't you at Heather's place when you don't come home until late at night?"

His brows angled, digesting what I had just said. Even I couldn't believe what I was saying, but I couldn't take it back. I was furious.

"Is that where you think I've been?" He looked disappointedly surprised. "Were you dancing with Nolan because you were jealous of Heather?" His lips protruded out, trying to hold in a smile or a laugh. I couldn't tell which one.

"No. I'm not jealous. I was just having fun dancing," I retorted and looked away. Shit! I couldn't help being jealous, but I didn't want him to see it. That didn't last long. I peered up since he hadn't said a word. He kept on staring, studying me.

"Are you done now? I'm cold. I want to go back in." I really wasn't, but I didn't want to stand there any longer.

"I'm sorry," he said softly when I started to head back. That made me stop.

"For what?" I asked. My back was still to him.

"For wanting to protect you." His tone was tender and it broke my heart. I could feel how much he wanted to protect his brother and his mother and he couldn't, but this was different.

"You don't have to feel like you have to protect me. I want you to be my friend, Elijah."

"A friend," he repeated, but it sounded more like a question. "I'm not sure what that means anymore." His words came out fast but soft. I wasn't sure if I had heard him correctly. When he walked away, I knew our little spat was over and everything would be fine in the morning like it always was, pretending that nothing ever happened between us.

Lexy and I didn't stay long since we had to work the next day. After she dropped me off, I went straight to bed, but I couldn't sleep. My mind wandered with thoughts of Elijah and Liam. I knew I wanted to end things with Liam, but what about Elijah? He never told me straight out that he was interested in me.

It was strange to have feelings for the type of guy I would never have considered dating. I swore I would never date a guy who smoked, although he hadn't smoked around me since he knew my dad passed away from lung cancer. Still, I couldn't help the way I felt. Every time I saw Elijah, my heart jumped and my sex drive had a mind of its own.

I must have dozed off for just a little while, because when I woke up it was still dark out. The need to quench my thirst was what woke me since the air from the heater made my throat dry. Groggily heading to the kitchen to get a drink of water, I walked out with barely anything on. Elijah was asleep since he came home shortly after I did. The lights were off, so it wasn't as if I had to worry about anyone seeing me.

My eyelids were so heavy that I was squinting as I tried to find the refrigerator handle. I'm pretty sure if anyone had seen me, I'd have looked like a zombie with my arms extended out as I opened the fridge door. Laughing at myself, I ended up grabbing the carton of milk since it was the first thing my fingers touched. As I was reaching for a cup, a shadow passed over me. The carton of milk went flying out of my hands, and ended up pouring all over me when I jumped up screaming bloody murder.

Chapter 24

Elijah

Whiteboard:
I cleaned the bathroom
since you vacuumed.
-Alex

    Unable to sleep on my bed, I decided to lay on the sofa, hoping I could fall asleep there. I was thinking about Alex and what I could do to distance myself from her. I knew that I was probably the cause of her fights with Liam, which wasn't right, even though I couldn't stand the dick. I had to do something about the situation since I could never give Alex what she needed and wanted.

    When I saw a light from the kitchen, I tossed my blanket aside and headed in that direction to see if Alex needed anything. Whoa! I was surprised to see her wearing nothing but her panties and a plain white T-shirt. Hot damn! She was beautiful.

    I didn't mean to scare her. In fact, I didn't say a word. I was going to walk away, but when I saw that she was half-naked, I couldn't take my eyes off her. The fridge door hadn't closed all the way, so there was just enough light for me to get a clear view. When Alex jumped and screamed, the milk carton went flying and the milk spilled all over her, from her chest to her toes, pooling around her.

Her shirt was soaked and I could see her hardened nipples through it. The sight of her had my dick stirring in my boxers. I was going to have this image burned in my mind forever, and I knew that I'd be dreaming of this moment for a long time to come. I grabbed the kitchen towel and reached out to hand it to her. Looking horrified and embarrassed, she slipped on the puddle of milk when she moved away from me.

Trying to stop her from falling, I slipped myself. It happened so fast, I didn't even know how we both landed on the floor with me on top of her, the same positions we were in on the ice. Only this time we were wet from the milk that was all over the floor.

My left hand was supporting her neck while my other hand had a mind of its own, and so did my dick. It did not help that I was only wearing my boxers.

"Alex, are you okay?" I whispered in her ear breathlessly, feeling my heart pound rapidly against my chest. It took every ounce of my willpower not to bury myself deep inside her, but I couldn't stop myself from rubbing my hand in a circular motion on the side of her breast.

"Yes," she breathed softly. Her breath quickened as she lay stiffly, and she didn't make a move to get up. Her eyes bore into mine in surprise and something I couldn't describe, but I was pretty sure it was the same look I was giving her. The look that screamed...I WANT YOU NOW!

What possessed me to do what I did next was beyond my control. I had totally lost all of my willpower. Being in this position and with no one around, I let my selfish need for her take over. The need I had the minute I laid my eyes on her. I wanted her and I was going to have her.

"Alex," I murmured. "I'm going to taste you now."

I didn't let her respond. After I heard what sounded like a whimper, I sucked on the wet spot on her neck that was splattered with milk. That was just the beginning. I couldn't stop there. While I licked my way down, my hand slipped underneath her T-shirt and headed toward her breast. She arched her back and let out a sexy little moan that made me even more excited.

After pulling up her T-shirt to expose her breast, my tongue circled around it, and I sucked and teased her nipple until she felt the need to take a fist full of my hair. I knew I was driving her insane. Thinking she would push away and knowing I should end this before it went too far, I started to slow down. But when Alex started to spread her legs open for me—Holy shit! There was no way in hell I could control it now.

"We shouldn't," she groaned. "But don't stop."

That was all the confirmation I needed. I crushed my lips on hers hard from all the sexual tension that had built up for so long. I slid my hands underneath that fine ass of hers and teasingly rocked on top of her, obviously giving her what she wanted.

Alex moaned louder, putting me over the edge. I was desperately trying to control my urge. Everything about this felt so right and yet so wrong. I had to stop. I knew she would let me have her and if we gave into temptation tonight, we would both be screwed. There wasn't going to be an "us" after this. I couldn't give her the good things in life she deserved.

Alexandria

I dreamt about this several times, but I never knew Elijah would feel this good. When his mouth was over my nipple, I had utterly left all reality behind and floated blissfully away. When his lips were on mine, every single nerve in my body jolted, awakening me. I couldn't understand why his touch excited me more than Liam ever could. Maybe because I knew Elijah was off limits or because I got a taste of what so many women wanted. Maybe it was the way he was caressing me with such need and passion.

I knew Elijah was slowing down and was probably thinking that this wasn't a good idea, but it didn't stop him when I moaned louder. When he pressed down on me, I nearly exploded. My body temperature changed drastically, and I stopped shivering from the cold milk. Having his hard body over mine, I completely came unglued. I withered under him and allowed myself to be taken. Surrendering to him, I didn't care what tomorrow would bring. I just wanted this moment with him, but at the same time, I had a feeling we were making a mistake.

Elijah suddenly stopped and let out a heavy breath. "Alex, what are we doing?" We can't. You know how this will end up." He had finally let go.

The truth was, he was right. I had let my desire and want take over. The fact that I was a virgin was another reason to stop, even though Elijah had no clue.

I didn't know how to answer his question as I continued to stare at his sexy smile and enjoy his hand caressing my cheeks. "Eli...jah," I hesitated, not sure how much I should tell him. "I'm not really that...what I mean to say is I'm not...." I was really making a mess of this, but how do you tell a guy you're a virgin? I sucked in a deep breath. Here it goes. "I'm a virgin," I blurted before I could change my mind.

Elijah nodded, looking at me blankly. Suddenly, I was lifted off the ground. He carried me to the bathroom and turned on the water.

"Take a shower," he directed, unable to look me in the eyes. "I'll clean the kitchen."

His tone told me that what happened between us would never happen again. Apparently, it didn't mean much to him. Whether one of us would end up moving out because of this, I didn't know.

Chapter 25

Elijah

I slept in as long as I could, purposely avoiding Alex after what happened last night. My mind kept on racing, thinking about how good she felt in my arms, but at the same time wondering how I had let it go that far. Now knowing she's a virgin, I'm glad I stopped. Since it was Saturday, I knew Alex had gone to work. Stretching and yawning, I went to the kitchen to get something to eat. My heart softened when I saw a plate covered with clear plastic wrap and the note on the whiteboard.

Elijah,
Hope you win this race.
Please be careful.
I made this breakfast for you.
Liam is coming over to talk.
P.S. Don't dunk your pancake in a glass of milk.
It will fall apart. I know you want to. Lol!
-Alex

Laughing aloud at her words, I lifted the cover. I let out a quick chuckle to see a racecar-shaped pancake. Cute! How could I eat this? I was starving, so I did anyway. Enjoying every bite, I saw Alex's smile in my mind, but I couldn't help the pain in my heart thinking of her back with that asshole. He wasn't good enough to be in the same room with her. I guess last night meant nothing to her. That hurt more than I wanted it to. It didn't matter. None of this would be any good for either one of us.

I guess it was a good thing she wouldn't be at the race. At least she wouldn't be a distraction for me. I would constantly worry about her if she were there. Little did she know that I had told Lexy not to bring her. It was one of the most dangerous sites and the crowds were going to be worse than the last ones. It wasn't safe for any audience, but unfortunately, more people meant more money for me.

After I ate the pancake, I drank a glass of juice and washed the dishes. I headed to my room where I saw a gift bag with my name on it. How did I miss that?

Elijah,
Happy belated Birthday!
Everyone needs a home, even pictures.
Hope you like them.
-Alex XO

The two picture frames were simple, just like how I like things. They each had a black border around them and that was all. My friends and I didn't exchange birthday presents, so it had been a while since I received one. Not only was I very touched by her gesture, I felt like crap about last night. I wished she could be mine.

Alexandria

"So you and Liam made up for the one hundredth time?" Lexy asked, leaning against the counter. It was so slow today. All we did was talk. Occasionally, my mind drifted off to last night and I could still feel the heat lingering from Elijah's touch. I wanted to tell Lexy what had happened mostly out of guilt, but knowing nothing good would come out of me telling her, I decided to keep that topic to myself. The fact that it would never happen again was another reason.

I frowned at her. She was right. Liam and I had been fighting more and more since I moved away to college. "To tell you the truth, I told him to come over so I can tell him in person that it's over. I just need the courage to do it. My feelings for him have changed. Maybe we're both changing. It's also this long distance relationship. It's difficult and he doesn't like that I'm living with Elijah." Talking it over with Lexy helped me sort my thoughts.

"Can you blame him?" Lexy said quickly. "I mean, would you want Liam living with a hot looking girl?"

Once upon a time I would've cared, but I didn't anymore. And how do I even know he wasn't with other girls? Who knew what he was doing? He was the one that had the car. He never invited me to his place. "I guess not. He wants me to meet his parents during Christmas vacation."

"Wow…that's pretty serious."

"I'm not going to. I'm not sure if it's because he's older, but I feel like I don't have a say in the relationship sometimes. It's like I need to accommodate his needs and his wants before mine. Am I being selfish?"

"Of course not. Relationships should be give and take."

"He wanted me to spend Christmas and New Year's Eve with him, which is fine, but what about my family? What about getting to know my friends?"

"Did you talk to him about this?"

"Yes, but he always gets his way."

"Hmmm…acting like a true lawyer already. Didn't you say he wants to go to law school?"

"Yup."

"You should have done what always works. If he's not giving in, then don't put out." Lexy's face was so serious; I thought she was joking at first.

"Does that work?" I only asked since I didn't feel like telling Lexy that I was a virgin.

"Hell yes. All guys ever think about is sex."

I let out a chuckle. "What are you doing for Thanksgiving?"

"I was going to go home, but I may just stick around and go home during Christmas break instead. It's costly to fly to New York. I might as well go for a week instead of a weekend."

"How about Elijah? Does he have any relatives nearby?"

"Why don't you ask him?"

I looked away. "Sometimes, he can be so complicated. I don't know if he likes me. I mean...like a friend." Oh God! I didn't even know what the heck we were after last night.

"Elijah is complicated, but he has a huge heart. He cares too much, but at the same time, he tries not to show it. For example, he doesn't want you at the race tonight." Lexy stiffened. "Shoot. Please don't tell him I said anything, okay?"

"He doesn't want me to go?" I don't know why, but that hurt my feelings. I wished I hadn't made him that racecar-shaped pancake. What the hell was I thinking? Feeling bad for causing a fight between Nolan and him, it was my way of apologizing for everything, including last night.

"Don't take it the wrong way. The crowd will be worse tonight and even I'm not going. It's not a safe place to be. And Liam is coming over to see you right?"

"Yeah, if he doesn't cancel. I wouldn't blame him. The drive is really long. I want him to come over so I can let him go. I don't feel right doing it over the phone or in a text."

"Wow, you are seriously going to break up with him?"

"Yes."

"Well, it happens. You grow, you make mistakes, and you change. You also see things in a different light. Not only will you make a lot of mistakes with your first, he will also be the hardest to let go. That being said, if you're sure he's not the one, then let him

162

go. You have yet to meet your Mr. Right, the one who was meant for you."

Letting Lexy's words of wisdom soak in, I knew she was right, but it was easier said than done. Letting go of someone was always difficult. It's as if they took a piece of you with them and you couldn't get it back.

"When will you know if Liam is coming?" Lexy asked.

My phone vibrated in the back pocket of my jeans. "You must be a psychic." Taking it out, I read the text from Liam. "He's not coming," I grumbled.

Lexy gave me a sympathetic smile. "Let's go out, just the two of us. What do you say?" Lexy must have seen the disappointed expression on my face.

"Sure." Then I had an idea. "Have you ever baked a turkey?"

Lexy grimaced. "Are you kidding? I can't even stand to touch one."

After letting out a small chuckle, I suggested, "Since you're not going home for Thanksgiving, how about I roast a turkey?"

"You know how?" Her mouth opened wide in surprise.

"Yes. I'll ask my friend, Emma, to help me."

"You're not going home?"

"No," I said wearily, texting Emma to ask her to come for Thanksgiving. "It's the first Thanksgiving without my dad. I don't want to spend it with my mom and my stepdad. I'd rather spend it with my friends."

"Girl, I will help you with everything else but the turkey."

"Deal."

Chapter 26

Alexandria

Lexy drove me to another place after dinner when she got a text from Seth, letting her know where they were going to celebrate Elijah's win.

"Are you sure I should be there?" I asked worriedly. After last night, I knew we were trying to avoid each other, but I guess now would be as good a time as any to face him. Having friends around would help me, like what happened between us was no big deal. It obviously meant nothing to him.

"Why not?" Lexy gave me a strange look.

"Elijah didn't invite me and he didn't want me at the race."

"I already told you why. Don't be ridiculous. He's just your roommate." Lexy tugged me inside.

The air was filled with music and excitement as we walked in, and seeing all the people I recognized was comforting.

"Lexy, it's good to see you," a plump lady said, pulling Lexy into her arms.

"Mama Rose," Lexy squealed, returning the hug. "This is Alex."

"So this is Alex. It's so nice to finally meet you." She gave me the same tight squeeze.

"Thank you," I smiled, unsure what to call her. "It's nice to meet you, too."

"Mama Rose is Seth's mom," Lexy explained. "She's the owner of this restaurant."

Seth had his mom's green eyes and similar facial structure. "Seth's mom," I repeated.

"You girls here to party with the boys and all those girls?" She gestured with a nod of her head.

All of those girls? Surely she didn't mean...oh yes, she did. I'd never seen so many girls at any of their parties before.

"If Elijah keeps winning races like that, he's going to have a line of girls at his doorstep. He'll be famous like a rock star. Shoot, if I was younger, I would be first in line."

Lexy and I snapped our eyes at each other. We started to laugh, but we held back the loud cackle that wanted to burst out of our mouths.

"It's true," she continued. "I may be old, but I have eyes."

Looking through the crowd, I saw Elijah standing with a bottle of beer in his hand. With his signature leather jacket on, he leaned back against the wall, looking cool and collected. His lips deliciously curled into a sexy, irresistibly wicked grin. He was thoroughly enjoying himself.

Blood had drained out of me and an icy chill suddenly shivered through me from seeing all those girls' hands on him. I knew girls were attracted to him, but why did it bother me this much? There was a sting in my heart, and it got worse when he kissed one of them. I had no idea who they all were. I didn't remember ever seeing them before on campus. Knowing last night meant nothing to him for sure now, I pretended, too, but I couldn't help the tears collecting in my eyes or the pain in my heart.

"Alex, let's go." Lexy broke me out of my trance.

The closer we got to them, the harder my heart pounded against my chest. The room suddenly felt small and it was difficult to breathe. I needed air. What I needed to do was to pull myself together. What made this worse was that he didn't even acknowledge me. He had to have seen me. There was no way anyone could have missed Dean's greeting.

"Lexy. Alex!" Dean slurred his words. He was thoroughly wasted. When he draped his arms around us, I got a good whiff of his breath. "You missed a good face...no." He shook his head. "Pace. No. Race." He laughed at his own words and so did we. "He almost boom....twash...no...cwash."

I flashed my eyes at Elijah. The thought that he could have been injured made me feel sick. I could vividly picture his car smashed, or even worse, tumbling into the crowd, killing some spectators. At that moment, I caught his eyes, but he turned away so fast I knew for sure he was purposely ignoring me.

I tried to snub him as best as I could, but I couldn't help my curious eyes shifting to him, wondering what he was doing. I knew I had seen enough when his hands and lips were on another girl.

For the first time, I felt like I didn't belong here. Everyone at our table was chatting away and I sat there listening. Lexy was sweet for bringing me, but I should have gone with my gut and gone home instead. No! It was a good thing I saw Elijah with another girl. He never did care for me in that way, and whatever fantasy or whatever thought I had about the possibility that maybe...just maybe...there could be something between us was gone. He killed it big time. My heart ached mercilessly and I was tearing up.

Tonight, he validated why I didn't date someone like him. He validated that what I wanted was someone stable, who knew what he wanted. Sure, Liam may be domineering at times, but at least I knew he loved me, didn't he? Even then I wasn't sure. Not that I was thinking of working things out with him. To me, we had broken up already. To hell with guys!

Why did my heart ache so much? Had I fallen for Elijah? What was wrong with me? I could never date anyone who smoked, that looked dangerous, and especially not someone who raced for a living. Oh God! I needed to snap out of it.

Feeling the dagger twist deeper and not wanting to be in the same room with Elijah, I texted Lexy, who had excused herself to the restroom. I wrote that I was catching a ride home. Turning around one last time, I noted Elijah was gone. That only meant one thing and I felt disgusted at myself for being this jealous…for letting it get this far…for letting it get to me.

Since our condo wasn't that far, I flung my purse over my shoulder and walked out the door. The sting from the cold breeze awakened me as I ran. I could see the mist puffing out of my mouth with every ragged breath I took. When I got home, I saw all the lights were on. I heard the muffled sounds from his room, and I knew Elijah had brought his date home. He was breaking my heart everywhere I turned tonight.

I suddenly recalled Lexy's words, when she told me if Elijah brought home too many girls and I couldn't stand it, I could sleep at her place. Then I remembered Cynthia, who had asked me in class if Elijah brought home a new girl every night. There was a reason my friends had said these things. I found out tonight that Elijah was a big time player. He had been hiding it from me. I felt like a huge fool for almost falling into his trap.

Elijah knew how to weasel his way into a girl's heart. Everything about him screamed trouble, but how could a girl ignore his charm, his charisma, his…everything? Wanting to prove that he had no effect on me, I went to the bathroom and made my appearance known by flushing the toilet, taking a shower, and making loud banging noises with the cabinets. There was no way he could miss me now.

After I got into bed, I texted Lexy again to let her know I was home safe. I also saw Emma's text letting me know she was coming down early to help me bake the turkey. I was just about to tell her not to bother, when I changed my mind, thinking about how excited Lexy was. Why did I open my big fat mouth?

It was difficult to sleep when all I could think about was what they were doing in his room. Now that I had a taste of Elijah, I could imagine what he was doing to her. I was just another girl that didn't make it on the one-night stand list. I meant nothing to him and apparently, our friendship meant nothing, either. At that moment, I hated him. Anger, frustration, confusion, love, lust, want, need, and sadness were all mixed up, jumbled into one messed up me. I never felt so many emotions all at once.

Putting a pillow over my head so I couldn't hear them, unexpected tears fell. They were tears for missing my dad, and tears because I didn't want to fall for Elijah, but I knew deep down inside, I already had. I would fight this feeling with everything I had and be strong, because I had a wake-up call tonight.

Elijah

I almost freakin' crashed the car. Death looked me right in my face, but it let me go. I was almost certain the car had been tampered with, and my only suspect was no doubt, Nolan. But holy shit! I had never been afraid of dying before, and I knew something had changed in me. I needed a reality check or more like an "Elijah doesn't give a fuck" check. That was the attitude I was used to.

Street racing was dangerous. I was willing to risk my life for fast cash. It was easy. Desperate measures meant desperate calls. If I died in the process, I didn't care, but a part of me did tonight. That scared me more than dying.

Seeing Alex tonight made me feel guilty for racing. She was like the angel on my shoulder who was shaking her head, telling me that this was not the way. I knew it wasn't, but it would have to be for now.

I assumed she was with Liam tonight, but when I saw her walking in with Lexy, my heart not only jumped out of my chest for her, but there was an ache I didn't want to feel. It was raw pain, deeper than the ocean; a pain I hadn't felt in a long time. And I knew what I had to do.

Being surrounded by girls was something I was used to, but being surrounded by them and not flirting back was not. When

Diane had her hands all over me, I responded by kissing her. I'd never kissed a girl in front of Alex before and I had no idea why. She was the one who was with someone. Why would she care and why would it matter to her?

Ever since she entered my life, I was adapting for her. I stopped bringing girls home, except for that one time. I said no to having parties at my place since I had to share with Alex. I even made sure to clean up after myself and to keep our place clean. This was not what I was used to doing. Not wanting to smoke in front of her caused me to smoke less. It also made me feel uncomfortable, since her father had died of lung cancer and it would remind her of that. I had even stopped flirting with all those girls that threw themselves at me.

I had become someone else. What was next? But I did it for her. My worries, my anger, and even the loss of my family was forgotten when she was around. I swear she would be the destruction of me.

I could tell Alex was trying not to look, but I could also tell she was curious at who I had in my arms. A part of me felt good that she bothered to look, but when she turned away, I felt like an asshole. Why should I care? She was the one that was taken, not me. I was playing games and I would play even harder tonight, just so that whatever she thought she felt for me would be gone completely. I wanted her to be disgusted with me so it would be easier for me to move on.

I took Tracy home with me since Diane was wasted. Yup, that should do it. Whatever feeling Alex had for me was out the door tonight. It was better this way.

Chapter 27

Alexandria

Whiteboard:
My friend is coming over today.
She will be spending the night.
I will be sleeping on the sofa.
-Alex

The best thing to do was pretend it never happened. That is what I did for the next couple of weeks. I went to work, went to my classes, and did my own thing. I even started looking at "roommates wanted" ads. Elijah was out most of the time, too.

I did jot on the whiteboard that I was making a turkey dinner several days ago, and that Seth, Lexy, and Dean would be here for Thanksgiving. I didn't know if he saw the note or not, but at this point, I didn't care. That whiteboard was his idea and if he didn't bother to look at it, then it was his problem. Whether he chose to be here or not would be his decision.

Liam texted me to let me know he wasn't going home for Thanksgiving. I asked him if he wanted to come just to see what he would say, but he opted out, knowing it would mean being with my group of friends. If there was any doubt in my mind about breaking up with Liam, he just gave me one more reason to do so. I don't know what I would have said if he had agreed, but I couldn't wait for Christmas break so I could finalize our breakup. I also couldn't wait to see Emma. When the doorbell rang, I ran knowing who it was.

"Emma," I cheered as I opened the door. But it wasn't her. The girl who stood before me was someone I had never seen before. She was tall and beautiful with long dark hair. The look she gave me summed up her personality. She was not to be messed with.

"Who are you?" she asked. Her tone was not sweet. In fact, it was more like how dare I be there.

"I'm Alex, Elijah's roommate. Can I help you?"

"Can you tell Elijah that I came by?"

"Who should I say stopped by?"

"Clara," she replied quickly and left.

Clara…why did that name ring a bell? Then it came to me. Lexy's brief discussion about how Clara was Elijah's disaster and the initials on his tattoo. C-L-A-R. The missing letter must be A.

Almost immediately after I went back inside, the doorbell rang again. This time I was careful to check and I was rewarded with the sight of my friend.

"Emma," I squealed. She grew out her auburn hair and she looked cute in her jeans and striped sweater.

"Alex." She threw herself at me and I happily held her tightly as the tears of missing her came crashing through. She was my comfort, my warmth, and my home.

Wiping any evidence of the tears I had, I welcomed her in. "So…what do you think of my place?"

Dropping her bag, she glanced around. "It's cozy, just enough furniture, nothing fancy. For a place with two girls, you sure didn't decorate this place the way you and I would have." Emma curled her lips and lifted her brows. "I'm just giving you a hard time 'cause

I'm jealous." She nudged me, breaking me out of my thoughts, wondering if Elijah would be home tonight. "Did you remember to defrost the turkey?"

"Yeah, I got your text. Follow me. I'll show you to my room. I'll sleep on the sofa." Emma trailed behind me.

"You don't need to sleep on the sofa." Emma gave me that pity eye look.

"Of course I do. You're my guest. It's too bad I don't have a bigger bed. Hey, I didn't make anything for dinner, so I thought I could take you out and show you the campus."

Emma didn't answer, her eyes swung to the sound of the door being opened. When her eyes grew wide and she sucked in air, I knew who had entered. She was taking in all his hotness, seeing his fine sculpted chest as he peeled off his leather jacket and set it on the sofa.

With her eyes still on Elijah, she smacked my arm lightly and mouthed, "Where on Earth did he come from? Tell me you see what I'm seeing. Or did my dreams just come true?"

When Elijah turned at the sound of our voices, he gave a shy sexy grin to Emma, but when he saw me, his smile faded. I'm not sure what I did to deserve this cold treatment from him, but it made me want to move out even faster. Needing to be polite for Emma's sake, I introduced them.

"Emma...this is Elijah. Elijah...this is Emma, my friend from home."

Emma giggled like a schoolgirl. "Hi," she waved.

"It's nice to meet you, Emma." Elijah shook her hand. "You're the one who's going to bake our turkey. That's very sweet of you."

"You're coming?" she squealed too happily.

"I'm pretty sure I am since I live here." He let out a short chuckle.

"You live here?" She sounded completely surprised and that's when Elijah looked at me. Now he knew I hadn't told her about him. Good! He'll seem less important and his ego might come down a notch or two. Or maybe he won't care.

"I guess Alex didn't tell you." His tone sounded somber, almost as if he was disappointed.

"I did," I butted in. "She knows you as Ellie."

Emma looked confused, looking at me with those big eyes of hers, asking me for clarification.

"Emma, Elijah's nickname is Ellie. I didn't know before. I didn't tell you because...." I paused, flicked my eyes at Elijah. "Anyway, I won't be staying here too long. Also, Emma and I are on our way out so you can bring home whomever you want." I don't know why I said what I just said, but it was too late to take it back. "And by the way, someone named Clara stopped by." After I said those words, I headed to my bedroom without making eye contact with him. I needed to get our jackets and purses and get the hell out of there. It was too hard to be in the same room with him.

Elijah

Seeing Alex without a smile made me feel guilty, but why was I feeling this way? If she had a fight with her boyfriend again, that was not my problem. She shouldn't be with someone who made her that miserable. When she said she wasn't staying here too long, it gave me a little jolt to my heart. I hoped she didn't mean she was planning to move out. Then again, if she did, maybe it would be good to give us some distance, but I felt bad that she felt like she had to. Maybe I should consider moving out instead.

When she mentioned Clara's name, my heart took a leap. She had been calling me, and I knew the reason why. It was always the same. Go out with a loser. He breaks her heart, and she comes running back to me. I wasn't going to play her game anymore. I only hoped she didn't say anything to Alex, like telling her I had cheated on her when it wasn't true. Clara used that excuse to leave me for another rich guy, but as usual, she came back to me when he dumped her. Enough was enough.

Alex and Emma went out. I didn't ask where they were going. I assumed they were going out to dinner since it was around that time.

I hated to admit it, but I missed Alex's cooking and the leftovers she would save for me. Though she never admitted it, I knew she cooked extra just for me, and that touched my heart deeply. I had to remain strong. She was still seeing someone else. To me, that was an indication she didn't want to let him go. After all, they had a history together and he'd been there for her through her father's death. At least I could give him credit for that. I just hoped I could make it through Thanksgiving dinner.

Chapter 28

Alexandria

Emma blasted her iPad and music filled the air. Cooking the turkey with Emma reminded me of the days when my dad was still alive. Every other year, I got to spend Thanksgiving Day with my dad, and when I did, Emma would come over just to help me bake the turkey. Everything else I could handle.

Elijah either went for a run or to the gym, I didn't know which, but I knew he had gone to work out since he came through the door all sweaty. Emma's jaw dropped and she was practically drooling. She almost dropped the turkey.

"Emma," I snapped. She broke out of her trance and stuck the prepped turkey into the oven.

"I can't help it. I don't blame Liam for asking you to move out. Regardless, I'm so happy you're going to break it off with him. But holy crap, Alex. How do you sleep at night, knowing that hottie is sleeping in the other room?"

I rolled my eyes. I'd heard that question way too many times. "He's just a guy, not a god," I stated and started to cut the potatoes.

Emma closed the oven, turned on the timer, and stuck her head in the fridge.

"Everything we need is right here," I reminded.

"I know. I need to cool down."

"Seriously? Shut up." I tugged her out.

"I'm just playing around. I've missed you so much. I missed those days when we used to talk about boys and sneak out to parties. You know your father knew you were sneaking out, right?"

"What are you talking about?" I dumped the potatoes in the pot, placed the pot on the stove, and set it to boil.

"I didn't tell you so you wouldn't feel nervous about doing it. I saw him peek out the window several times."

"He did?" I started to peel the onions while Emma trimmed the beans.

"Yeah. Your dad was cool like that. He understood. We came home at a decent hour, which was probably one of the reasons why he didn't say anything to you."

"Yeah, he was the best," I agreed and started to tear up. For a change, it wasn't from what Emma had said; it was from cutting the onions. The aroma shot through my nostrils and burned my eyes. I had no choice but to shut them and let the tears pour out.

"Alex, you should have let me cut the onions. I forgot how cutting onions affects your eyes."

Emma shoved the napkin in my hand. I wiped the tears and headed to the bathroom with my eyes still shut. Just as I took a step out of the kitchen, I bumped into something hard.

"Alex, are you alright?" Elijah asked. I had my hands pressed against my eyes as he took hold of my arms. His tone was sweet and sounded genuinely concerned. He cleaned up real fast.

"It's the onion," I sniffed, still unable to open my eyes. "It stings. I've never had it this bad before."

Elijah led me to the bathroom and told me to bend over the sink. He splashed cool water on my face. After hearing the sound of the cabinet being opened and closed, I heard the water running again. Then, he placed a cool towel over my eyes.

176

"Does it feel better?" He could be so sweet when he wanted to be and that calmed my anger toward him.

"I'm okay." The burning sensation lingered somewhat, but it was much better. Trying to adjust my vision, I blinked several times. "Thanks."

"Freckles, are you winking at me?" He cracked a joke and my heart stung when he called me Freckles, but he made me smile. That was unexpected.

"Did you need something from the kitchen?" I asked, changing the subject.

"Looks like both of you were having so much fun in there, I thought I'd help."

I couldn't believe how he was warming up to me as if nothing ever happened between us. Maybe this was the best way to move forward. I had to try to get everything back the way it was because I missed this. I missed our friendship, the talks, and the closeness between us.

I missed HIM.

"Lexy is coming over to help. You don't have to. Emma and I have done this many times before with my dad. We haven't burnt the turkey yet," I snorted.

Elijah nodded in understanding and he even gave me a sympathetic look when I mentioned my dad.

"Want to know a little secret?" Elijah took a step forward and I tried to take a step back. With nowhere to go, I was backed against the sink. His muscles flexed and his hands rested on either side of the sink, making me his prisoner. I couldn't breathe and he gave me no space when he leaned in. His lips brushed against the tip of my ear as if to reveal a top secret. "I can make one hell of an order of mashed potatoes."

"You can?" I asked, feeling dizzy by his proximity. His lips were way too close. I could almost touch them with my own. Recalling our first kiss, how they tasted and felt, I thought I was gravitating toward them.

"And you know what else?" he continued.

I nodded because speaking was out of the question. A minute ago, I was extremely mad at him. Now, I was totally melting into him. How does he do that to me? It's unnerving. I had to snap out of it.

"I make really good beans, too."

I bet he could make anything taste good.

"That's what my little brother always told me anyway." His flirty eyes became soft.

I felt his pain when he mentioned his brother, and my eyes shifted to his dragon tattoo. Without thinking clearly, I reached for his cheek and gently stroked it in a circular motion. Surprisingly, Elijah closed his eyes, pressed his cheek into the palm of my hand, and let me comfort him.

We both jerked and flashed our eyes to the door when there was a knock. I didn't realize Elijah had shut the door behind us.

"Are you guys okay in there?" Emma asked. How long were we in here? I had no clue. Time always seemed to stand still when Elijah and I were alone.

"We're fine. We'll be right out," I managed to say, feeling my pulse escalate.

"We're done making out...I mean...." Elijah shook his head and snapped his eyes at me. I think he blushed. "making up...I meant...cleaning up." He let out a quick snort.

Emma said nothing. She was most likely back in the kitchen already.

"We should get going," I said, still held captive. My eyes shifted to where he had Clara's name tattooed by his heart. I assumed he loved her enough to have her name imprinted on his body like that. Knowing he could never love me like that, I needed to guard my heart.

Elijah looked down to his shoes for some time, and then gazed into my eyes sternly. "Alex." He let out a soft sigh. "I'm sorry. I shouldn't have done what I did that night. I was buzzed and we were in that position and...."

"Please, stop." I didn't know why he felt the need to apologize. I wished he hadn't. He made me feel cheap and worthless, as if I

178

was just a snack he wanted to have before bedtime, and all because he wasn't himself. Elijah looked at me like he wanted more of an explanation, so I lied. "That's okay. I had already forgotten about it." I tried to play it cool, but he had no idea how much I was hurting and I couldn't believe it got this far.

"Cool," he said with a nod. "We're fine then."

He might have been, but I wasn't. "Yup, we're fine," I nodded, trying not to tear up, but I knew I had an excuse if I wanted to just cry. My eyes were still burning from the onions.

"Alex...," he added, dragging out the word. "I didn't have a chance to thank you for my birthday gift. You really didn't need to do that, but I thank you. My pictures thank you."

"It was nothing," I said, trying to give him a smile, but I could only give him half of it.

"Alex." There was something different about his tone this time, like he was about to confess. I didn't say a word. I waited for him to continue. "That night when I brought home that girl...."

Why did he have to bring it up? My heart was breaking all over. I didn't know if I could hold myself together. I wanted to drop to the floor and cry. Swallowing down a hard lump in my throat, I listened, but every single nerve in my body was alert. I was jealous and in pain. I wanted to hate him, but I had no right.

"I should have stuck to our agreement and told you I was bringing someone home. I mean...she didn't mean anything to me. Whatever you thought or heard...." he sighed somberly. Whatever he was trying to tell me took much effort. Surprisingly, he looked down and nestled his head lightly on my shoulder. He couldn't look at me. "Nothing happened. I swear nothing happened. I sent her home. I couldn't. I just couldn't."

Tears poured down my face. He might be telling me the truth, but why was he telling me this? What was the point? He had hurt me to the point of no return anyway, though a part of me was happy that he didn't sleep with her. Regardless, I knew he did it to prove a point, to prove to me that he didn't care about me that way. Before he looked up, I quickly wiped my tears. "This is your place. You don't need my permission. Don't be silly." I tried to play it off like it was no big deal, but it was difficult when my lips were trembling and my heart wouldn't let go of the ache.

"Okay." Elijah finally looked up, matching his eyes to mine, searching, wanting to read my expression. Whatever he saw, he looked satisfied. "Great." He paused. "We're okay?" He paused once more for my answer, giving me a crooked grin.

"Yup," I said it as if I meant it.

"I'm going to give you a hug now since friends hug after they make up."

Suddenly, he embraced me before I had time to register what he had said. I sucked in air when my body pressed against his. God he felt so good. I needed him off me. But when he pressed his face into my hair, around the space of my neck, I was reminded of that night and pleasurable heat infused through every part of me. My heart hammered faster and the arms that dangled down by my sides refused to push him away, no matter what my mind told them to do.

"I think the gang is here, Freckles," he murmured in my ear, sending electric shivers through me again.

Next thing I knew, he released me. The cold air took his space when he headed out the door without looking back. As for me, I stared at the wall to get a hold of myself.

Chapter 29

Alexandria

Emma got along perfectly with my friends. I knew she would. Her personality was just like Lexy's. Being the social butterfly that she was, there was never a doubt she wouldn't be loved. If I wasn't mistaken, Seth was paying extra attention to her.

Looking at the table full of delicious food made me smile. The turkey came out perfect, plump and juicy. Elijah wasn't kidding when he said he made the best mashed potatoes and beans. I hadn't tasted them yet, but they looked wonderful. Lexy made rice and steamed corn, Seth brought salad and yams, and Dean brought gravy, cranberry sauce, and pumpkin pie for dessert. The dishes, utensils and drinks were on the table. We were all set.

"Before we slice this baby up, let's go around the table and say what we are thankful for," Emma suggested.

"What?" Dean chugged his drink. "I thought we were done with that when we left home."

"That's 'cause you've got nothing to be thankful for," Seth scowled. "Where's your manners?" He lightly socked him.

"Up my ass," he snorted.

"Shut up and sit down if you want to eat," Lexy scolded playfully. Since there weren't enough seats, we stood around the table. "I'll start first," she continued. "I'm thankful for my new friend, Alex." She gave me a sideways hug, making me smile.

"I'm thankful for this feast," Seth added. "The turkey looks delicious. Great job ladies." Seth was looking right at Emma when he spoke.

Emma lit a shy smile. "You're welcome."

It had been a long time since I'd seen her gush like that. Oh no! I knew what it meant.

Emma was next. "I would like to thank all of you for taking good care of Alex. She's like a sister to me. I was very worried about her, especially since she left her hometown so soon after her father passed away."

Emma made me teary-eyed and I did my best not to let them flow. It was very sweet of her to say, but I wished she would have told me that in private. I didn't want the others to feel uncomfortable about it. Like always, she tried to lighten things up after something that sounded so somber. With her elbow, she nudged me. "Your turn."

I rolled my eyes at her, but she knew I was being playful. "I'm thankful for all of you, for making me feel like I'm home. For helping me get through the most difficult months of college."

"That's because you're easy to take care of," Dean started to say. "I mean, you're easy going and nice." Dean shrugged his shoulders sheepishly, probably wondering if he'd said the right thing. After a pause, he continued. "I'm thankful for nice people. Thanks for the invite."

"It was Alex's idea," Lexy added quickly.

All eyes flashed to me. "It was Lexy's idea, too." I wanted to say that to get the attention away from me, but it didn't work, so I tried something else. "What are you thankful for, Elijah?" It was his turn anyway.

He took a moment to pause, as if searching for words. "This is easy. I'm thankful for good health, a roof over my head, great friends that are like family, picture frames for my photos, and milk and cookies."

Elijah arched his brow and raised his lips in a mischievous grin. His answer tugged my heart. Everyone gave him a baffled look but me. I knew he was trying to let me know that he appreciated his birthday gift again, but I wasn't going to give him any satisfaction. He wasn't going to weasel back into my heart. I preferred to be mad at him. It was safer for me this way. As for the milk and cookies, that made me blush big time.

"Since when do you like milk and cookies," Seth challenged with an unbelievable tone.

"I never disliked them," he retorted.

"Well then," Lexy coughed, breaking the conversation. "Let's eat."

After Seth carved the turkey, we filled our plates. The girls sat around the table while the guys sat on the sofa.

"The turkey is so juicy," Lexy gushed, showing us the slice she just poked. "You'll have to give me your recipe."

"Sure," Emma agreed. "You just have to make sure to keep basting and buy the right brand of turkey."

"How long are you staying?" Lexy mumbled, chewing.

"Just over night. I'm scheduled to work on Saturday. It's crazy after Thanksgiving. I'm just glad I'm not working on Black Friday. It's like a zoo."

"Alex, if you didn't plan anything for tomorrow, let's go see a movie." Lexy looked at me, waiting for an answer.

"Sure, if Emma is up for it." I stuffed the mashed potatoes in my mouth. They were so smooth and creamy. I couldn't stop eating. Looking at Emma, she couldn't stop eating them either.

"Yeah. I'm up for a movie. I haven't seen one in a long time," Emma said.

"Great. I'll come pick you guys up before lunch," Lexy smiled.

Elijah

After having one of the best turkey dinners I'd had in a long time, we all helped clear the table while Emma and Alex did the dishes.

Standing next to Alex while she rinsed the dish that Emma just soaped, I spoke to her. "Alex, you missed a spot," I joked, pointing to the dish in her hand.

"Thanks," she replied in monotone.

Alex wasn't making eye contact with me and that made me feel like shit. Even when I tried to have a conversation with her, she was very short and to the point. She purposely avoided me. Yeah, that hurt. And worse, I think I screwed up our friendship. I thought she accepted my apology in the bathroom, but maybe she said it just to get me off her back. I had to fix this, but how?

Just as I came out of the kitchen, Seth dragged me to the hall and whispered bleakly, "You kissed her didn't you?"

"What? What are you talking about?"

"Elijah, I can read you like a book. We are like brothers. Don't give me that shit," he huffed. "I can tell."

"How can you tell?"

"You're desperately trying to get her attention and she's desperately trying not to look at you. There's something going on between you two."

I shut my eyes, and then opened them slowly. "Look. It happened once. It won't happen again."

Seth's eyes grew wide and he backed me against the wall in anger. I didn't want to hurt him and I didn't want to bring any attention to us so I did nothing. "You're not supposed to touch her," he growled through his teeth. His words were so soft, not wanting others to hear. "You know our code. What the hell were you thinking? Whatever is going on, stop it. She's not the kind of girl you have a one-night stand with. She deserves better than that. Jesus, Elijah. Jimmy is coming down for our graduation. Don't mess with the little family we've got here, okay? I don't mean to tell you what to do. From what I can see, she's into you. You know how I know? She's trying so hard to ignore you. You're almost invisible to her right now. Whatever you did, you hurt her. If you really like her then make it work, but knowing your track record...." He paused. "Look, just do the right thing."

"Hey, you two making out back there?" Dean chuckled, peering in from the living room. "Hurry up, I've set up the table. It's poker time."

"Yeah, we are. Jealous much?" Seth headed toward him.

As I followed behind, I took a peek into the kitchen. Alex was smiling and laughing at whatever they were talking about. When she caught me watching, she became a different person. The smile vanished and so did her laughter. Had I hurt her that much?

We sat around the coffee table. I didn't know Alex and Emma could play, but then again, I'd never asked. I was sort of surprised. Alex didn't seem like the type that would know the game, but she did say she was close to her father. Perhaps they played together.

"What's the bet?" Dean asked.

"How about the winner can request one thing from anyone at the table." Lexy looked at each of us for confirmation.

"Deal," we all said in accord. Simple enough.

Dean exchanged chips for cash and dealt the cards while explaining how much the color chips represented. "The red is worth fifty cents. The blue is worth a buck. The green is worth five bucks."

Everyone nodded.

"Seth, it's your bet," Dean directed.

Seth tossed in the red chip and everyone took turns looking at their cards. After a few rounds, everyone folded except for Seth and me. I knew Seth was bluffing. Even with that poker face, I could see right through him because he wasn't making eye contact with me. I never told him I knew his tell. This was my secret. Sure enough, I called his bluff and I won that hand.

It had been a couple of hours. Everyone was out of the game except for Alex and me. She continued to make minimal eye contact with me. When she did, it was very quick, as if looking at me burned her eyes. I had to make her smile again.

I didn't know if Alex was getting tired or if she didn't want to be in the game with me anymore, but she shoved all her chips in the center. "I'm all in," she said.

I gave in. "I'm all in, too."

Everyone else gathered around us again, waiting...anticipating. Seth tried to see my cards, but I wouldn't let him. Alex looked shocked and worried. Wringing a strand of hair in her finger reminded me of the first day I met her. "Show me what you've got," I said.

Alex placed her cards down and bit her bottom lip. "Three tens."

Those were pretty good cards, but mine were better. I had a full house. Looking at my cards again, I waited to give them a good show. "I was bluffing. You won," I said quickly and shoved my cards with the other used ones.

"I won?" Alex beamed a real genuine smile. That made me smile big time and my heart felt warm seeing her happy. Everyone congratulated her and Dean gave her the wad of cash.

"Thanks," she cooed, but sheepishly accepted it. I knew she felt bad for taking our money. She had a good heart. "Dinner's on me next week. I'll make my famous spaghetti."

"No, no Alex," Lexy said. "You keep the money. You don't need to spend it on us."

"Save it for the down payment on your car," Emma suggested, "so you can come home anytime you like." She gave Alex a hug, then let go. "Or you can go shopping where I work and I'll get you a discount."

The girls laughed, but were soon interrupted by Dean.

"Before I forget, Alex. Cynthia told me to tell you that she may need a roommate as soon as Christmas break. She asked me to let you know since she went home for Thanksgiving."

"You're moving out?" Lexy asked Alex, and then turned to me with a questioning look. Now I was going to hear it from her.

It occurred to me that Alex might move out after what had happened between us, but I thought that was a very slim chance. I didn't know it bothered her this much. I also didn't know the idea of her moving out would cause a tremendous sting of pain in my heart. Maybe it was for the best.

"I was going to let you know," Alex started to tell me, keeping her eyes glued on her fingernails as if she was being scolded. "Cynthia told me she needed a roommate. This way you could have your place back. You can smoke whenever and wherever you want. Or bring girls home so you don't have to ask me and feel weird about it."

"Liam must be happy about that," I slithered in that comment and headed to the kitchen without letting her answer back. I don't know why I said it, only that it pissed me off knowing he got his way. This also confirmed she was still with him.

Chapter 30

Alexandria

Whiteboard:
Going home. I left the rent on the table.
-Alex

The bus ride home wasn't too bad. Mom picked me up at the bus station, and I settled into my old room. It was strange coming back home after being gone so long, especially since my father passed away. Besides seeing Emma and few of my others friends, I didn't have much to look forward to.

"You're not eating much," Mom said, sitting across from me. "Is everything okay?"

"Do you remember Liam?" I asked, twirling my fork through the rice pilaf. I hadn't opened up to Mom in a long time. We rarely talked about this type of thing. Actually, I was the one brushing off the subject every time she would bring it up, so I was surprised at how open I was tonight.

"Of course I do. Are you two having problems?"

"To make a long story short, we are. I don't feel the same about him anymore. Actually, I want to tell him that I think it's best we don't see each other anymore, but I'm so nervous."

What I really wanted to tell Mom was that I was attracted to a guy who smoked, who had not one, but two tattoos, didn't believe in commitment, and was street racing for a living. Yeah, that would go over really well with her. Even though these were things I normally avoided in a relationship, somehow, it seems I was falling in love with him. I wouldn't want to change anything about him. Elijah is who he is because of what he'd been through in life. It was ironic. I never thought I would fall for someone like him. I guess the old saying is right; you can't help whom you fall in love with.

"To tell you the truth, I really didn't like Liam. I'm sure he treated you well, and I know I don't have the right to judge him since I didn't get to know him, but he reminded me of your dad."

Anger flared like a shotgun blast. "What do you mean? How could you say that? Dad was the best. He did so much for us." I could feel my face burn with fury. He wasn't here to defend himself. How could she say things like that?

Mom took a deep sigh. "Alex, you always blamed me for the divorce and I never said anything in my defense because I never wanted you to look at your father any differently. And you shouldn't have to. What you two had was very special. You were his sunshine, but I was his rain. He was a great father, but a terrible husband. He was domineering, controlling, and mostly selfish. I'm sorry to tell you all this, but you have to know. I felt like I lost you when I left your dad."

Her words shocked me. I never knew how it was for her. Then it hit me. Of course, I didn't know. I was their daughter, but I knew very little about their relationship. What they wanted me to see compared to what really went on was completely different. I had never heard them arguing. I couldn't recall my dad ever acting the way she said he did, but how could I? Looking in from the outside, everything was perfect. I always thought mom was being selfish and just wanted out of the marriage. I thought about Liam. None of his friends would think he was controlling, demanding, or selfish. Then I understood.

"I'm so sorry, Mom. I never knew."

"Of course you didn't. It was our problem and not yours. Your dad and I were good at arguing when you weren't around. But when it was the three of us, we were a happy family. We did it for your sake. To tell you the truth, I was miserable. I stuck it out as long as I could. I'm so sorry that I couldn't make it work for all of us. Don't suffer the same fate. You can't help whom you fall in love with, but you can be smart about it. Liam was your first real relationship. It doesn't mean he has to be your last. Don't feel like you have to make it work because dad and I couldn't. You're not married. Play the field while you can, and figure out what kind of man you want."

Just as she finished her words, William walked through the front door. Mom stood up, her smile beaming. I could see how happy she was with him. I rarely saw that smile when she was with dad. I got up and gave William a hug. I promised myself that I would stop thinking negative thoughts about him and be more open-minded.

My eyes were truly opened today. I didn't know why I made snap judgments instead of looking at all the evidence. Maybe I just refused to see the truth that was right in front of me. I was Daddy's little girl and I only saw what he wanted me to see.

Liam picked me up. I had a feeling he knew something was up when I had stopped calling him or returning his calls, especially when I texted him to let him know I was not going to spend Christmas with his family. I knew it was childish of me, but that was one way of letting him know we were done.

Liam didn't even get out of the car when he came to my house. He just honked the horn several times to let me know he was here. Jerk! I knew he wasn't happy with me, but he gave me all the confirmation again that I was doing the right thing.

"I'm going to drive to the park nearby so we can talk." His tone was not friendly.

"Sure." I nodded, trying to keep it cool. My heart was pounding against my chest. I was not good with confrontation. It also saddened me that the feelings I once had for this guy could vanish just like that. I guess I really didn't love him, but what did I know about love anyway?

After a couple of blocks, he pulled over to the curb. All the beautiful leaves had fallen, leaving the branches bare and decorating the grass with colors of orange, red and yellow. It was a beautiful sight. I purposely focused on them, trying to figure out how I should tell him without hurting his feelings. I was also anticipating his loud, angry tone.

"Why didn't you answer my calls?" His eyes set on mine with disappointment and anger.

"Liam—"

"Alex. Let me talk first," he cut me off.

There he was being all about him again.

"I don't think we're right for each other. I think it's best we go our separate ways. The distance isn't helping either."

I was disgusted. All this time I had been worrying about how he would feel about me breaking up with him, worrying about hurting his feelings. Obviously, he had been thinking about it, too.

My anger began to boil. Was I angry because I had wasted all this time on him, or because I didn't see what a real jerk he was? Or maybe it was the fact that he wanted to make it sound like he had broken up with me. Why? Probably so he could save face in front of his friends—who knew which one.

"You know what? I was going to say the exact same thing," I retorted. Liam didn't look surprised.

"I was right. It's because of him, isn't it?" he huffed, raising his voice. "You slept with him, didn't you? You let him be your first when it should have been me. Well, I hooked up with someone else, too, so I guess that makes us even."

I knew I should have been hurt, but truthfully, I didn't care. I was just glad I never gave him all of me; I didn't want him to take the best of me, either. I wanted him to know I wouldn't be thinking about him after I left. I wanted him to know that he was not going to push me around anymore.

"Where do you think you're going?" he demanded after I opened my side of the car.

I thought about the time Elijah asked in front of Liam if I wanted his big dick, referring to the Big Stick popsicle he was holding. They didn't know I was listening. They didn't know I was laughing at Elijah's question. I bore into Liam's eyes so he would see the sincerity of what I was about to say.

"We're done. Oh and by the way…I kissed Elijah. He's a great kisser." Going in for the kill, I added, "And his dick is a lot bigger than yours." Then I slammed the door. The look on his face was priceless. I wished I could have taken a picture of it and sent it to Emma. Running across the park, I felt the cold breeze brush against my face. It felt good to run the rest of the way home. It felt even better to be free of Liam, but a part of me was sad. He would no longer be a part of my life. I guessed that was a good thing.

Elijah

Everyone had gone home for the holidays. Though my friends invited me to their homes, I didn't feel like going anywhere. It had been a week since Alex left, but it felt more like a month. When Jimmy was gone, I'd missed him, but not like this. I kept telling myself that it was the fact that there was another body here again so it made it less lonely, but I knew that wasn't the real reason. What made this situation worse was knowing Alex was seriously considering moving out, or maybe she had already made up her mind.

Standing against the cool breeze, I tugged my leather jacket closer together as I stood before my mother and my brother's graves. The cemetery was always crowded and beautiful this time of the year. Most people brought either a small, decorated Christmas tree or poinsettias, but I brought something different. From afar, the color red stood out and it was an amazing site to see.

It didn't matter that it had been a little over a year. The pain was just the same. "Merry Christmas, Mom." I placed a dozen red roses on her stone. "I've brought your favorite flowers. If you were here...." I choked and paused. "I would've placed them all over the house for you."

Turning to my brother's headstone, I placed down a huge stuffed dragon. "Merry Christmas, Evan. I saw this and I knew you would like it." I took a moment to collect myself. "You know, it's not fair. You and Mom are together and I'm here alone. I miss you both very much. I have good friends, but it's not the same." I exhaled a heavy sigh, taking another moment to collect myself.

"So what are you two doing up there?" I tried to lighten my mood. "Not much for me. The same old thing except, I have a new roommate now." I smiled at the thought of Alex. "She's a girl, Mom. A really nice girl. I know you would have loved her," I snorted. "I can tell you this without worrying about you lecturing me."

"It's kind of complicated. I think I really like her and I think she likes me, but she's seeing someone. So, my dear brother, nice try. You really did send me a hot girl, but too bad. It just wasn't meant to be," I said, remembering his words at the hospital, when he told me he was going to ask God to send me a hot girl to make me stop smoking. Yeah, right.

Kneeling down, I brushed the cut grass off their headstones and ran my hand across once more, as if I could touch them. The stones felt cold and rough, but I didn't care. It was a painful reminder that I was alone and they were gone.

Knowing I had to leave soon, I had my own moment of silence and took in their presence. The gut-wrenching pain sucked me in, holding tightly against my heart, tearing piece by piece, slicing layer by layer, until there was only an empty space...until I felt nothing. Every time, it was the same. I started to heal only after I let the pain out through my tears and through the ugly, horrid sound that escaped my mouth. Only a few could understand how much I was missing them, aching from their absence. I didn't bother to wipe away the tears. They continued to fall as I headed home.

Alexandria

Emma and I had a blast, shopping and hanging out for a couple of days before Christmas. We tried to spend a lot of time together, and I made sure to spend quality time with my mom, as well. The visit with her was different this time around. There was a misunderstanding between us that was cleared up now. I felt closer to my mom than ever before.

School didn't start for another week, but since I was scheduled to work, I had to cut my vacation short. I also needed time to get my things packed to move out. Elijah had no clue I was actually moving. I didn't think I could do it face-to-face. Knowing he wasn't home, I packed up quickly and left a note.

Chapter 31

Elijah

When I walked through the door after being at the gym, I didn't know if my mind was playing tricks on me. Strangely, I inhaled Alex's perfume, the flowers I loved to smell. I was happy she might be back home so I quickly showered. When I headed to the kitchen and saw a letter addressed to me, I knew it wasn't good. My heart sunk and I didn't want to read it.

Elijah,
I'm sorry to give you such short notice. By the time you get this letter, I'll be at my new place. I've left you the rent for January as well, since it wasn't fair of me to leave without giving you at least thirty days' notice as you requested. I also added my share of the monthly utility bill in the check. I hope it's enough. If not, please let me know. I hope you had a nice Christmas and I guess I'll see you around.
-Alex

I stared at the letter after I'd read it twice. I crumbled it up and chucked it across the dining room as if I was throwing a baseball. FUCK! I messed up. I messed up BIG time. Gripping my hair tightly with both of my hands, I walked in circles, trying to calm myself down. There was so much anger, frustration, and regret bottled up. I could've fought for her, should've fixed whatever came between us. Now I lost her friendship and HER!

She had moved out...she had really moved out. It repeatedly echoed in my mind. This was my fucking fault. I knew it was coming. I was almost certain Liam had forced her to do it. I guess it was better this way, but why did it hurt so much? It was as if we had broken up. A blanket of emptiness settled around me, and it refused to let go.

It got worse as the days went by, especially when I'd lay alone in my bed at night. I could almost see her laying with me, asking me to sing to her. The feel of her smooth skin was imprinted on my mind and it haunted me. Not to mention the sweet taste of her lips and the softness of her hair. I loved to bury my face in her hair.

It was difficult to concentrate on anything else, especially at home. My mind was consumed with thoughts of her. Everything in this place reminded me of Alex, especially the milk carton and her favorite popsicles. I was even daydreaming about the meals she would purposely leave for me.

I could say without a doubt that I missed her. I missed everything about her. I didn't have Art History class with her anymore, but I knew where she worked. I couldn't go there. It seemed desperate, even though a part of me wanted to go. Maybe it wasn't a good idea. I had a race in a couple of weeks. It was going to be on the streets, one of the most dangerous ones, and we'd be drawing a lot of attention.

A soft knock broke me out of my thoughts. "Lexy?"

"Hey, Elijah. Got a minute?"

Squeezing into the small space between the door and me, she didn't give me a chance to answer, so I asked her a question instead. "Did something happen to Alex?"

She looked at me like I was an idiot. "Seriously? You're like my brother and you're asking me that question? I know something happened between you."

"Alex told you?" I nervously ran my fingers through my hair.

"Shit," she mumbled softly. "Something did happen."

She had tricked me! Crap! Alex hadn't told her anything. "We just kissed. I didn't sleep with her."

"Were you wasted at the time or—"

"No, I wasn't. I told her that I was. I know I shouldn't have, but—"

"You like her don't you?"

I didn't answer.

"I'm here because there's a rumor Clara is pregnant. I thought I should give you a heads up. I've seen her a couple of times around campus. She doesn't look pregnant so I'm wondering—"

"It's not mine," I snapped. "I haven't seen her in at least six months. She calls me all the time, but I don't answer. I have nothing to say to her."

"Good. Just don't let her weasel her way back into your life."

"Don't worry. I've been burned before and it's not going to happen again."

Lexy paused, peering into my eyes. "You really like Alex, don't you?"

"It doesn't matter. She's with someone else. Besides, she shouldn't be with me. I can't give her the things she deserves."

"You think she's materialistic?"

"No, I didn't mean that."

"You think Alex left because of that kiss?" Her tone was slightly raised. "Boy, guys really are stupid and clueless." Lexy crossed her arm, shaking her head. "I'm going to tell you straight out. She moved out because she feels something for you, too." Then she headed for the door. "Sorry, I gotta go. Someone called in sick."

"Have you seen Alex lately?" I asked hesitantly. I didn't know why just saying her name gave me both joy and pain.

Lexy stopped after she opened the door. "No, but we texted. Here is my advice. Either you two stay away from each other for a

197

while, or shape up to be the man you think she deserves and go fight for her. Elijah, life was very cruel to you before, but it's about time for payback. You deserve happiness now. And, by the way, Alex broke up with Liam. Thought you might want to know," Lexy winked and closed the door behind her.

Chapter 32

Elijah

Knowing Alex broke up with Liam was the best Christmas gift ever. As I looked at my phone, debating whether to text or call her, there was a knock on the door.

"Clara," I said, raising my brows in discontent. She still looked as beautiful as I remembered. Her dark hair was longer and she looked like she'd gained some weight. Regardless, she was still gorgeous and dressed to turn guys' heads with her short skirt, tight top, and killer heels.

"It's good to see you too, Elijah." Her tone was sarcastic. "Why didn't you answer my phone calls?"

"Really?" I crossed my arms and leaned back against the doorframe.

"Are you going to let me in? Or is there another woman in your life?"

I didn't answer her or budge. She continued. "Listen. I'm sorry to bother you, but I'm pregnant." Her eyes welled with tears. Crap! Why does that get to me all the time? I hate seeing women cry.

"Don't even lie to me," I said sternly. "And don't you dare tell me it's mine." I paused to examine her stomach. "You certainly don't look pregnant."

"I'm only a few weeks along. Don't worry. It's not yours. The father doesn't want anything to do with me. I just...I don't know what to do." Tears streamed down her face. "I don't have any friends." Her lips trembled.

I knew better than to let her in, but I couldn't just slam the door in her face. "I think I know who you can talk to."

"Thanks, Elijah. I don't know why I ever let you go. You're the best." She walked in when I moved out of the way.

Funny how she saw it that way, when it was I who left her. "You can eat, take a nap or do what you need to do, but you can't stay here. Do you understand?"

Clara nodded.

"I'll make some phone calls to get you some help. I'm going out to take care of a few things. I should be back in two hours. I want you to be ready to leave by the time I return."

"Fine," her tone was bitchy. "We have a history together and you're going to kick me out, even when I'm pregnant."

Anger rushed through my veins and I could feel my muscles tighten. I would not give in to her manipulating ways. "Like I said, be ready to leave in two hours." I slammed the door behind me.

I made a phone call to a friend who worked at the hospital, and she provided me with some phone numbers where someone in Clara's situation could turn for help. If I was going to make this right between Alex and me, I needed Clara out of my life.

Working at the Administration Office had its perks. Having access to personal information, I jotted down the address for Cynthia's apartment, assuming Alex was living there.

Nervous feelings shot through me as I stood in front of the door. I had no idea what I was going to say to her. After a few long, deep breaths, I knocked on the door.

"Uh...Elijah? Do you have the right address?" Cynthia blinked.

"Hi. Is Alex here? She lives here now, right?" My heart was thumping too fast.

"Yes, but she isn't here right now. Would you like for me to tell her you stopped by?"

"No, I'll come back later. Do you know when she'll be back?"

"She might be at work."

"Thanks," I said quickly and left.

Alexandria

I'd been debating for a while whether I should give Elijah his Christmas present, even though it wasn't Christmas anymore. After all, he had been my roommate. It was only a small friendly gesture. With the wrapped box in my hand, I headed to his place. I didn't know why I felt so nervous. We were friends, after all. I also needed to give him my set of keys.

Knowing this was not my place anymore I knocked on the door. I was completely surprised to see a girl open the door. It was Clara. I had not expected to see her and worse, I didn't expect that stab in my heart, especially seeing her wearing Elijah's sweatshirt. "Is Elijah home?" I asked. He sure moved quickly. Not that it was any of my business.

Clara gawked at me just like she did the last time. "Aren't you the girl that was living here?"

"Yes. I don't live here anymore. I moved out."

"Oh," she nodded, happily. Her facial expression softened. "What happened? He kicked you out knowing I would return?"

Ouch! That was mean. "No. I moved out on my own." I narrowed my eyes at her. "Can you give the keys to Elijah for me?"

"Sure," she shrugged. "I'll let Elijah know you stopped by. He should be right back. He went out to get something for me. I'm pregnant."

The shock of her words shot through me so fast that I thought I was going to drop dead. I guess I hoped in the back of my mind that if Elijah knew Liam and I had broken up…just maybe there was a possibility for us...a very slim one, but this news just killed it. There was never going to be a chance.

"Congratulations." I tried to sound excited for her, but I couldn't help the way I felt. "Anyway, I better go. I guess the keys will be yours now." I don't know why I made that comment. I gave a quick fake smile and walked away.

"Hey, did you need me to give that gift to Elijah?"

I stopped and looked at the box in my hand. "It's not for him," I replied and left with a crushed heart.

Elijah

I swung by the dining hall to see if Alex was working. I couldn't find her anywhere. Lexy was at work so I assumed Alex wasn't at her place. Then all sorts of thoughts flooded my mind. What if she was with Dean or some other guy? I was probably the last one to find out she had broken up with Liam. They're probably all over her. First things first, I needed Clara out of my life. When I entered my place, I saw Clara all comfortable, laying on my bed with one of my favorite sweatshirts on.

"What are you doing?" My tone was not friendly. "I told you to be ready to leave."

"I didn't think you meant it," she whined, sliding off the bed. "What's your problem?"

I never thought I would be this cruel, especially to a pregnant woman, but I figured her being pregnant at all was questionable. I didn't answer her. Instead, I handed her a slip of paper. "I've already made contact for you. She's expecting you when you're ready."

"You want me to go see some woman I've never met?" She started to take off her clothes. When she came toward me seductively, I walked out of the room.

"Fine. Just kick a pregnant woman out," she stammered, standing in the living room looking all pissed off, as if this was my

202

fault. "By the way, the girl that used to live here stopped by and asked me to give you her keys."

My heart and stomach did a somersault. Shit! I just missed her. "When?"

"About thirty minutes ago, I guess. I don't remember. I'm not your secretary."

"Where are the keys?"

"On the kitchen counter."

"She saw you in my sweatshirt?"

"Yes, but so what?"

I knew Clara better than anyone else in this world. I backed her against the wall, towering over her, looking at her with a deadly look in my eyes. "What. Did. You. Tell. Her?" I seethed through my clenched teeth slowly so she could hear the conviction in my tone.

Clara shuddered and wouldn't look me in the eye. "Nothing. I mentioned that I was pregnant, but I didn't tell her it was yours."

"But you didn't tell her it wasn't mine either, Clara. When are you ever going to get it? I don't love you. I will never love you. We're done. I don't ever want to see you again. Don't call me. Don't stop by. Don't even text me. If I ever see your face again, you better run the other way because I don't know what I will do to you."

Clara nodded with a whimper. I had never spoken to her like that before. She got out of my place so fast, it almost made me feel bad.

Not knowing when Alex would be home, I decided to head to her place after dinner. Hopefully, she would be home by then. I texted her, letting her know I got the keys, but she never texted me back. When I stopped by her place, nobody was home. This only made me more desperate.

I was about to text Lexy and ask her if she knew where Alex was, but I knew how girls tended to stick together. I didn't know if Lexy would talk to me on the phone so I went to her place instead. Talking in person was a great way to read peoples' faces.

"Lexy," I hollered, banging on her door. "I know you're in there. I heard your television. I'm going to keep knocking until you open up."

Lexy opened the door, but not all the way. "Elijah. What's the matter with you?"

"Do you have a guy in there with you?" I asked sheepishly.

"No. What gave you that idea?"

"'Cause you won't open the door."

"Maybe I don't want to see your ugly face." Her lips perked up, playfully.

"Who wouldn't want to see my face," I joked back.

"I know one person for sure."

There was my answer. I looked at her for a second with a wicked plan, and without her permission, I picked her up. Lexy screamed. "Put me down." That's when Alex ran out of the bedroom, then froze when she saw me.

Our eyes locked for a split second, but I swear I just saw heaven. There was no need for words. I felt my heart thump happily, radiating toward her. I might have given her a dorky grin. I wasn't sure. Seeing her made me realize how much I cared for her and missed her. Afraid I would drop Lexy since she wouldn't stop squirming, I gently placed her down.

"Did you need something?" Alex tried to give me a smile, but it was faint, and there was something different about her. She didn't have that glow, the liveliness about her. It was dead. I was sure I was the reason it was gone.

"No, I came by to ask you a question." That was such a stupid thing to say but seeing her after all these weeks, my tongue was twisted.

"I'll be right back." I heard Lexy say with the sound of the door closing. I didn't bother to look. My eyes were deadlocked on Alex. I didn't even want to blink. I was so afraid she would disappear.

"So, what's your question?" Her tone was a bit cold.

"Why didn't you text me back?" I asked softly.

Alex shifted her eyes to the dining table. That's when I saw not just her phone, but a wrapped package with my name on it. "Is this mine?"

"No," she snapped, reaching for it, but I was faster.

"Can I open it?" I held it like it was the most precious thing,

"No. It's not for you. It's…it's…for my other friend," she stuttered.

"Alex. We've been roommates for the past five months. I know your likes and dislikes. You slept in my bed. We shared the same bathroom. I've seen you practically naked. I've heard your beautiful voice. We shared milk and cookies. I know when you're not telling me the truth." With each word, I took another step toward her as she took another step back, until there was nowhere to go. "So don't lie to me because I can read you."

Alex gulped as her back hit the wall. "It's just a stupid gift. You probably already have it." She tried to make it sound like it was no big deal, but when you go out of your way to buy something for someone, it means you were thinking of them. And knowing Alex was thinking of me during the Christmas holidays tugged at my heart.

When I unwrapped the gift, it was a 'Grease One and Two' DVD set. That put a huge smile on my face. She was the only person that knew how much I liked them. I had never told anyone else. "I don't have these. Thank you."

That put just a hint of a smile on her face.

"Maybe we can watch them together?" I asked. She didn't answer so I asked her another question. "You broke up with Liam?"

Alex blinked her eyes. "You knew?"

"Of course I did. I've been waiting a long time for you to leave that bastard so I could make my move."

She looked at me disconcertedly.

"Don't tell me you had no clue?" I turned my head to the side as I trapped her with my hands planted on either side of her waist.

"But…but…."

"Clara?"

She nodded, trying to look anywhere but at me. "You love her. I know you do. You have her name tattooed over your heart." Her eyes started to tear.

"I think it's time I showed you my tattoo." I took off my jacket, then my sweater. "I won't lie to you. I did get a tattoo of her name, but when I saw whom she really was, I had the letter A altered and added the letters…T and Y. I changed the word to Clarity."

Alex's eyes grew in wonderment. When she traced the word with her fingertip, I shivered from the contact. Her simple touch always made me feel electrified. It sparked through my body, making me crave her even more.

"Why? What does it mean to you?"

"It's everything I want in my life," I started to say after I pulled back my sweater over my head. "I don't need material things. Ever since I lost my family, that is all I ever wanted back, to have a home, a family. All I wanted was clarity in my life. Something that made sense, something that I could hold onto, someone I could love without a doubt and be my home. Alex, you're my clarity. You. Are. My. Home."

Tears streamed down her face, but I knew she still needed more convincing. I could see the uncertainty in her eyes. What was it? Then it came to me.

"Clara's not pregnant with my child." I framed her face with my hands and smeared her tears away with my thumbs. "She was my past and I'd like to keep it that way. As for you, I'd like you to be my future. Alex, I'm going to shape up and be the man you deserve. I've stopped smoking, and I promise no more racing. I want you more than the things that may kill me. I've missed you. Please come back home with me." I paused. "I know we're doing this all backwards, but who cares." I nuzzled the tip of my nose to hers. "Freckles, please be my roommate again so we can start dating."

I thought Alex was going to faint. Seeing her knees bent, she was sliding down the wall. I caught her before she touched the ground, and held her tightly in my arms. Oh, how I missed her body molding perfectly into mine, her scent filling my nose, and her hair on my face. "Alex," I whispered. My heart pounded against my chest, afraid of the possible rejection. "Say something."

Chapter 33

Alexandria

I couldn't believe the beautiful words coming from Elijah. I was utterly speechless. Never imagining this scenario as a possibility, I was in shock. Minutes ago, I thought Clara was pregnant with Elijah's baby and there was no chance of us ever being together. I had no idea he had all these feelings for me. "Am I dreaming?" I asked softly.

Elijah's body shook with mine when he chuckled. "No, but I can make your dreams come true if you'll let me." He released me and wrapped his arms around my waist. "Let me in, Alex. I swear I'll make it up to you every day. Let me be the one who gets to say you're mine, the one who gets to take care of you, the one who gets to take your sadness away and replace it with happy memories. Let me be the one who gets to hold you at night and tuck you into bed. I want to be with you."

Clarity

I didn't need too much convincing after that. "Okay, Elijah," I nodded as my lips lifted, trying to hide the enormous smile and not look too desperate. Feeling the need to say something to him after he poured out his feelings, I did the same. "You were always the one I wanted. My heart was already set on you from the moment we met. I just didn't know it. I just didn't know how to let Liam go."

"Sometimes we don't know how to let go of what's comfortable. We just need a little push. But I also know I pushed you away. We can make this better now. Come home with me."

I gave Elijah the biggest smile that I could, no longer holding anything back. That was my reply, but it was cut off when his lips began savoring mine. He pulled me tighter to him as his arms traveled up my back.

"You taste like milk," he said, giving me sweet little kisses on my lips while speaking.

I laughed at his comment. "I just had some."

"With cookies?"

"Yup."

"I don't taste the cookies. Maybe I need to reach in deeper."

There were no more words. His tongue slid into my mouth, reaching deeper. With hunger and desperation, he conquered me, sucking me in, making me want more than just a kiss. Panting, he pulled away.

"I'm going to do more than just a kiss if I don't stop," he said breathlessly. "And I'm sure Lexy would like to come back inside."

"Where did she go?"

"I bet she's outside, waiting."

"Oh, no. We better let her in."

"We can tell her the good news on our way out." Elijah gave me that mischievous grin. He was up to something. "Do you have a warmer jacket? I need to take you somewhere."

"Where? And no, I don't have one."

"To your Christmas present." He twitched his brows playfully.

"I don't need a Christmas present. You already gave me you," I said, and I really meant it.

"Oh, no." He shook his head with a grin. "You're not getting out of this one."

"What?" I walked to Lexy's room and grabbed my purse. Elijah reached for my hand. "I'm not going until you tell me where you're taking me," I said with a playful scowl.

"Remember when you told me you wanted to do something for your dad, but you were too chicken to do it."

My eyes grew wide with excitement and a whole bunch of nerves flooded through me. "I'm still a chicken."

"But you want to, right? You just need a little push, right?"

"Elijah, I don't know if I'll ever be ready."

"I'll be right there. I'll hold your hand."

I paused to think, but no matter how much I wanted to do it, I was scared. "I need a push."

"You got it, Freckles."

Next thing I knew, Elijah picked me up off the ground and threw me over his shoulder as he walked out the door.

"Put me down, Elijah," I laughed, smacking his ass. It was nice and firm, just how I thought it would be. "I didn't mean this kind of push. And what about Jimmy and your frat code?"

"I don't care. He can kick my ass a thousand times. I'm not letting you go. No fucking way. You're mine."

Lexy had great timing. She was headed back to her place from wherever she had gone. "Everything okay there?"

"We'll call you later, Lexy," Elijah said, passing her. He didn't even stop. "Don't wait up. I'm taking my roommate back."

Chapter 34

Alexandria

"I'm not getting on that. That thing is huge."

"That's what all the ladies say," Elijah said, teasing in a sultry tone.

"Hey, I wasn't talking about…." I stopped and giggled, not knowing whether he was thinking I meant something perverted. With Elijah, it was easy to think that way. His bike was shiny silver, with a black leather seat; and it was the coolest thing to know he actually drove one. He had made my ultimate bad boy dream come true.

"But I was," he winked. He placed his leather jacket over my shoulders, helping my arms through the sleeves. "I'm guessing you've never ridden before. I need you to stay safe. After my leather jacket, this Harley Davidson is my other pride and joy."

The sleeves of the jacket hung past my fingertips and it looked like a dress on me. Laughing, I flapped them as if they were wings.

When I looked up, Elijah was giving me a naughty grin, checking me out. "What?" I looked at myself.

"Sexy. I'm imagining seeing you naked underneath my pride and joy leathers."

"Maybe one day you will." I shyly turned away with a smile, only to look back again when I felt the helmet slip onto my head. It fit perfectly. Then he put on his.

After Elijah swung over and sat on the seat, he helped me settle behind him.

"I can't believe you had one all this time and I never knew," I said.

"You never asked and I never said." He touched my hand, making sure I was steady. "We're not going that far. I'll go slow."

"Okay," I replied, holding tightly around his waist. I pressed my head against his back, ready for take-off. Though I was nervous, I knew I would be safe. It felt good to hold him this way, but more than that, I couldn't believe we were together. I'd have to take a picture with Elijah and me on his bike and send it to Emma. She was going to flip out.

The cool wind whipped the loose strands of my hair back and the ride wasn't nearly as scary as I thought it would be. Elijah was sweet to drive as slow as he said he would, but I couldn't help my heart hammering faster the further we drove away from the parking lot. I couldn't believe I was going to get a tattoo.

Stretching my arms, I felt a body next to mine. I immediately flashed my eyes open and set them on Elijah's smiling face.

"Good morning, Sunshine." Elijah froze. "I'm sorry. It was—"

"It's okay, Elijah. You can call me Sunshine. It reminds me of my dad, but it's not painful to hear it like before."

I snuggled closer to him and Elijah kissed me tenderly on my forehead.

"How's the tattoo?"

I sat up and looked at my right ankle. "It's still a little red, but it feels fine." I brushed my fingertip over it. "I can't believe I have one." A giddy feeling shivered through me, but I was squealing loudly inside.

"The sunburst is perfect, a wonderful memory of your dad."

I plopped back into his arms. "Thank you." I caressed his cheek. "That was the best Christmas present ever," I said sincerely, looking into his eyes. We were connecting on a whole different level. It was as if we had been a couple for a long time. There was a level of comfort that would normally have taken months to build, but then again, we were roommates before and had that familiarity. "So are you going to show me your new tattoo now?" I pouted.

"Don't pout like that, or I'll be doing things to you that I shouldn't...I mean...not yet anyway."

"I'm glad I waited. I want you to be my first."

"I'm glad you waited, too. I hate thinking about you with anyone else," Elijah stated, running his fingertips down my arm, causing a tingling sensation.

"Mr. Cooper, are you trying to seduce me, or are you just trying to distract me so you don't have to show me your tattoo?"

"Why, Ms. Weis, I would never dare. First, you'll have to take off my T-shirt."

"Really? I don't mind that part at all."

"I bet you don't." Elijah curled his lips into that sexy smirk. "Before I show you, I need to explain why I got it."

I gasped when Elijah suddenly straddled me and pinned my arms above me on the pillow. Though I knew it was not his intentions, he was turning me on, making me hot all over.

"Alex, the tattoo is about you. I got it because of you, to show you how much I'm committed to us." Elijah took off his T-shirt. It didn't matter how many times I had seen his chest, it called to me, beckoning me to surrender to him.

"Do you see the moon?" he asked.

I nodded. "Yes." I traced the small crescent moon above the 'Clarity' tattoo. Elijah slightly shuddered from my touch.

"I'm the opposite of you. You are day and I am night. We complete each other. You are my clarity, Alex."

213

My hands glided over his hard, toned pecs. I couldn't help myself. It was the most romantic and the sweetest thing I'd ever heard, not to mention getting a tattoo because of me. "I think I'm falling in love with you, Elijah Cooper," I said softly, in a dream-like state, lost in his eyes.

"Good, because I'm already in love with you." Elijah's eyes became dark with lust and want. He slipped his hand under my waist and lightly pressed his body onto mine. Heat infused throughout me, blistering with every breath he released. Elijah let out a soft sigh. "I'm sure this line has been said many times before, but I mean it. I love you to the moon, Freckles," he whispered tenderly against my ear.

"And I love you back," I said, laughing, thinking how silly our words were.

Elijah pulled away to look at me. His grin expressed surprise and amusement. He paused for a moment as if gathering his thoughts, his eyes dancing, searching for the perfect words. "Oh yeah, I love you to the moon and back. The universe isn't big enough to compare how much I love you. It's impossible."

He left me completely speechless. I stared back at him. "I...I...." I wanted to say something that expressed something bigger, but there wasn't anything more. He didn't let me finish.

Elijah slowly moved in for my lips. As I watched, I was sinking into the mattress from the anticipation and longing. When his lips brushed mine, fireworks exploded from the simple touch. He kissed me tenderly, taking his time, but it only intensified the burning, needing sensation that his words had already built up. My breath became ragged as I ran my hand along his back. I wanted his naked body on mine, but before we could get there, he stopped.

"Alex," he said breathlessly, still caressing me. "We need to stop before I can't control myself."

"I don't want you to stop." I looked into his eyes, trying to read his thoughts.

"I want to make it special for you. Since I will be your first, we have to do this the right way."

I smiled, appreciating his charisma. "And that is why I fell for you."

"Is that the only reason?" he asked playfully, nipping on my shoulders.

"Nope, your chest. I'm in love with your chest," I teased. Elijah pulled at my T-shirt to trail his kisses down to my breast. I closed my eyes and released a soft moan. "And your tattoo," I sighed, unable to thinking coherently.

"Is that all?" he mumbled through his kisses against my skin.

"Ummm...your bike," I managed to say as his hot breath purposely skimmed down to my stomach. He lifted my shirt to expose my flesh.

"Is that all?" he murmured. His words were muffled, as he worked his way along the top of my cotton pajama pants.

"Your voice." Oh MAN! "And your tongue," I whimpered, feeling the warmth of his breath between my legs. Elijah pulled down my pants just at that perfect spot. The things Elijah was doing, I was coming completely undone.

"Elijah," I called his name softly, a feeling building up inside me that I couldn't explain. It was growing until I felt like I was going to break apart. It was the most intense thing I'd ever felt. I wanted more, but I knew he wasn't going to give in. My lips parted and I heard sounds I had never made before. My head was spinning in ecstasy and time stood still, no worries, no pain, no thoughts, just in the moment with Elijah.

Digging my nails into his arm, I arched my back as I enjoyed every moment of his tongue devouring my clit, teasing the hell out of me. When he stopped, I collapsed, feeling dazed.

"Alex, are you okay?" Elijah got out of bed and I laughed at the curve of the bulge forming in his briefs.

Smiling, I propped myself up on my elbows to get a better look at him. "I'm great, but I don't think you're okay." I pursed my lips, trying hard not to laugh.

Elijah gave me a coy smile and wiggled his legs. Then he slowly turned his head with a wicked grin. "Don't worry about me. Is that the first time you've ever had an orgasm?"

"Yes," I said shyly.

"I feel so privileged that I could give you your first," he winked.

"I love you, Elijah."

"I love you, too."

Suddenly, he scooped me up and tossed me over his shoulder. "Elijah. You can't just pick me up like that. Where are you taking me?"

"We're taking a shower, Freckles. A really cold shower. I'm going to tease you even more. You can watch me make myself cum."

Did I hear him correctly? Oh God! Every inch of me was tingling from his words. This was going to be another first for me.

School started and everything was back to the way it was before break. I moved back in, but I slept in Elijah's bed. It felt strange to be living together as a couple when we had just started dating, but for us, it felt perfect. Elijah told me about his part-time job at the Administration Office, which took me by surprise. While he headed there, I went to my job.

"Hey, Lexy," I greeted her with a hug.

"How are things?" she asked, smiling.

"Great."

"Well, it's about freakin' time. I knew from the first day we met that you and Elijah would end up together."

"Really?"

"He generally smoked only when he was nervous. He had been trying to quit, but he picked it up again the first day he met you after going several consecutive days without a cigarette."

"So I was the cause?" I felt horrible.

"Don't feel bad about it, Alex. Think of it as a compliment. Anyway, how are your classes so far?"

"Good. How about yours?"

"Perfect. I can't wait to graduate."

"What happens next?"

216

"I don't know. I'm thinking of going to grad school, but maybe closer to home."

"Oh," I said somberly. It also reminded me that Elijah was graduating and we hadn't spoken about our plans for the future. I guess I would have to wait and see where this went.

Lexy turned to the students rushing in. "Time to work."

The line never seemed to end, but after an hour, it finally died down.

"Want to ditch your boyfriend and go on a date with me?" I heard someone mumble as I picked up a napkin I'd dropped.

"Elijah," I said happily, giving him my biggest, flirty smile. "It depends. Do you have a motorcycle? 'Cause I think guys who wear leather jackets and ride motorcycles are hot," I giggled. I couldn't help myself. Flirting with him was exciting. I couldn't believe we had finally gotten to this point.

"Sorry to disappoint you, I drive a car now." Elijah twirled a set of keys hooked to a keychain.

When I gave him a confused looked, he explained. "I can't take my girl out on dates on the bike. I leased a car…for both of us…so you can use it, too."

"You didn't sell your bike, did you?"

"It was getting old anyway. I can always buy another one."

I shot my eyes to the ground, afraid he would see my eyes water. This man, who had been through so much hardship, was not just generous; he was too good to be true. He put me first. He was concerned for my well-being. I was so lucky.

"Alex, are you mad?" He cupped my face and raised it until I set my eyes on his.

"No." I shook my head, unable to answer as a teardrop escaped. "Thank you. I'll help with the payments and gas."

Elijah understood without me explaining how I was feeling. He knew me so well. "I'm not asking you to pay, Freckles, but maybe we can work out a deal. You can pay me with something other than cash. I think that's fair."

"I think I can handle that," I toyed back, but my heart was breaking. I knew he loved that bike. But now, I knew he loved me more.

"I'm going to hold you to that offer," he winked. "Come home as soon as you can. I have plans for us tonight."

"Okay," I cheered, anticipating tonight.

"Bye, Lexy," Elijah said out loud, never taking his eyes off me as he walked away.

"Remember what I told you?" Lexy reminded. "Elijah has a huge heart. But he'll have a bigger one for the one he loves."

"You're right, Lexy. And to think I almost gave him up for Liam."

"Well, you can't help whom you fall in love with."

And she was so right.

Chapter 35

Alexandria

Whiteboard:
Can't wait to take you out.
-E

"Freckles, we're not going anywhere fancy." Elijah knocked on my bedroom door. "I told you it was causal, and don't forget to bring a jacket."

"I'm coming out right now. I promise." Putting on my jeans, sweater, and jacket only took me a second. It was my hair and make-up that took longer than I had planned. I wanted to look my best for Elijah on our first real date.

When I swung my door open, Elijah was standing there, blocking my way. "Hey gorgeous. You don't need to get all dolled up for me. I already love you the way you are, but I have to say…." He pulled me into his hold. "you look deliciously sexy." He nibbled my neck.

"You don't look bad yourself," I smiled. Elijah wore jeans, a sweater, and his leather jacket. It didn't matter what he wore, he always looked good.

"Thanks, Freckles, but I always look good."

"Aren't we a little arrogant?" I punched him lightly.

"But you like me that way." Elijah chuckled aloud and gave me a long, tender kiss. "Now we need to go." Taking my hand, we rushed out the door.

"We're going to the hospital?" I panicked when he pulled into the parking lot. "Elijah, are you sick?"

"Relax. The hospital is on the way to where I plan on taking you. I want to show you something first. Remember when you were mad at me and thought I went to Heather's place when I wasn't home? Well I know I already told you I hadn't gone there, but I'm sure you wondered where I actually was when I didn't have class, because I wondered about you. Anyway, let me show you."

Elijah took something from the trunk when we got out of the car.

"Is that a guitar case?" I asked excitedly.

"Yup." Elijah swung it over his shoulder, grabbed my hand and strolled to the entrance.

"I didn't know you played guitar. How come you never played before?"

"I like to hide my talents," he muttered with a wink.

The glass doors slid opened. "Ms. Parker," Elijah greeted the lady sitting behind the front desk. She was probably in her mid-fifties with curly light brown hair.

The lady peered up over her reading glass. "Mr. Cooper. It's good to see you again. I see you've brought a friend."

Elijah's hand was still in mine. "This is Alexandria Weis. She's going to sing with me."

My blood pressure skyrocketed from the shock.

"That's so sweet of you," Ms. Parker said with a smile. Opening her drawer, she pulled out a couple of visitor stickers, wrote our names, and handed them to Elijah.

"Thank you," Elijah said, leading us to the elevator. After he placed my sticker on me, he did the same with his own.

"Elijah, what are we doing here? And you didn't ask me to sing," I pointed out as we waited for the door to open.

Elijah let me enter first. "You don't have to sing. I just said that so you could come with me. Sorry, I should have told you first."

"Where are we going?" I nudged, since his mind seemed to drift somewhere else.

"Sorry. It's just that my brother died at this hospital. It still gets to me coming here, but every time I do, it gets a little better. It's not so bad. You never forget, but the pain becomes bearable."

My heart softened and I squeezed his hand to let him know I felt his pain and that I understood. The door opened on the seventh floor. When we stepped out, the ladies at the front desk smiled.

"Elijah, welcome back. It's been a while," one of the nurses said.

"I've been busy, but I brought someone special with me. This is Alex."

After the introductions were over, we entered. The first thing I realized as we walked down the squeaky white tiles was that all the patients were young. Then after putting two and two together, I soon realized we were on a special floor for kids with cancer. My heart was breaking. I tried to smile as I followed behind Elijah into a room, and I couldn't help the memories of my dad that came crashing through.

"Hey, Marcus," Elijah greeted cheerfully.

"Elijah." The little boy suddenly looked alive. I guessed he was about ten years old, but it was difficult to tell, especially since he had no hair. Then he looked at me and gave me a huge smile.

"Hey, why does she get a bigger smile," Elijah joked, giving Marcus a high five. "Marcus, this is Alex. Alex...Marcus."

"Hi, Marcus." I shook his hand.

"Elijah has a girlfriend," he sang, and paused. "Well, for one thing, she's prettier to look at," he laughed shyly, making me laugh, too.

"That's so true," Elijah agreed. "So how was your week?"

"Same old thing. I wish I could go outside. I love the winter." Marcus looked out the window. His eyes were full of dreams. "It's going to rain tonight. I wish I could stand in the rain and jump in the puddles. That would make my day," he sighed.

I thought my heart would fall out of my chest. We take simple things in life for granted. It's human nature to do so. But to see a young boy who only wanted to play in the rain…he should be able to do anything he wished, but couldn't. It was heartbreaking.

Marcus changed the subject. "Is Alex going to sing with us?"

Elijah looked at me for an answer.

"It depends. If I know the song," I replied.

Elijah gave me a wicked smile. "I know just the one."

As Elijah strummed his guitar, we sang. "I'm the one who wants to be with you…." Surprisingly, Marcus knew the song, too.

"That's Elijah's favorite song," Marcus commented after the song ended. "I think I know the reason why now." He lightly socked Elijah's arm.

"You know I'm going to wrestle you hard when you get better. So be prepared."

"Yeah." Marcus's tone suddenly became somber.

"Anyway, I'm sorry we were a bit late today. Want me to read you a story?"

"I want Alex to read to me."

Marcus looked at me with those innocent eyes, so how could I refuse? "Of course I'll read to you," I said quickly.

When Marcus fell asleep, we headed out. I was so touched seeing Elijah interact with Marcus that I was sure I couldn't respect him any more than I did right now. Most people felt sorry for themselves for their loss, but Elijah did something good. He took that pain and replaced it with something to honor his brother. In the process, he was helping others.

Elijah drove us to the top of a hill, pulled out a picnic blanket when we got out of the car, and draped a light blanket over my shoulders. The sun had set and the stars and moon appeared, illuminating the dark sky with their magic. The city lights below shone in multiple colors, looking like lights on a ginormous Christmas tree. It was a marvelous sight; one that held your attention so you couldn't look away. It was so peaceful here. Being the only ones here was like being in our own world within a world.

"I didn't make dinner. I bought it from a restaurant. I know the owner. She let me borrow these containers to keep the food hot for hours," he explained, placing them in front of us.

"Elijah, you didn't have to go to all that trouble. Sandwiches would have been fine or I could've made something. Just sitting here with you, looking at this view, I don't think I could think of food."

Elijah let out a chuckle. "I know you're starving, you barely ate lunch. Of course, I had to do this. I only want the best for you. You've seen just a part of who I am. You haven't seen anything yet," he winked.

"I can't wait," I gushed.

Sitting side by side, we finished our seafood linguini, salad, and we even shared a big hunk of cheesecake. Then we cuddled together with a blanket around us. Though occasionally, the cool wind would brush my face, making me shiver, I was warm from the heat of Elijah's body.

"How did you find this place," I asked, tracing his facial features with my finger. I started from his thick brows, across his long eyes lashes, glided down his nose, and curved around his cheekbones. When I reached his lips, he kissed my fingertip.

Elijah closed his eyes and took a deep breath. "It was by accident. When my brother passed away, I took off for a few days to be alone. That's when I found this place. It gave me peace. I would sit here for hours just staring at the stars, the moon, and the city lights. I needed something to balance the pain. You are the only one I've ever brought here."

I tenderly kissed his lips to thank him.

Elijah gave me a kiss on my nose and continued. "I still come here a lot. It's what gives me hope. It keeps me grounded so I won't do anything I might regret. Besides my friends being there for me, it's how I survived the loss of the only family I had. I brought you here so that I could share this special place with someone I would do anything for. You know I'll be graduating this year, but what I didn't tell you is that I'm going to take an internship with Professor Kelp. There is a good chance I may get into the MBA program. I'm even thinking of becoming a stockbroker."

I blinked at the realization he was thinking about the future...our future, and the feeling was incredible. "Elijah, I don't know what to say. I'm so proud of you. You don't know how happy you just made me. I was worried about our future."

"Don't be. I told you I would shape up so I could be the man you deserve, the man you need me to be. I want to be able to provide for you and the family I hope we'll have one day."

"I love it when you say things like that." I wrapped my arms around the strong nape of his neck and pressed my body to his. "My dad would've loved you. If you're up for it, I'd like you to meet my mom and my stepdad. I'm glad I went back for Christmas. Mom and I had a long talk. There were misunderstandings that got in the way before, but it's all good now."

"I'm happy for you, Alex. Life is too short. Don't dwell on the bad."

"Okay," I nodded and blinked when I felt a drop on my nose. "Is it going to rain?" Then it was apparent when the drops fell faster.

"Looks like Marcus was right."

We both stood up, gathering the items from the blanket. "Why Marcus, Elijah? Why did you pick him?"

Elijah stopped what he was doing and looked at me. "He took over my brother's room. It's my way of being connected to Evan. My brother's name was Evan."

224

His words gave me chills. "Do you sing for any of the others or just for Marcus?"

"Sometimes, I sing to a group of patients."

The rain started pouring faster, interrupting our conversation. Elijah gathered the last few items, threw them in the trunk, and opened the door for me.

"What are you waiting for, Freckles? Get in."

I closed the door, and pulled Elijah to me. We were getting drenched, but I didn't care. Rain fell on Elijah's face and soaked into his sweater. The way he was staring back at me reminded me of when we showered together. Pushing my naughty thoughts away, I curled my lips into a mischievous smile. "I want to dance in the rain. I want to do it for Marcus."

Elijah looked at me for a second. His eyes twinkled with approval. Rewarding me with his sexy grin, he swung me around. "We can do more than dance. Alex, you feel like heaven to touch."

He sang "Can't Take My Eyes Off You," an oldie by Frankie Valli and the Four Seasons. It was one of the songs my dad used to sing.

Trembling, my body felt like it had turned to ice and the wet clothes clung uncomfortably to every part of my skin, but it was worth it—worth this moment—worth it all. We jumped in puddles together like children, all the puddles we could find, while Elijah bellowed at the top of his lungs singing. "I love you, baby!" As the rain poured down on us, we both sang our hearts out, laughed out loud, jumped as high as we could, and danced like we'd never danced before without a care in the world.

Chapter 36

Elijah

Whiteboard:
Thank you for the most
amazing date!
-Alex

It had been a while since the gang got together. I told everyone that it was potluck, so we ended up with all different types of food. Alex offered to cook, but she had her job and her classes. I didn't want that kind of stress for her.

"Are you ready for the race of your life?" Dean asked, lazily sitting on the sofa next to Lexy.

I wanted to punch him for spoiling my plans. I knew Alex would disapprove, especially when she glared at me without a smile. I was going to charm my way into convincing her and let her know it would be my last race, but it looked like I was going to have to do a lot more than that.

"Why don't you back away from this race," Seth suggested, sitting across from me at the dining table. "I mean, you don't need the money. The risk isn't worth it. You know the cops are going to be swarming the place, especially after all of the unavoidable complaints."

"I have to agree with Seth," Lexy added.

"That's strange, Elijah told me he wasn't going to race anymore." Alex's tone was sarcastic.

"I had already signed up for this one before we agreed that I wouldn't race." I couldn't look at Alex. I was doing this for her, for us. She may not understand, but as a man, I had this need to provide and take care of her. With the amount of money I could win, I could buy her a car and save the rest for the future.

When Alex went into the kitchen, I followed and snatched her before she could get away from me. I was holding her so tightly that she couldn't even struggle. "I promised you that I wouldn't race anymore, but this is different."

"When were you going to tell me?" she frowned, darting her eyes at me in anger. "And when is it?"

"The race is next week. I had this whole speech ready for you and I even thought about how I was going to convince you."

"You did?" Her tone softened, looking amused.

I rocked us back and forth. "I did. I was going to tell you that I went two weeks without smoking, even after telling myself I would never stop smoking for anyone but myself. Now you know that I would do anything to make you happy."

Her eyes glowed and she gave me that smile I loved so much. "I'm so proud of you. Thank you."

"And I was also going to do this." I leaned into that special place I like to nibble on her neck. Thank goodness Dean had the television on and they were watching the Lakers game. When she moaned, I trailed my kisses lower, down to her breasts.

Backing her against the cabinet, my hands explored her body as I continued to consume her mouth with my lips and tongue. I anchored her right leg around my waist and grabbed her ass. When she sucked in air, it drove me to another level of excitement.

"You know that's not going to work. Safety. Comes. First," Alex managed to say between kissing me back, lost to my touches. I didn't reply because I was way too into what I was doing.

"You have a bedroom. Actually two," Seth hollered, chuckling. "Pick one."

Alex turned her body away shyly with a soft giggle before I could release her. I dragged my hair back and watched her walk away. I could tell this was not over.

Alexandria

It was late into the night and everyone had gone home. While I washed up, Elijah was already in bed, studying his notes. Trying to look as seductive as possible, I inhaled a deep, nervous breath and rested my hand on the doorframe with my hip leaned to one side.

"So you thought you could convince me with your speech and charm, but you see I also have a speech ready. I even thought about how I could convince you. So here I am." Still standing by the door, I made sure the leather jacket opened just enough so he could see that I was completely naked underneath.

Elijah's lips curled deviously and he tossed his notebook on the floor. Putting his arms behind his neck for support, his muscles were cut and defined. He was shirtless. Actually, he had nothing but his cotton shorts on, and he looked way too sexy.

"Are you trying to seduce me, Ms. Weis?" His eyes raked over my body while he bit his bottom lip.

"It depends on your answer, Mr. Cooper." I swayed to him seductively, allowing the jacket to slide off my shoulder, exposing my breast.

Elijah gasped slightly as he stood in front of me, cupping my face. "If you take that off, something will happen. I won't be able to control myself. You don't have to do this if you're not ready."

"I've been ready. I was just finding the right time." I gave him a wicked smile. "A night with me or the race?"

"That's not fair, Freckles. I had signed up for this race long before we met. It's a once in a lifetime chance. If I win, we could use that money for a down payment for a house. One day soon, I'm going to marry you, and we're going to have a minivan full of kids. I want to take care of us, our family."

I stared at him as his words soaked in, touching me to the very depth of my heart. My body tingled hearing the thoughts I never knew were running through his mind. I knew he loved me, but I hadn't realized just how much until this moment.

Tears pooled in my eyes, feeling grateful for his love and devotion. I couldn't be happier than I was right now. There was nothing more I could say. I would have to talk him out of it tomorrow. I still had time.

"I'm ready, Elijah," I whispered, letting the jacket fall to the floor. We hadn't been together that long, but I felt like I'd known him a lifetime.

"You're absolutely beautiful, Freckles," he said, taking a moment to study me. Then he scooped me up and hovered over me on the bed. "I'm going to make you remember this night forever. I promise you, it will be special. Baby, I'm going to give you all of me."

Elijah's lips brushed against mine and tenderly began to suck my lip. When his hand roamed over my breast, I gasped from the pleasure that shot through every nerve ending in my body. His kisses moved to my cheek, down my neck, and then his tongue ran deliciously over my nipple. He slowly tortured me as he sucked and nibbled on it. God, that felt so achingly good. Arching my back, I moaned as I felt the sensation between my legs burn with desire.

When Elijah slipped his hands under my ass, he pressed his warm body against mine. That sent another erotic jolt to my sex. It blistered with want and need, making me crave him even more.

"Elijah, please," I whimpered, turning my head from side to side.

"Not yet, Baby," he murmured between nipping down past my belly button until...oh God...his mouth was sucking my clit. His tongue circled, licked, and flicked in the most gratifying way. He was driving me insane. My hands gripped his shoulders, slowly losing all sense of motor coordination, especially when he pushed his fingers inside me. Closing my eyes, I took in the pleasure.

"I'm preparing you for something bigger," he groaned. "I need to make you as wet as I can." Elijah took my hand and placed it over his dick.

My eyes shot open. He was right. He was big. When did he take off his shorts?

"Are you sure you want this?" he asked as I stared at the beauty that was going to go inside me.

"Yes," I nodded, aching so badly from his fingers moving in and out.

After driving me crazy to the point where I was about to beg, he spread my legs wider with his knees. After putting on a condom, he was on top of me. "I'm going to go slow," he explained, cupping my face and looking lovingly into my eyes. "Tell me if you want me to stop, okay?"

I nodded again, but a little part of me was frightened. There was no doubt I wanted Elijah and I wanted this, but it also would mean that I was giving him all of me. I knew from the bottom of my heart that I belonged to him.

Keeping his eyes on me, he pushed in. I gasped as he penetrated a little deeper. Slowly, cautiously, he moved his hips back and forth, gliding in and out and each time going deeper. "You ready?" he asked as his eyes darkened with passion and love.

Before I could reply, I sucked in a big lump of air waiting for the burning sensation to pass.

"I'm in," he grinned, and then looked worried. "Does it hurt? Do you want me to stop?"

"Don't stop," I begged, pulling him in for a kiss. Oh how I loved the taste of him.

Elijah moved his hips slowly, looking into my eyes, giving me pleasure beyond anything I could imagine. He was filling me with his love and I knew he was right. I would never forget this moment.

"I'm going to go easy with you. I don't know how you'll feel after tonight. I'm so honored to be your first and I want nothing more than to be your last," he panted, running his hands through my hair. He had started to rock on top of me again, this time a little bit faster.

The tingling sensation started from my stomach and expanded, spreading up to my head, and down to my toes. I was full to my limit; there was nowhere to release it as foreign, breathless sounds escaped my lips. I never knew I could make sounds like that.

"God, Alex, you feel so damn good. I don't want to stop," Elijah said. "I want to make love to you all night, but I also don't want you to be sore. You're so beautiful. I love you, Baby." Those were his last words before he conquered my lips again. Slowly taking his time with his lips and tongue, he brushed them along my neck, my shoulders, around my breast, and every inch of my body, worshipping, caressing, and making me feel special.

Elijah touched me everywhere. He engulfed me with his kisses, his tenderness, and suddenly it hit me…I never knew what love was or making love was until tonight.

After who-knew-how-long, he entered me again, but he was very gentle. As our bodies rocked together as one, he held me as if I was the most precious thing in his world.

When I felt his body shudder and heard that unmistakable groaning of pleasure, I knew his will had been spent. After he examined me, he went to the bathroom and came back with a small wet towel. He gently wiped between my legs, cleaning me and tending to my needs. "You're bleeding a little, but you'll be fine." He kissed the area he wiped, then cuddled next to me and placed my arm across his chest.

"How are you feeling? Are you in any pain?"

"No, I'm okay. Better than okay." I released a soft sigh, feeling the warmth of him. How I loved to be here, right next to him.

"Did I ever tell you that this is my favorite time of the day?" he commented.

"What do you mean?"

"Lying in bed, having you next to me, I look forward to this moment every night." He kissed my forehead.

"Me too," I agreed and kissed him back.

Chapter 37

Elijah

Whiteboard:
Please don't race!
-Alex

Alex and I purposely avoided the topic of the race for the past few days. I assumed she was thinking that I wouldn't go ahead with it, but I knew what I had to do. There was no way I was going to back out. My mind was made up.

"Where are you going?" I asked, stepping into the kitchen. Alex was washing the dishes. "You don't have classes on Saturdays." I wrapped my arms around her waist from behind and nibbled the side of her neck.

"I told you I had to work this afternoon, remember?" She finished rinsing the last cup, then turned to face me and placed her hands on my arms. "I have to work until almost closing, so I'll be home about nine."

"I'm going to win that race so you don't have to work anymore. I'll take care of you."

Alex's smile disappeared. "What if I don't want to quit my job? You never asked."

I glanced to the side and looked up at her once again. "You're right, I didn't. I'm sorry. You don't have to quit, but I just wanted to let you know that I'll be home late tonight."

"So you're going to go through with it, even knowing how I feel." Her tone had changed, becoming more authoritative. "Please, Elijah. I'm begging you." She caressed her hands down my arms. "I don't feel right about this. I feel sick to my stomach. It's not just dangerous, the cops, and even your friends are against it. What if you get hurt or even kill someone?" she rambled. Her eyes pleaded.

"If we worry about all the things that could happen, then we might as well worry all the time. Anything could happen to either of us at any time. I could have a heart attack or get hit by a car. But that doesn't mean we stop living. That's just life. When it's your turn, it's your turn, and there is nothing anyone can do about it. Nothing is going to happen to me."

"Can you promise me that?"

When I couldn't, she pushed me away and walked out of the kitchen. "I don't understand," she started to say. "Why would you want to risk your life like that? Let me guess…is Nolan going to be in the race, too?"

"Yes, but that's not the reason." I followed her to the living room.

"Really?" she challenged, gazing at me as if she couldn't tell if I was telling the truth, and then she continued, "You say you love me and want a future with me, but that's all talk, isn't it?"

I wanted to go to her, but knowing how upset she was, she would only push me away. "That's not fair. I told you that I do and I meant it. Like I told you before, I signed up for this before I even met you. Speaking of which, you're not considering what I want. What I need to do for you, for us, as a man. You don't understand."

Alex crossed her arms. "That's different. You're putting your life on the line. And we don't need the money."

"That's easy for you to say when your parents provided for you. I had to do it all by myself." The words came out of my mouth so fast; I immediately regretted saying them. I couldn't even take it back. Shit! "I'm sorry. I didn't mean...."

Alex grabbed her purse and opened the front door. "You're right. Maybe we just don't understand each other. Maybe we are two opposites that don't complete each other. I have to go to work. Do whatever you want because obviously what you're really doing is thinking about your ego and your greed. You might as well sell your soul to the devil."

The door slammed behind her. I didn't know what to do.

It was close to dinnertime, and neither Alex nor I had texted or called each other. We were both being stubborn. Alex's words replayed in my mind like a broken record, but there was no turning back. I knew she would get over it once I brought home the prize money. After all, we wouldn't need to fight about me racing ever again since I promised her I wouldn't race after this. Looking at my watch, I grabbed my keys and headed to Seth's dad's garage.

"Sorry, I just got your text," I said, seeing the back of Seth's head. He was bent down, wiping the wheels on my bike. I made eye contact with the other employees, greeting them all with a little smile. The smell of grease and being surrounded by cars in various stages of repair always excited me, but I could never be a mechanic. I'd rather drive them, not fix them.

"You're early." Seth stood up and tossed the towel on the table against the wall.

"I can't believe your dad sold my bike already. Speaking of which, where is he?"

"He went out to run an errand. Besides, you sold it to my dad first, so you can't say it's your bike anymore," he reminded. "And of course he did. It's beautiful. I still can't believe you gave it up. You're really serious about Alex, aren't you?"

I shifted my body a little and waited a second to answer. "I am," I finally said. "I know for sure she's it. I don't doubt it at all."

Seth set some items in the toolbox. "Does this mean you're backing out of the race?"

"No," I snapped. I didn't mean to, but already feeling fired up from the fight with Alex, I was agitated that he was on her side.

Seth threw up his hands as if to surrender. "Whoa. I didn't know that question was going to upset you."

"Sorry. It's just that Alex and I already had a fight about it, and I feel like shit. I'm trying to decide what to do."

"Good. Think about it while you do me a favor." Seth threw a set of keys at me.

"What's this for?"

"Your last ride on your bike."

Alexandria

It was extremely busy today, which was rare for a Saturday, but I was glad. I didn't want to think about the fight Elijah and I had. Was I being unreasonable? I didn't think I was, especially when it came to his safety. I knew for a fact that if the roles were reversed, he would say and think the same as I did.

Regardless, in the end, I knew the choice was his. I never wanted him to bring this up later, wondering what would have happened if only I'd let him go. He might end up resenting me for it. I never wanted to be the controlling girlfriend, so I decided not to call him, though it was killing me inside. Ultimately, it was his decision.

Day had turned to night so fast I didn't realize that it was closing time. Since I wasn't closing tonight, I checked out with my boss and said good-bye to my co-workers.

Lexy's shift had ended earlier, so when I saw her coming toward me with a dreadful look on her face, I knew something was wrong.

"Lexy? What happened?"

Lexy grabbed both of my arms, holding me steady. "It's Elijah. He's in the hospital. I'm going to take you there. Seth was with him when it happened. That's all I know."

"What do you mean?" It took some time for my brain to register what she was saying. I just stood there in shock. I heard the words, but my mind refused to believe it. I didn't even know what questions to ask to complete the picture in my mind, this awful picture of Elijah inside his wrecked car. "I told him not to go," I mumbled. "Oh God!" I covered my mouth, thinking of the awful things I had said to him before I walked out on him.

I didn't remember getting in her car or how we ended up at the hospital. All I knew was that my heart was beating out of control and my hands were unsteady. I was back at the same hospital where Elijah had taken me the night of our first date.

Lexy looked at the text on her phone as we got into the elevator. We were both quiet on the car ride here and were still quiet now. When the doors opened, Seth was right there waiting for us with tears in his eyes. When a guy has tears in his eyes, that meant it was something serious. Knowing it was bad, I closed my arms around my chest. I tried to hold myself steady as we walked down the hall, but I couldn't help it, tears escaped.

"He's in a coma," Seth explained as he continued to lead us down the hall. "He's had a head trauma, so the doctors had to induce a coma to help him."

His words were like a stab to my heart. I felt my body tremble, but I didn't know how much until Lexy placed her arms around my shoulders.

"I tried to convince him not to go," I cried as tears poured down my cheek. "It's my fault. I should've tried harder."

Seth halted smack in the middle of the hall and turned to me. "He didn't go, Alex. He didn't go to the race. He changed his mind just before we left my dad's shop. Before he blacked out, he asked me to make sure that you knew he had changed his mind. He did it for you."

I was beyond relieved that he hadn't, but guilt punched through me. I had been mad at him for thinking he had gone to the race when he really hadn't.

Seth continued walking and talking. "My dad bought his bike and fixed it up a bit so he could sell it. Elijah said he didn't need it anymore, that it was too dangerous to drive you around on it. My dad sold it yesterday. We were on our way to drop it off to the buyer. I was driving behind him so I could bring him back home. Then some stupid ass car ran a red light…and…I'm so sorry, Alex. It—" Seth stopped when he saw how upset I was. He knew I didn't need to know the gruesome details.

"Can I see him?"

Seth guided Lexy to a chair after we turned left into a waiting area. She looked like a mess, too. "You go in first," she said.

"This is the visitor's room. We'll be right here. He's in room 512." Seth gave me a quick, reassuring smile. "He'll come out of it, Alex. He has to. He loves you too much."

Chapter 38

Alexandria

I couldn't do anything but stand there as I tried to grasp the reality of what I was seeing in front of me. A tube had been inserted through his nose and a breathing tube ran down his throat. Next to the bed was a machine that was breathing for him. There was an IV connected to his neck. His left leg was apparently broken and was in a cast. Seeing Elijah helpless and not knowing if he would wake up was shredding my world apart.

"Elijah," I sighed heavily as my lips quivered. "I'm so sorry. I wish I could help you. Tell me what to do?" Tears streamed down my face. I told myself to be strong, but it wasn't working.

Looking off to the side, I saw his leather jacket. Needing to hold it for comfort, I picked it up off the chair and put it on. "I'll hold your pride and joy for you, so hurry and come back to me, okay?"

Slipping my hand into his, I placed it close to my heart as my eyes outlined his handsome face—memorizing the curve of his brows, his long eyelashes, his perfect nose, his kissable lips—

memorizing him. I couldn't stop staring at him. It felt like any minute now, his eyes would open. I wanted to be the first one he saw.

Caressing his face, I spoke to him softly. "I know you can hear me. I'm right here waiting for you. You promised me a home, a future, a family. We've only just begun. Please, Elijah," I pleaded, bringing his hand to my cheek. As I kissed his knuckles, the tears escaped and I could taste the saltiness of them. Placing his hand down, I wiped my tears and gently snuggled into his shoulder.

"Seth told me what happened. What did I ever do to deserve someone like you? You amaze me with your voice, your talent, your generosity, and your love for life. There are no words to describe you and your beautiful heart. You took everything that was bad and turned it into good. You've taught me so much, and I don't want you to stop. I want to see more of who you are. I need you. Your friends need you. Fight, damn it. Fight for me. Fight for us."

Feeling drained, I closed my eyes and slipped my hands into his jacket to keep them warm. I felt something in the pocket crinkle. It was a sealed envelope addressed to me. Astounded by what I saw, I sat up and opened it.

My Dearest Alex,

If you're reading this letter, it means that I'm either in really bad shape in the hospital or I've passed on and there are no words to tell you how sorry I am. I don't even know where to start, so I'll just tell you that I wrote this letter just in case something happened to me during this race.

You see, Alex, I've never been afraid of death until I met you. I'd lost so much that I didn't care anymore. I lived day to day without a care in the world, but when you came into my life, you made me care.

We've both been lucky to be able to say good-bye to our loved ones, but sometimes you run out of luck. So just in case I never get to say good-bye, I thought this would be the best way. If I'm unconscious, just know I'll be fighting with everything I have to come back to you. I'm fighting, Freckles. I'm fighting like hell because you're everything to me. But if the worst has happened and I'm dead, I'm going to be so pissed that I'm not going to be the guy giving you everything you deserve. This also means that fate screwed me over again.

Alex, don't be afraid to let me go. It's okay to cry and let it all out. But you must promise me you'll live your life. Life is too short. Be happy and make many wonderful memories. I'm going to be so jealous of the guy who will give you what I wanted to give you, but at the same time, I'll be so happy for you. It will mean you've moved on and found someone new. I just know that no one will ever love you as much as I do. It's not possible. My love for you is bigger than the moon, bigger than the universe, and I can't imagine anything bigger than that.

I fell in love with you the second you said you were Alex. I fell in love with you more when you dunked your cookie in milk, and even more when you dumped water on me when you were mad at me. Who could ever forget that angelic voice and that smile?

Alex, I love everything about you. From the freckles you think are imperfect, to the faults I haven't found yet (you wouldn't be human if you didn't have any) and all that is good about you. Everything about you brings me happiness, so I thank you for that. I'm only sorry it might be short-lived. You are the strongest and bravest person I know. You are also the most beautiful girl I've ever laid eyes on. Don't you ever forget that!

I want the world for you, but I might not be there to give it to you. It hurts like hell that I might not be the one. Don't be afraid to live, and don't be afraid to let your dad go either. He'll always be in your heart, just as I will. Replace the sad memories with better ones so that you'll never have to be sad.

Sometimes life sucks big time. It takes you on a roller coaster ride, drags you through the mud, smears it on your face until it takes every bit of your air and you can't breathe. Don't ever let it take your beautiful smile away. Don't ever let it stop you from being the beautiful person you are. Don't ever let it stop you from seeing the beauty in the world.

You have one of the most generous, loving hearts and the best part is that you don't even know it. That is the part of you I fell in love with the most. I wanted to take you to watch the sunset and drive off like Sandy and Danny from Grease, but I guess we might not ever get that chance. And that thought tears me apart. God I wish I could hold you right now!

Alex, I want to thank you for being my sunshine. When my brother and my mother passed away, I was completely dead inside, and even though I got through the days with the help from my friends, it wasn't until you came into my life that I started to truly heal.

Knowing you were grieving just as much as I was made me want to help you, but in the process you were helping me, too. There is a saying that goes "People enter our lives for a reason. Some people stay for a short period and some people stay for longer. But no matter the length, they leave footprints on our hearts." I guess I was meant to pass through your life quickly, and you should see it that way. It only means that someone else was meant to be your last.

Our broken roads led us into each other's arms, but now it's time to let go. You'll always be in my heart wherever I may be, but I'll never forget your smile. I'll never forget cookies and milk. I'll never forget our love for Grease. I'll never forget how beautiful your voice is. I'll never forget you. You are my sunshine and I'm your moon and for too short a time, we were perfect and complete.

Seth has all my bank account information. I'm leaving everything to you. He will know what to do.

And before I forget. Remember when you asked me if I'd ever loved a woman after I sang the song, "To Love A Woman" by E.C., and I said no? The truth is, I hadn't until I fell in love with you. So, now you know my answer is yes. The song was written by me, E.C.—Elijah Cooper. 'A Woman' is you-Alexandria Weis. Yes. I wrote the song for you. The actual title is, "To Love Alexandria Weis."

P.S.

If I'm perfectly fine and you're reading this letter, shame on you. That means you had your hands inside my pockets or you

accidently found it by seducing me and wearing my pride and joy.
How I wish this could be true.
   All of me loves all of you, forever and ever.
   -Elijah

Tears poured down my face. My aching breaths came out as tiny gasps, causing me to hyperventilate. The little tremors inside me quickly became an earthquake. I was panicking. I was desperate. I needed Elijah to wake up. Reading this beautiful letter brought me to another level of grief and despair, and I was freaking the hell out. Suddenly, the little hope I was holding on to faded.

I didn't know I had dropped to the floor until Lexy started to lift me up. Feeling like my heart had been ripped out, I leaned forward and wrapped my arms around my chest to keep from breaking apart. "Elijah," I managed to say, gasping for air. With a trembling hand, I showed Lexy the letter. She didn't read it. She folded it, shoved it into the pocket of the leather jacket and embraced me.

"I need to tell him—" I started to heave. No air. I needed air. Oh God. I couldn't breathe. "We had a fight. He needs to hear it again," I cried. "I didn't say—" I made another aching noise.

"It's okay, Alex." Lexy rubbed my back, trying to comfort me, but nothing, absolutely nothing could ease the pain I was feeling right now. "Shhh…it's okay. He already knows you love him."

As I held onto her tightly, my body shook and gut-wrenching sounds escaped from my mouth. It hurt so bad. I couldn't feel anything else but the pain that controlled me. It sucked me into an endless hole, falling and never stopping. Everything I did took so much effort. I couldn't think, I couldn't breathe, and I had lost all control.

Lexy stroked my hair as she continued to comfort me. "He loves you so much, Alex. He's fighting with everything he has to come back to you. I know Elijah, and he never breaks his promises."

Unable to say a word, I nodded after I took a moment to calm down.

Seeing Seth walk in, I released Lexy and wiped my tears.

"You should get something to eat," Seth said. "Why don't you and Lexy get something to drink at least? There is a cafeteria on the first floor."

"Come with me, Alex," Lexy suggested, wiping away her own tears. "Elijah's other friends are here to see him. Let's take a walk, so we can give them some time with him."

I nodded in agreement, but I couldn't move. I didn't want to leave Elijah. Seth placed his hand on my shoulder. "I forgot to tell you, Jimmy is on his way. He should be here tomorrow."

"Okay," I nodded and headed out with Lexy. I don't know why, but knowing Jimmy was on his way gave me comfort and hope.

I knew I was dreaming and I didn't want to wake up. Elijah and I were in his bed, laughing and talking. He was telling me how much he loved me, while he held me in his arms. My dad appeared, standing by the window, smiling. I sat up thinking he was going to be upset seeing his daughter in bed with a guy she wasn't married to, but he just stood there without saying a word.

"Alex," I heard a voice say.

Lifting my head off the hospital bed mattress, I fluttered my eyes to clear my vision and rubbed my shoulders to ease the ache from the position I was in. I had scooted the chair as close as possible to the bed, so I could hold onto Elijah's hand.

"Alex." I felt someone's hand on my back.

"Jimmy?" I stood and practically jumped on him. "You're here." The tears poured out again. Jimmy held me tightly for a long time until I was ready to let go. With the same blondish short haircut, he looked the same. Though he was still lean, he had more muscle than the last time I had seen him. He wore a black sweater and a pair of jeans. His blues eyes shined with concern as he stared back at me, as if he couldn't believe why he was here.

"When did you get here? What time is it?" I asked.

"It's noon. I came here first thing. The gang is outside in the waiting room. They've been here all night."

I turned to Elijah with a look of admiration. "He's had a lot of visitors, not just from friends, but from the hospital staff. I think he gets special treatment from the nurses because they know him. They're letting things slip by that are against regulations. I wouldn't be able to spend as much time with him if it wasn't for the nurses pretending they don't see me."

"He's a great guy. He spent a lot of time at this hospital for various reasons."

"So I'm guessing you know about Elijah and me?" I asked nervously.

"When you told me what college you were going to, I thought it would be a perfect opportunity for you two to hook up."

"What?" I arched my brows in confusion. "You were hoping we would hook up?"

"I knew you were perfect for him, and he was perfect for you. Though we have rules against dating each other's sisters or cousins, I knew that he would go against it if he really fell in love with you. And I was right. He knew, without a doubt, that you belong together. It would be the only reason he would risk our friendship." Jimmy turned to Elijah. "You better get up so I can kick your ass, Ellie. Do you hear me?"

I had never seen Jimmy tear up like that. Jimmy turned away from Elijah and cleared his throat. "Does your mom know about Elijah?"

"She knows we're together, but I didn't tell her what happened."

"Alex, we need to talk about something. Elijah doesn't have a family, so I'm on his emergency contact as his health care proxy. If the swelling doesn't go down in his brain and there are more complications...." He paused. "I don't want to think about this, but—"

I knew what he was trying to tell me, but the thought never crossed my mind until now. "No," I said softy before he could finish his words. "He's going to be fine," I said with conviction, almost angrily. "Talk to him. I'll leave you two alone. I'll be back soon."

I left the room, heading away from the waiting area so the gang couldn't see me. Walking down the hall gave me some peace and it was exactly what I needed. After passing the patient rooms, I came upon the dimly lit open room. I hadn't been inside a church since my dad passed away, but I decided to go into the chapel anyway.

Sitting in the last row, I glanced around. It was small, with ten pews on each side, lit candles off to the left, and statues of Saints off to the right. I didn't know what I was supposed to do as I stared at the cross. I felt so guilty to be in here to pray for something for myself when I hadn't prayed in so long, but I needed hope.

"I know it's selfish of me to be here and to ask something of you when I don't even pray like I should. There are people with worse problems than me, but right now, this is all I can think of. You took away my dad, who meant the world to me, and you've already taken so much from Elijah. I don't mean to question why, but I'm asking you for a second chance...please. And Dad, I know you can hear me. I miss you. I know you're watching over me, and I know you're listening right now. Please don't let anyone take Elijah away. I need him. If God takes him, I don't know how I'm going to survive. My heart can only take so much."

That was all I could say before I lost it again. The tears poured, taking every ounce of strength I had left until my eyes hurt like hell, until my muscles felt like they were on fire, and until I could feel nothing more. I don't know how I got back to Elijah's room. I could only recall how heavy my body felt and how tired I was. Jimmy reached out for me. I think I collapsed in his arms.

Chapter 39

Alexandria

Voices spoke to me as I drifted in and out of consciousness. They were mostly mumbled sounds, but I heard words like—swelling is down—breathing on his own—full recovery. They all sounded so good, I was afraid the dream would end. I wanted to wake up and hear it from the doctor. I didn't want it to be a dream.

Lexy and Jimmy woke me up a couple of times to eat. I tried to take a bite here and there, but my stomach couldn't handle solid food, so I drank some juice instead. Sometimes I drank coffee when I wanted the caffeine, but it didn't help much because I was utterly exhausted. Besides, after drinking the same hospital coffee day after day, it left a lingering bitter taste in my mouth.

Though they already knew the basics from Lexy, I had to call into work and let them know the full extent of my situation. There was no way I could even function right now. As another day turned into night, I got as comfortable as I could in a chair by his bed, still wearing his jacket.

It was my fourth night here. Many of the nurses stopped by and reassured me that he would be fine since the swelling had gone down. I was comforted by all their positive words. I really needed to hear them.

Lexy came back with some clean clothes for me so I could shower and wash up in the bathroom that was in Elijah's room. Getting the good news that there were no further signs of swelling in his brain and that they had stopped the medication to induce his coma made me practically giddy. He was expected to wake up any time now.

Being as impatient as I was, I started to kiss every part of his face and his hands, trying to coax him into waking up. It was easier to do now that the tubes were out of the way. I even threatened to sell his leather jacket. I tried everything to get him to open up his beautiful eyes, but—nothing.

Elijah made it through the most critical stage, but the waiting was driving me crazy. Even with the good news, I would have to see him with his eyes open to know for sure that he would be okay. Slipping in the bed beside him, even knowing I shouldn't, I wrapped my arms around him gently. I missed laying with him like that.

As I breathed in his scent, I felt his chest rise and fall. It put me in a hypnotic state. I found myself drifting off to sleep.

Elijah

I tried to get my eyes to open, but they were so heavy. It took some time to clear as I blinked numerous times. Every muscle in my body felt achingly painful, like I had been hit by a truck—wait—no. I had been hit by car—my poor bike. I realized I was in the hospital. What happened? Then it all became clear. It was like a scene from a movie. I was thrown off my bike and landed on the cement.

Something was on my chest—an arm—a thin arm—Alex? Craning my stiffened neck, I saw the most angelic face, fast asleep. The joy of my vision was enough to put a smile on my face. Though I couldn't make my face cooperate, I felt it. It was pure ecstasy, warming my heart. I stayed in that position and stared at her as I wondered how long I had been here. My eyes became heavy again and I couldn't keep them open any longer.

Alexandria

I had a wonderful dream, but when I opened my eyes, I was brought back to reality. Feeling something warm brush against my cheek, I looked up. The overwhelming joy of seeing Elijah's eyes opened, his lips smiling, looking at me through those beautiful long lashes made me sob. I couldn't help myself. My face dug into his shoulder, and I bawled like crazy out of happiness. I thanked God for giving us this chance.

"I'm sorry." He wiped my tears away. "I didn't mean to make you suffer like this."

I couldn't believe he was worried about me when he was the one in pain. When I tried to get out of bed, he held me tighter and wouldn't let go. "Don't get up. I'm okay. The doctor has been in here already. I asked him not to wake you."

"How long have you been awake and how long was I asleep?"

"For a couple of hours."

"Do you remember what happened to you?"

"Yes."

"I need to call Seth and Lexy. Oh, and Jimmy is here. All your friends and all the nurses came by to see you. Jimmy came as soon as he found out."

"He did?" Elijah looked so happy, but then his vision fell to what I had on. "You're wearing my leather jacket?"

"Of course."

"Did you, by any chance, come across something?"

"I did. Your letter," I sighed. "It was very sweet and heartbreaking, but don't you ever put yourself in a situation like this again where you feel like you need to write me a good-bye letter."

248

"I won't. I promise. Life may be short, but I'll never do anything stupid enough to be apart from you." Elijah's serious eyes became flirty. "Are you naked under my pride and joy?"

I laughed and held him tighter. Yup, my Elijah was back. "Why don't you take it off and see for yourself."

"I will when I don't feel like an old man," he groaned. "I ache all over. Nurse Alex, I think I'm going to need a lot of tender loving care." Then he looked at his casted leg. "My leg, too." He rolled his eyes.

"Don't worry, patient Elijah, you're going to get lots of attention from me. I mean tons of it."

"With milk and cookies?"

I laughed out loud. "Whatever my kinky patient wants. But right now, it's not fair for me to hog you all to myself. I think you have a few guests still waiting for you in the visitor's room."

I jumped out of bed and rushed out the door. "Thank you," I shouted. I didn't care who had heard me. "Thank you for this second chance."

Chapter 40

Alexandria

Whiteboard:
Welcome home, Limpy!
-your friends

"We're going to have to call you Limpy," Jimmy curled his lips into a smirk. Sitting with his feet on the coffee table, he leaned back against the sofa.

"Limpy?" Elijah narrowed his eyes at him, sitting in the same position as Jimmy.

Seth placed a cookie in his mouth and mumbled, "You should be glad he didn't call you something else. Hey, these cookies are good. Where did you get them?"

"Alex baked them." Elijah turned his head sideways and gave me a wink. "She's a great cook…hell, she's good at everything she does."

"I should've invited her over when I lived here," Jimmy said.

Lexy headed to the kitchen and picked up another cookie. "I wish you would've. I only have three more months to eat her spaghetti before I graduate and who knows where I'll be then."

"You'll just have to come back and visit me," I said.

Lexy came back with a soda in her hand. "You know I will." Then she turned to Jimmy. "When's your flight?"

"Tomorrow, about ten. Seth offered to take me to the airport. But hey, I'll be back to see you all graduate. Elijah, you're all good?"

"Yup. Being in the hospital for a week didn't set me back too much, and my professors have been accommodating. I'll be on schedule to graduate."

"That's great news," Jimmy said. "I'm glad it all worked out."

"I hate to break up our little reunion, but I have to go. It's almost midnight. I have the breakfast shift tomorrow and so does Alex," Lexy reminded.

I nodded, producing a pout, letting her know I didn't like the morning shift.

"Elijah also needs his rest," Lexy added.

"I'm fine," Elijah intervened.

"No, Lexy is right," Seth agreed. "We should all get some rest."

"Sorry about that." Elijah looked sympathetic.

"Don't worry, not your fault," Jimmy said. "I'm just glad you're here. I don't think Alex...well...it was just meant to be." Jimmy got up and gave Elijah a hug. "I'll see you in three months."

"Thanks."

After the hugs, the gang left, and Elijah and I headed to our room.

"Come on, Limpy," I teased, walking alongside him while he used the crutches to help him move.

"Not you, too," Elijah chuckled. "You're lucky I can't do what I wish I could do."

"Oh yeah?"

As if the crutches were an extension of his arms, he wrapped them around me, pulling me into his chest. "Much better. I'm a little handicapped, but it doesn't mean I can't show you I'm still a man."

"There was never a doubt, Mr. Cooper," I said, enjoying his lips brushing against mine.

"I have something for you. I bought it before the accident. Take out the big box inside my closet."

"Really? You got me something?" I started to walk backwards to his closet, keeping my eyes on him. Upon opening, sure enough there was a box. Opening my gift, I took it out and the smell of leather tickled my nose in a pleasant way. "This is beautiful, Elijah. I don't know what to say." I held up a black leather jacket.

"Try it on. Let me see it on you."

I stood up, slipped it on and modeled for him. "What do you think?"

"It's perfect. I knew it would be, but I think it would fit better if you were naked underneath it. What do you think?"

I practically jumped on him, causing him to plop onto the bed. "Thank you so much. I never had a leather jacket before. I love it," I said, kissing all over his face. Straddling him, I pinned his arms over his head. My hair cascaded down the side of my face. It created a tunnel and I saw nothing but his beautiful, happy smile.

"I can really get used to this," Elijah chuckled. "I should buy you gifts more often."

I let out a laugh. "No need for a gift. I can do this every day. But it's time for you to get to bed. Nurse Weis's order."

Elijah shifted his body while I helped him get into a comfortable position by plumping pillows behind his back. "There, that should do it. I'm going to wash up. I'll be right back."

"I'm so tired." Elijah closed his eyes and yawned. "I may be asleep by the time you get back."

"That's okay. You had way too many visitors for your first day back home." I pulled the blanket up to his chest and gave him a tender kiss on his lips. When I stood up from the bed, Elijah pulled me back down. "One. More. Kiss."

With a smile, I happily obliged and then walked away. "Before I forget," I started to say, but stopped speaking when I looked back. His head was tilted and his eyes were shut. Elijah was already fast asleep.

Chapter 41

Alexandria

"Freckles, give me my backpack," Elijah ordered. Stepping out of the car, he used his crutches to help himself up, and then slammed the door.

"I'll hold it for you."

He raised one of his crutches up, preventing me from moving ahead. "Alex," he said calmly, "If you don't give me my backpack, I'm not moving. I'm standing right here. There is no way in hell I'm letting you carry my pack and yours. I may be a gimp right now, but that doesn't mean I'm not capable."

I raised my brows. "You just don't want to look like a wimp in front of your friends," I teased, helping him sling it over his shoulder.

"That's right," he chuckled. "They'll be calling me Wimpy Limpy."

I snorted loudly. "Come on Wimpy Limpy. I'm going to be late for class."

"I may be limpy, but I can still be speedy."

He was.

Just like on the ice, he maneuvered the crutches gracefully, as if they were an extension of his legs. He moved faster than me. We didn't have any classes together, but Elijah insisted on walking me to class.

"I guess this is where I drop you off," he said. "I have a class after you get out, so I'm going to hang around here for an hour. I might be sitting in the campus café." He looked to his left at the small structure.

"Okay, don't miss me too much." I tippy toed to give him a quick kiss, but my lips never left his.

Elijah held on tightly, giving me a kiss I would dream about all through class. It was the kind of kiss that made me tingle everywhere, making me see shooting stars. I lazily opened my eyes, feeling dazed when he let go, and planted my feet firmly on the ground.

"But I want you to miss me," he growled in that low sexy tone against my ear.

"I don't think I'll be able to concentrate in class after that kiss." Taking a deep breath, I looked into the warm brown eyes that held so much love for me.

"Hey, Alex. Hey, Limpy," Seth called, breaking our connection. He slapped Elijah lightly on his back. "It's good to see you out and about."

"You have class, Alex?" Seth asked.

"Yes, I'm on my way." I pointed at the door.

"Doesn't it start at ten?" Seth looked at his watch.

"Why? What time is it?" I panicked, taking out my cell from my back pocket. "Shit. I better go. I'm ten minutes late." I gave Elijah another quick peck and ran.

"I'll take good care of Limpy," Seth cracked up.

Elijah

My class ended at twelve. I told Alex to meet me at the school's dining hall. I felt like eating Lexy's super-sized burrito. When I got there, Alex was sitting down at a table with Lexy, Seth, and Dean.

I nodded my greeting to everyone, dropped my bag, and sat on the chair next to Alex. Sliding my crutches under the table, I settled in, getting as comfortable as I could.

"I'm going to order lunch now. I'll go get your burrito," Lexy said, gazing at me with a questioning look.

"That's okay." I held up my hand to stop her. "I can go order one."

"I'm not working so you can't get what you want," Lexy informed. "I know the workers."

"Good point," I said, looking at Alex. She gave me a huge smile.

"I'm going with Lexy so I can order mine, too."

I smiled with a nod. Alex had waited for me before ordering her lunch. That was the way she was.

"I'll go with you guys." Dean stood up, turned to Seth. "I'll get your burrito, too. You can keep Elijah company." Dean followed behind them.

"Thanks," Seth said.

"Did you get into UC Berkeley Graduate Business School?" Seth asked, slurping his drink through a straw.

"I did," I nodded. "How about you?"

"Me too," Seth grinned. "But you're not going, right?" There was a hint of disappointment in his tone. Though he tried to hide it, he couldn't. I knew him too well.

"I can't leave Alex. I got into Grad school here, too. It's good enough. Jimmy will be happy you're joining him soon. Did you tell him?"

"I did." Seth paused. "He's excited, but it would have been great if we were all together again in one place."

"I know. It would have been cool, but—"

"I know," Seth nodded with a sigh. "The only reason Jimmy and I would understand."

"Hey."

255

Seth looked at me.

"I'm here, your parents are here; we can visit. You'll come down to see them, won't you?"

"True. Speaking of which, my parents want to invite you and Alex over for dinner this weekend."

"Sure, I'll ask Alex, but I'm not sure if it was this weekend or next weekend that we are supposed to meet up with her mom and stepdad." I changed the subject. I had brought this subject up before, but I needed to bring it up again. Clearing my throat, I found my courage. "I need to pay your dad for the damages to the bike."

Seth looked at me with a frown. "I already told you for like the millionth time. The bike wasn't that badly damaged, but I'm beginning to think your brain was." Seth let out a chuckle, trying to steer away from the topic.

I never got to see the damage to the bike. Seth told me many times before that it just needed a new handlebar, new grips, and some paint, but for some reason, I didn't believe him. His dad was kind enough to allow me to borrow his car to race. Though I would give him a very small percentage of my winnings for the loan, he was always generous, which was the reason I felt guilty. Sometimes he even gave me guidance like a father. Our conversation was cut short when Dean and the girls came back with our lunches.

"Here you go." Alex placed my lunch in front of me.

"Thank you." I gave her a wink.

Her beautiful blue eyes radiated as she bit her bottom lip with a coy smile. I knew that wink would cause all sorts of sensations to flutter through her, which was naturally the reason why I did it. There was never a doubt in my mind. I would never leave Alex even after I saw the acceptance letter from Berkeley. There was no way I could leave her behind. I couldn't even go a day without seeing her. How was I supposed to make it through a week without her? Living together had its perks, for sure. We were almost like an old married couple.

Nolan and his group walked in and got in line. After buying their lunches, they sat at the opposite end of the dining hall. Choosing to ignore them, I continued to focus on the small talk at our table, but it didn't last long. Nolan strutted over. Seth and Dean released a short sigh and Lexy rolled her eyes.

"You ready for the next race?" Nolan didn't bother to let me answer, he just continued speaking as his eyes shifted to my cast. "Isn't it too bad that you can't? I guess I'll win by default."

"You can't beat me when I'm not even in the race, shit-face," I retorted. He was pissing me off, interrupting our lunch just to gloat. His face turned red. I guess he didn't like his new name. "I've retired. I'm not racing anymore." I craned my neck to Alex. She looked very pleased with my answer. I could also tell she was holding in her laugher. I bet she liked Nolan's new name.

"What do you mean?" Nolan asked, raising his brows in confusion.

"I'm graduating in a couple months. I have bigger and better things to do." I looked at Alex when I said those words. Her eyes were gleaming. I probably looked as if cupid had struck me with his arrow, but I didn't care. Alex meant the world to me. I would tame my ego and swallow my pride for her.

Nolan started laughing, really laughing. He was laughing so hard that the echoes of it bounced off the walls. "You're shittin' me." When I didn't respond, he spoke again. "You're serious? You've been doing this for a couple of years and suddenly you want to stop." He shifted his eyes to Alex and pointed at her. "Because of her?" His tone was degrading toward Alex, and I didn't like that at all.

I got up so fast, my chair slid out from under me. The unsteady balance from my cast almost caused me to fall backward, but I didn't care if I fell. Seth was right beside me, ready to catch me. "Don't fucking point at her," I seethed, slapping his hand away.

Nolan shook his head. He raised his hands to surrender. "Whoa. Have a nice life. As for me, I'll happily take first place. I'm going to the top."

"That's going to be little tough since you didn't even place in the street races." It was the race I would've gone to, but didn't for Alex. It was one of those crossroads situations. Had I gone instead, would I have ended up in the hospital? Maybe I would have been injured at the race. Who knew? But that was life. This was my chosen path.

Nolan let out a defeated laugh, and then walked away. He knew I was right. He'd never have what it takes to become a professional.

I sat back down and looked at Alex. Her face was slightly red. Was she embarrassed by my actions? After watching the way she blinked, then closed her eyes completely, I realized something was off. Seeing how she hardly touched her lunch, too, I became worried.

"Alex, you okay?"

"She looks sick," Seth commented.

"Maybe we should take her home," Lexy added.

"I don't feel so good," Alex mumbled, placing her elbow on the table while her hand supported her head. Her eyes were closing again. She looked so drained. When I touched her forehead, it was scorching hot.

Chapter 42

Alexandria

Lexy and Seth helped me get into Elijah's bed. Not wanting Elijah to get sick, I had asked them to take me to the other bedroom, but Elijah refused. It had been a while since I had been sick like this. It was probably from all the stress of Elijah being in the hospital and trying my best to take care of him after he came back home. I guess it finally all caught up to me.

"I'll take good care of you, Baby. Don't you worry about a thing," Elijah said sweetly, caressing my hair. He sat on the bed. "You've been through a lot. Taking care of me wore you down. Now it's my turn."

My eyelids were so heavy and every part of my body ached, as if I had been beaten. Though it was difficult to move, I turned my body to snuggle into his warmth.

"I know you don't feel like eating, but I'm going to make some fresh chicken soup. Lexy and Seth went to the store for me. They'll be back with some medication to help you feel better."

"That so sweet," I sighed and shivered. "You have wonderful friends."

"I sure do, but they're your friends, too"

"I know." I paused. "Elijah."

"Yes." He placed his cool hand over my forehead. It felt so good, but it made me shiver again.

"When you're feeling better and your cast is off, will you come somewhere with me?"

"I would go to hell and back if you asked me." Elijah tenderly stroked my cheek with a loving smile.

"You would?"

"Anywhere, Freckles, as long as we're together. Where would you like to go?"

"Somewhere I should have gone a long time ago, but I was too nervous."

"Ahhh," he said softly. "I think I know where. I would be honored to go with you."

"Thank you."

Elijah planted a long kiss on my forehead, my eyes, my nose, my cheek, and then my lips. "They're here. It's time for this Limpy to cook. I'll be back soon."

"Thank you." I wasn't sure if that was what I said. Exhaustion took over and I fell into darkness.

Alexandria

Two months later

The sun managed to peek through the dark clouds. It poured this morning, but the rain died down quickly. Though the leather jacket kept me warm, feeling the cool breeze against my face reminded me that it was still early spring.

"This is my first time here since we buried him," I explained to Elijah. He squeezed my hand, letting me know he was here for me.

"I didn't want to come back here. I thought it would hurt too much, but I think I'm going to be okay."

"Talk to him. It will help. You want me to leave you alone for a bit?"

"No," I pulled him next to me. "I want you to stay."

With a nod from Elijah, I looked at my dad's headstone. I hadn't said a word and tears already started to flow. All I could do was stand there.

"I'll start first," Elijah said, surprising me. I gazed at him wondering if he was joking, but he wasn't. "Hello, Mr. Weis. My name is Elijah Cooper. It's a pleasure to meet you. I want you to know that Alex is in great hands. I love your daughter with all of me and there isn't anything I wouldn't do for her. I'm going to show you time and time again so you can rest in peace."

Elijah's words made me tear up even more. Taking out Kleenex from my purse, I blew my nose and wiped my eyes.

"Your turn, Freckles. I promise it gets easier. The first time is the hardest."

"Okay." I took a deep breath. "Hello, Dad. I'm in college now, but you already knew that." I paused, wondering what I should say next. "Umm...I want to thank you for listening to my prayer. I would have given up anything for Elijah, so thank you for that. Mom and I are closer now. We got our misunderstandings out of the way. We're actually going to get together with her and William this weekend. Not that you needed to hear that."

"Anyway, I want to tell you that I miss you." My lips quivered as I let out more tears. "I wish you were here with me." I took a moment to pause while Elijah held me in his arms. When I composed myself again, I continued. "Hey Dad, I found him. I found the one who loves me with all of him. The one who loves me for my goodness and my faults. I didn't understand what you were saying back then, but I do now. Now—" My lips trembled as the words I wanted to say were very clear in my mind. "I can let you go now. I found the one you said would one day replace you. You'll always be in my heart. Oh, and on my ankle. I got a tattoo in honor of you." I snorted at the thought that my dad actually would have flipped if he saw me with one.

Holding onto Elijah, my body relaxed as I let go of my sorrow, my pain, and my dad. Elijah held me tenderly until I was ready to be released. Wiping my tears, he gazed into my eyes. "Doesn't that feel much better?"

"Yes," I nodded. And it did. I felt a little bit free, like a brick had been lifted off me.

"You ready to go?"

"Yes," I said, glancing at the headstone.

"We'll come back, Alex. Anytime you want to come back, I'll come with you."

"Thank you." I snuggled to him. "I must have done something good to have you in my life."

"You were just being you. That's all. Plain and simple." Elijah changed the subject. "Hey Alex, you see the rainbow and the sun peeking out of the clouds?"

I glanced in the direction he pointed. Nodding my head, I was rendered speechless. The colorful arch was a mesmerizing site, gracing the Earth with its presence. It was a reminder that even after a heavy storm, there was hope and beauty in life. Seeing the rainbow reminded me that there was something great out there…something powerful, something beyond our control. Next thing I knew, I was being lifted off the ground.

"Elijah, put me down." I lightly spanked his ass.

"I'm taking you out of here. Sorry, Mr. Weis. Time for me to take care of your daughter."

"Where are we going?" I asked, watching my dad's headstone get smaller in the distance.

"We're riding off into the sunset Freckles, just like Danny and Sandy. I'm going to make your dreams come true."

What could I say after that? My heart was filled with his words, his love, and his devotion. I would return them back to him just the same, if not more. I loved Elijah with all my heart. Though I didn't think it was possible to love him even more, he continued to show me that there was no limit to that love. It grows every day, with every new experience, with every new hope and dream. Sometimes the broken road does get fixed. It just needs time to mend…just like broken hearts.

Epilogue
Elijah

Five years later

Whiteboard:
I love my wife to the moon and back.
That is all I have to say today.
-E

"Thank you, Babe. You make the best breakfast burrito. You don't have to wake up to fix me one, you know." My fingers softly tugged under her jaw. Inhaling the scent from her lotion, I kissed her on the lips. She always smelled divine, like she just stepped out of a floral garden.

Alex started to rub her tummy. "I had to wake up anyway. I've been so hungry lately."

"Well, of course you are. Our babies are growing." I bent down, placed a hand on her as if I could touch them, and kissed her belly. Feeling a push on the palm of my hand, I took in the moment. "You want to come out, don't you?" I said. "I can't wait for you and your sister."

"Hey." Alex tugged my tie, forcing me to stand up. "Maybe the one that kicked you is Elizabeth and not Evan. Don't underestimate the strength of a woman."

I chuckled, embracing Alex in my arms. "You're so right. I have one right here to prove that theory."

"Don't you forget it," she said with a sassy attitude. "Just three more months until we get to hold our twins in our arms, or maybe sooner. I already feel like I'm going to explode."

"I can't wait," I said. "But right now, I better get to work. What are you going to do while I'm gone?"

"The painter is coming back today to do the touch-ups on the sun, stars, and moon in the nursery."

"Okay," I nodded. Please be careful when you go up and down the stairs."

Holding Alex's hand, I led her to the garage. Glancing around, I looked at our amazing house. We had moved into an over-priced, two-story house in a gated community, but with a stockbroker's salary, it was within our budget. I wanted to give Alex the best things in life, even if it meant I had to work like a dog. I would do it for her, for our children, for my family.

"By the way, Lexy, Emma, Seth, Dean, Jimmy and his wife will be coming over this weekend," Alex said, rubbing her hand on my arm, over the area of the dragon tattoo.

Hand over hand, I held hers tenderly and kissed every knuckle. "Have a good day, Freckles. I'll call you later to check up on you."

"Drive carefully. I'll be waiting for your call, Mr. Cooper."

"I will, Mrs. Cooper. Oh, before I forget. I'll be a little late tonight. I'd like to swing by the hospital to check on the wing our company donated in Evan's name, to make sure they're on schedule."

"Okay," Alex nodded.

Alex leaned against the door, watching me while I headed to my car. Upon opening the garage, I glanced over at my collection of motorcycles parked next to my car, then covered my eyes from the light. The sun shone brightly and the sky was covered with the fluffiest clouds. I took a deep breath and thanked the heavens for the life I had today. Never would I have imagined myself to be in this moment. Never would I have imagined finding someone like Alex, who loved me as much as I loved her.

Life presents you with many roads, but two remain constant. You're born, and when it's your turn, you die. The other roads are presented along the way, and which ones you decide to take is up to you. Sometimes, you don't get to decide and the roads take a turn for the worse. I was one of the lucky ones. My broken road led me to Alex and the life I have today, and I don't regret a thing—not a single thing.

"Elijah," Alex called, tapping on the window just as I started the car.

I rolled my window down, gazed at her beautiful smile and waited for her to speak.

"I forgot to tell you that I love you." She reached in and I pressed my lips to hers.

"I love you to the moon and back," I told her. As always, that put a huge smile on her face.

Ever since the accident, Alex has always said she loved me when we parted ways. I knew the reason why. There were no guarantees in life. There was no happily ever after—only reality. So I promised her on our wedding day that I would show her that every day with her was a blessing. We would always find our sunset, sing our hearts out, dance in the rain, jump in puddles, and make mad, passionate love. For every new day was a new beginning, a new experience, filled with new hopes and dreams—one that should always be lived as if it were your last.

Tempting Sydney, A Tempting Novel, Book 1
By Angela Corbett
May 28, 2014

The light from the setting sun glared off the truck door as it opened. The person was in shadow, but his outline showed a large, tall, imposing frame. Wide shoulders, narrow waist. I thinned my eyes. Since Red was just a little above hobbit size with grey hair, I figured this must be one of his employees, and not one I recognized by silhouette. I lifted my hand to block the light and try to get a better view. It didn't help. He kept walking toward me and was five feet away before I realized who it was.

Confident, gorgeous blue eyes held mine. It was *the* guy. And he was standing in front of me...about to work on my engine. I had a momentary hot flash and took a deep, steadying breath to try to calm down.

"Hey," I said, shoving my hands in my front pockets. There was no telling what my hands would do if I gave them freedom— but I was sure it would be mighty embarrassing, and perhaps illegal.

His eyes raked over me, dark and with purpose. I felt like I was being undressed with each shift of his gaze. "Hey," he said back, his voice deep and smooth. Shit. Even his voice seeped testosterone. Why couldn't he have sounded like a chipmunk?

After what felt like a thorough inventory of my assets, his gaze slowly made its way up my body to meet my eyes. I felt like I'd been measured—and was suddenly completely self-conscious about my clothing choice: low-rise jeans that made my ass look great, a rose pink sequined tank that complimented my cleavage, fair skin, and blonde hair, and a beige moto jacket. I'd been pretty happy with the ensemble when I'd left the house, but wasn't sure how I felt about it now. I wished I was one of those confident girls who could grab a guy's attention with a smile and keep it for as long as I wanted. But I wasn't Brynn, and there was no point in pretending I was. Mindless flirting with guys I couldn't care less about was one thing—that sort of flirting I could do. But this guy was hot. Like, break-the-rules-and-to-hell-with-my-goals hot. This guy was in a whole different ballpark, and I was completely out of my league.

He'd practically had eye-sex with me at the Soup and Spoon, but I didn't want to make it obvious that I remembered who he was. Though, really, who wouldn't remember him? He could star in an ad for muscles. So, I went with something utterly stupid instead. "You're not Red."

One eyebrow went up like he was contemplating my lack of IQ. "Nope."

I nodded, feeling like an idiot for beginning the conversation that way. At least I hadn't started with an ode to his eyes and bicep circumference—because that had been on the tip of my tongue. I decided to try again. "I think I saw you the other day at lunch. Do you go to college at Easton?" There, that was good. An acknowledgment that I recognized him, but not an affirmation that I'd thought about him in seriously inappropriate ways that required me dipping into my secret naughty box on several occasions since I'd ogled him earlier this week.

He eyed me again. "Nope."

"Then you live in Winchester?"

"Yep."

And he wasn't talkative. So we'd established that.

He stood back and looked at the curvy lines of my car, almost the same way he'd looked at me. I took that as a good sign, since my car was pretty damn hot. "She's gorgeous."

"Thanks."

"A '69?"

I was impressed he identified the year with a glance. Though cars were his job, so I shouldn't be. Maybe my impression of his probable chest measurement was seeping into my impressions of him in general. "Yeah. And she exploded."

I explained what had happened, and he followed me to the front of the car. He put his tools down on the gravel next to the road and started checking the radiator.

"Any idea what's wrong?"

He didn't answer for a minute. "A few."

He was a man of little words.

We were quiet for what seemed like eons. I felt awkward just standing there, watching him inspect my car in silence. I'm not good with awkward—I tend to just make things more awkward. But I couldn't stand the no-speech zone any longer. "Have you lived in Winchester long?"

Again, he waited more than a minute to answer. "A few weeks."

"I'm surprised I haven't seen you before." I would have remembered. Those eyes. Those arms. It was suddenly much warmer than it had been a few minutes ago.

"Because you're an expert on all the men in town?" My cheeks flamed and I was about to respond when he said, "I just started working at Red's, so it's not really that surprising."

Okay. So we weren't friends, and there was a good chance he thought I was an absolute idiot. Or maybe he just wasn't interested in talking. In any case, I already felt dumb enough, and I had no further interest in talking to a man who didn't want to talk to me, regardless of his criminally low levels of body fat, or tight jeans and shirt that fit him like a second skin. He worked in silence, and I watched in silence. It was even more awkward than before. He seemed totally fine with that.

I felt deflated. Why wasn't he talking to me? Or even attempting to flirt? We'd flirted during our eye-sex encounter, so what was his problem now? He'd barely said a word, which made him so difficult to read that I couldn't tell what his issue was. But his issue was giving me issues, and I didn't like it. I toed some gravel on the ground, wishing I could speed up time and get this service call over with.

"Why isn't your boyfriend helping you with this?"

I started at his voice, surprised he was instigating a conversation. I was even more surprised he was instigating a conversation that was fishing for information about the state of my relationship status. Since it seemed he'd already put me in the epic loser category, I decided not to give the Superman body double any other ammunition. Instead, I lifted a shoulder, non-committal—

which was how I felt about my dating life—and pretended I was actually in a relationship, "The guys I date don't do cars."

He placed his hands on the front of She-Ra and looked at me sideways, his lips lifting. "What *do* they do?"

I shrugged.

"So…not you?"

I felt my cheeks redden.

He smiled wider, turning his attention back to the mess under my hood. "With a car like this, you should really have someone who appreciates it, and is willing to help you put in the work."

That whole statement seemed like it had a lot of double-meaning attached to it. I wasn't sure what to make of it, but I wasn't the type of woman who wanted a man to take care of me, and I didn't want him to assume I was. "I can do the work myself. I don't need anyone else."

He braced his arms against the edge of the car, his muscles even more defined than usual with the added strain of his weight. He held my eyes. "You definitely needed me tonight." My eyes widened and he grinned. It took me a second to realize he was talking about my car, and not about all of the other ways he thought I needed him.

Whispering Wishes
By Jennifer Miller
May 28, 2014

"Hello beautiful ladies, I'm Wes. Can I start you off with something to drink?"

I look up and take in Wes, and holy cute waiter batman. He's super cute. No, strike that. He's hot. Before I even realize what I'm doing, I'm completely checking him out. He's wearing black pants that must be uniform for the bar. But he wears them very well. Tucked into his pants is a white button down shirt that's rolled up his forearms, one of which is covered in tattoos. As I run my eyes up that arm, wondering what other tattoos his shirt hides, I see a strong jaw, and full lips upturned into a wide smile and the best pearly whites. They are the kind of lips that make a girl think dirty thoughts. I flush when my mind flashes to what I'd like those lips to do to me. When I meet his eyes, I blink at the impact. They are swimming pools of a green so beautiful, I find myself lost for a moment. As if the rest of him isn't enough, his head is completely shaved except for the dark thick strip of hair that runs down his scalp — a Mohawk. As if he knows exactly what I'm thinking, those amazing lips form a smirk, and ends with a rather smug look on his face.

"I'd like a glass of chardonnay, please," Mischa says, making me blink and come to my senses.

"Umm," I feel flustered. Geesh, I'm an idiot. I fumble with my menu and battle the embarrassment wanting to make its way across my face. "I'll take a glass of merlot, please, thank you."

I chance a glance at his face again, and find his eyes on me. "You got it ladies. I'll be back in a few." I'm not proud of the fact that I totally stare at his ass as he makes his way to the bar to get our drinks. And what a fine ass it is. I look at Mischa with widened eyes, "Woah. No wonder your client likes this place."

She laughs and the sound makes me smile. I can already feel the remnants still clinging to me from my awful day — start to disappear. Becoming serious once more, Mischa gently asks, "Do you want to talk about what happened today?"

"No, and yes," I give her a sad smile. "We had our staff meeting as planned and at the end of it, Steve made the announcement. I could feel myself lean forward and I even started to grin in anticipation; certain that it was going to be mine. Then, he announced that big fucking boob Brandi got the job."

As I make that statement, having emphasized "fucking boob," Wes picks that precise moment to drop off our glasses of wine. I hear a laugh, and then a cough that is an obvious attempt to cover up the former. I look up and see Wes trying, but failing to cover a grin. Given my somewhat snarly mood, I can hardly believe myself when I say, "Yes, you heard me right. Big fucking boobed Brandi got a promotion over me. You ever have someone get a job over you because their dick was bigger?"

"Aspen!" Mischa gasps in horror but also covers her mouth as a giggle escapes. The look on her face is funny. She doesn't know whether to be embarrassed or find it hilarious.

I look at Mischa, shrug my shoulders, and give her my best innocent face, "What?"

"I'm not usually in the habit of talking about my super huge dick with people I don't know."

"Hm, that's too bad."

"Well here's your wine. Hopefully this will help ease your pain," Wes states with a knock out grin. I feel my girly parts jerk in response. Man, but he is pretty. "I'll be back to take your order."

"Thanks." Mischa says, and I just stare until he walks away.

"That boy is almost too pretty. Down girl!"

Mischa raises her brows in confusion, "Down girl? I'm not the one salivating."

"I wasn't talking to you, I was talking to my vagina."

She giggles "Did it work?"

"No, she won't listen. She's been neglected too long."

She laughs again, but then sobers, "So big boobed Brandi, huh?"

"Yeah. She got the promotion. Can you believe that? She's worked there for what, three months? She has absolutely no experience. Un-freaking-believable. But that isn't even the worst part."

Mischa raises her eyebrows in confusion, "How is that possible?"

"Lisa brought me into her office after the announcement and told me that they want me to train her."

"What?!"

I raise my glass of wine in a sarcastic salute and take a sip before answering. "Yep, my reaction exactly. I'm not good enough to get the job, but yet, they want me to train her? Are you fucking kidding me?"

"I don't even know what to say. Should we call our people who know people?"

"I think we should seriously consider that possibility."

"I'm so sorry. What did you say to Lisa?"

"I told her just how stupid I thought that suggestion was. Then I told her I needed time to think about it." I sigh and drop my shoulders feeling defeated, "How the hell do I do that, Mish? It's an insult."

"It is, and I wish I knew what to tell you, but I really don't. I can tell you that you are right to feel that way. I would feel that way too."

"Well that's something. At least I know I'm not just being a jealous bitch and overreacting."

"No, that's at least not the whole reason," she gives me a small smile because she knows of course a part of me is jealous, as much as angry, and hurt, and insulted, and... well the list could go on.

"What I'd like to do is quit, and leave them high and dry, fucking them in the ass like they did me."

And because the universe can be a cruel mistress that is the precise moment Wes once again makes an appearance at our table. I hear his laugh and look up. "I'm not even going to touch that one," he says with a wink. Oh lord, he winked at me. I think my uterus just skipped a beat.

"Thank, God." I hear Mischa mumble. I'm sure it isn't the first time — and likely not the last — she's wondering why she's friends with me.

I laugh out loud because what else can I possibly do?

Wes blesses me with a full out grin, and I'm pretty sure I'm about to ask him to be the father of my future babies when he thankfully asks a question, and stops me from having word vomit. "Did you decide what you want to eat?"

"Oh, I didn't even look at the menu," I confess.

"No worries, I got this," Mischa states and then proceeds to order a sampler appetizer plate for us to share and various kinds of bruschetta.

"Works for me. She knows what I like," I grin at Mischa.

"Okay then, I'll go put that in now. It shouldn't be too long."

"Thanks," I say with a smirk, which Wes returns. He stares at me for a minute and it almost looks like he's going to say something, but then the hostess walks up to him, "Hey excuse me Wes? Can I ask you a question?"

"Oh, uh sure, Kimber. I'll be back soon ladies." He walks off and I look at his ass once more with a sigh, then turn my attention back to Mischa and see her smiling at me.

"What? I said he's cute. Whatever. He's the best thing about my day. Don't judge me. And speaking of which, I have a bone to pick with you."

"With me? What did I do?"

"You know, I made my list to the universe last night during the new moon like you told me to and so far, if today is any indication, the universe hates me."

"The universe does not hate you. You can't blame this on her — everyone has a bad day. Now just relax, and give it time," she admonishes. "I know what you just said, and can only imagine all you are feeling, but you do need to think about what you are going to say to Lisa tomorrow."

"I really don't know. I guess I will just play it by ear. Maybe I'll be lucky and she will have mercy on me and ask Dave to train her instead. He would probably like that, although he would probably walk around with a semi erection all day long from training her. You know… considering her tits would be in his face all day."

"Wow, I have the best timing ever today."

If I was a better person I would flush, but I just look at him and shrug.

"I just want to apologize for Aspen, she's had a bad day and the filter between her brain and mouth is obviously out of order at the moment."

"Hey! Sitting right here, Mish! Besides, filters are overrated."

"No worries. I find it refreshing," Wes says with a smile. "Here's your food, and a couple plates. Would you like more wine?"

"Yes, please." Both Mischa and I say together.

"Okay, I'll be right back. I can't wait to find out what I will hear next."

Bite and Release
By Cory Cyr
May 31, 2014

#1

His pants hung low on his hips and his abs were indented and cut. Shea had a very serious looking six pack. His hips narrowed into a sexy "V" with a line of dark hair that trailed beneath his waistband. His chest was smooth and chiseled, along with muscular arms, and....He had tattoos. How did I not know Shea was hiding this perfect work of art beneath his clothes?

I felt my breath hitch and my mouth go dry. My purse and bag slipped out of both hands and fell to the walkway. I'd seen hundreds of tattoos in New York, but I had never seen any like this. It looked like a large vest of intricate tribal lines woven together in black and gray, so tightly inked that it almost appeared to be clothing. They went half way down on both sides of his chest, curved over each shoulder onto his back, and then the pattern extended to the elbows of each of his arms. I'd never seen anything so beautiful. I couldn't tear my eyes away from it and I had to fight myself from reaching out and licking each line. The tattoos were hypnotizing. I just stood there and stared.

Shea looked carnal and all male. I felt my nostrils flare slightly and suddenly I became territorial. I hardly recognized the emotion; I had never felt it with anyone. He was mine, and I wanted him— to possess him. The silence was deafening and the cold was paralyzing. I finally looked up from his chest and our eyes locked. He reached for me, his arms circling my waist and picking me up. As his lips crashed into mine he let out a moan, and I greedily sucked on his tongue, inhaling him into my mouth. He moaned again as his tongue probed every corner of my mouth, and I could feel his hardness against my belly.

As he held me, he closed the front door with his foot. He set me down, frowning slightly as he cracked the door back open, grabbing my purse and bag, then closing and locking the door securely. Taking a quick look around, I was surprised to see that Shea's

276

apartment was not what I expected. I thought it would be some single guy's lair, but it clearly was a *home*.

#2

"Irish coffee?" he asked as he opened a cabinet, getting a bottle of whisky down.

"I'm so cold, maybe just the whiskey," I chuckled as I rubbed my hands up and down my arms trying to circulate blood back into them.

He poured me a small glass of whiskey. I took it gratefully as I watched him walk back into the living room and throw another small log into the fireplace. He then moved over to his stereo and turned the music back on, which was classical jazz. I sat down on the sofa, sipping my drink, realizing that I really didn't know anything about Shea the man. Everything I had based my decisions on had been because of him as the eight year-old I used to babysit. Thirteen years later, Shea was an intelligent, hardworking and wickedly sexy man. He was kind, funny, and charming; he was the kind of man that any woman would want. Shea sat next to me, Indian style, on the sofa. His height and his leanness made his body look perfect. He had not one ounce of body fat, and as he sat there, I could see that everything from his shoulders to his abdomen looked rock hard, smooth skin stretched over heavily defined muscle. Inches of intense tattoos covered his strong chest and entwined his arms.

"Are you still cold?" he asked, as his eyes drifted to my coat.

"No, I'm finally beginning to warm up," I replied. In all honesty, I was still kind of chilled, but extremely hot at the same time. Between the drink and Shea's scantily clad body, my pulse spiked; I felt the thumping in my neck, my wrist and in between my thighs. Shea looked at me, his eyes sensual and intense. I felt my body begin to quiver as my breathing began to quicken.

Shea moved his hands over to the front of my jacket and began undoing each button. Once they were all undone, he positioned me so he could remove the coat. I was still wearing my maid of honor dress.

"I really like this dress," he remarked as he pressed a kiss to my bare collar bone. I blew out a breath and the touch of his warm lips on my body made me shudder. I felt like this was my first time with a man because I was so nervous and excited.

"Did I tell you how much I like this dress?" he repeated as he pressed small kisses over my shoulders and neck. Each kiss made my nipples stiffen into hard points, pressing against my bra, heightening their sensitivity. I closed my eyes and licked my lips as his hand went to the back of the dress and I heard the zipper coming down. His breathing sounded slightly faster as he took the glass out of my hand and stood up. As he pulled me up to him, my dress slid down to my ankles. I heard him hiss. I stood there in my strapless bra and panties. I kicked off my shoes, which now made him over a foot taller.

"Jesus, you take my breath away," Shea murmured. "You're the most beautiful thing I've ever seen."

 Author Mary Ting resides in Southern California with her husband and two children. Writing her first novel, Crossroads Saga, happened by chance. It was a way to grieve the death of her beloved grandmother, and inspired by a dream she once had as a young girl. When she started reading new adult novels, she fell in love with the genre. It was the reason she had to write one-Something Great. Why the pen name, M Clarke? She tours with Magic Johnson Foundation to promote literacy and her children's chapter book-No Bullies Allowed.

Website: http://www.authormaryting.com/
Facebook: https://www.facebook.com/AuthorMaryTing
Twitter @MaryTing
Instagram: http://instagram.com/authormaryting
Email: authormaryting@outlook.com
Blog: http://www.marytingbooks.blogspot.com
Follow Mary Ting & M. Clarke on Goodreads.

34754677R00158

Made in the USA
Charleston, SC
18 October 2014